I KNOW NOT

THE LEGEND OF FOX CROW

Book One

JAMES DANIEL ROSS

Winter Wolf
PUBLICATIONS

| CINCINNATI OHIO

Copyright © 2017, James Daniel Ross
First Edition: 2011 Dark Quest LLC
First Winter Wolf Edition: 2017
Cover Design & Art © 2017, by Miriam Chowdhury
Interior Image Art © 2017, by Miriam Chowdhury
Edited by T.R.Chowdhury
Interior Design by T.R.Chowdhury

Published by CopperFox,
an imprint of Winter Wolf Publications LLC

ISBN: 978-1-945039-05-8 (paperback)

RADIATION ANGELS
The Chimerium Gambit
The Key To Damocles

THE DEFENDING THE FUTURE ANTHOLOGY SERIES
Breach the Hull
So It Begins
By Other Means

CHRONICLES OF RITHALION
Elvish Jewel
The Fireheart
(release June 2018)

THE TROUBADOURS INN ANTHOLOGY SERIES
Tales from the Hapless Cenloryan

The Whispering of Dragons
The Last Dragoon
The Echoes of Those Before

To those that are told they can't:

You can. You will.

TABLE OF CONTENTS

IT BEGINS...

SCREAMS flew like arrows, stabbing into the ground and splashing in pools of blood. Limbs thudded into the earth, hewn from bodies without mercy or thought, creating the drum beat of armies at war. Men died by the dozens underneath a cold sky crowned by a distant moon that watched on and didn't give a damn. Balanced on the very edge of civilization, the castle was being gutted.

But outside this chaos a poison flowed through the veins of the castle. It cloaked itself in righteousness, but those that saw it pass made signs to ward off evil, for it had lost the mask of civilization. Its eyes burned with madness. Those that knew the name whispered it was a ragman, but no one would survive to warn the outside world. It was made of blades and death. It flew past defenders and turned attackers into disconnected piles of muscle and bone. It laughed as it did so.

The ragman, hands tight on the hilt of his sword, made it to the gates of the main hall. It stood like a rock over the surging crimson surf of bodies. Eyes sharpened by the presence of so much death, he saw his prey bobbing in the fray. Blood fanned into the sky, turning into black droplets that flew and called out with the voices of crows. He tasted the bowel flavored wind and growled like murder incarnate as he sprang into action. He hacked at a living wall of bodies that kept him from his target.

Like the tip of a spear, he created a wake of blood and gore, penetrating into the very heart of the squirming mass. One man, only one hero, managed to turn and meet his fury. But then, a voice in the sky screamed.

The ragman turned, too late.

ONE

THE WOMB I DESERVE

I AWOKE.

Actually that's really oversimplified. I would rather say that I came to be awake like a spark struck to tinder, sizzling and sliding along from inert to aware. On the other hand, sizzle is probably the wrong word; it denotes far too much speed. It would be better to say I awoke like the tide, a slow but steady progress. There wasn't any black-fading-to-light part or opening-of-eyes as of yet. In fact, the first thing that struck a chord in any coherent part of my soul was the smell; it reeked of death. Then again, I haven't even mentioned the pain.

There was a lot of pain.

If any other part of me was severed, I doubt I would have noticed it for the lancet of fire in my head. It was as if someone had ripped out an eye and filled my skull with molten lead.

That's when the functioning parts of my mind got together and realized that there were pieces missing. In reality, whatever pieces of me there were supposed to be inside my head were gone. I searched for me and only found this white cottony cloud where I used to be. I once knew my name, I once had a family, friends–at least I hope I did, but it isn't as if I could really know could I? I had in-conveniently lost myself as I lay in this perpetually dark place that stinks of rotting flesh and excrement.

My thoughts slipped through my fingers and went on a brief sojourn about the disgusting nature of defecation at death. The last thing any creature does is reveal its last meal through its rectum. To spoil the appetite of whatever is trying to eat it, I'm sure. Kind of a final insult: 'Go ahead! Try to eat me with that smell following you around!' It lacks a certain amount of dignity; but I suppose you have to take what victories you can get when you can. I started

11

to giggle, a high pitched, eerie sound that created echoes of pain that ricocheted inside of my skull.

To say I was only 'nearly' insane is kind; to say I had totally lost my grip on reality is much more accurate.

Then, very quietly, the darkness pressed inward. I felt it in my brain, past the fuzzy Void that used to be me– two halves. One half was urging me on to madness, wishing to let go of every pain and pressure to the exultation of ennui. The other was dark, sharp and foreboding. It simply stalked forward and seized the reins of my mind. Without a word as to its identity, it wrapped thorny hands around the neck of my weaker self and strangled it determinedly until it shut its festering gob. This murderer in my mind brought me back to the here and now.

It was then I learned a lesson known by precious few men: sometimes you choose whether you go insane. It's all a matter of giving up, really. I get the feeling I'm not the giving up type. Now I have confirmed my suspicions, but I am ahead of myself.

I tried to open my eyes, and failed. With monumental effort and not a little confusion, I raised my hands to my face and probed my eyes to see if they were still there. I got an image of my fingers exploring empty sockets that had been picked clean by crows and my skin was instantly sheathed in freezing ice. My fingers paused, trembling as they hovered a few fingerlengths away…

I don't know how long I sat there, frozen in terror at the possibility of permanent blindness, but that dark thing in my head jabbed me sharply. My hands finally moved and found a thick, sticky crust covering both lids. It felt like old paint, mostly dried. I tasted it. It was sweet, metallic, bitter, and sour all at the same time. It was surely old blood, dried over at least a day. Relief eased the ache across my shoulders as I realized my eyes were just gummed shut.

Perhaps I should have been wondering how in hell do I know what old blood tastes like? But I was busy. I didn't remember that I was carrying a canteen, but thankfully my hands did. They grabbed it and Left poured it in my eyes as Right scraped at the dry, scabby mess. I sat up shakily and pried my eyes open to finally look upon the cause of the great stench.

I was in a keep, well the courtyard actually. Forget the tales you may have heard of white walls, graceful towers, and airy passages. This building was a weapon of war: short, squat, dirty, and functional. Of course I noticed that much later than the carpet of bodies that littered every free stride of space. Men and pieces of them lay sprawled out across the parade ground like the vomit of a colossal monstrosity. Faces screamed at me, berating me for drawing breath even as they pleaded for me to remember their names. The Fog circled in to cut me off blocking all but the shallowest parts of me.

I shook my head to clear it and nearly passed out– white light, ghostly noises, and smells attacking in crashing riots as I went to my knees. Long moments passed before the world came back into focus. I heaved once, and spit out a mouthful of stomach acid.

Let's...let's not do that again.

I agreed with myself and gingerly levered to my feet. Right Hand was thinking on its own again; it had picked up a sword from the bloody soil. I stared at the thing, thick and heavy and crusted with the leavings of its last job. Right tested the balance and I sneered, thinking it was half a waterweight heavy on the blade side. It was less a weapon than a cleaver.

Am I a swordsman, then? Darker and more powerful voices argued between my ears, *Not now, later. Get safe, and then vivisect your head.*

Again, I agreed, heartened that I would give myself such good advice. My eyes again drank in the scene, looking for a clear path through the swamp of hewn human flesh. Amidst the broken bodies and shattered bones, I began to pick out vaguely familiar features. A nose here, a shock of red hair there, battle standards, heraldic heater shields lying cleft next to round. The picture clarified very quickly inside my mushy head: I was in a border keep and Westerners had raided the outpost, slaughtering all the Norian Kingsmen inside.

Well almost. Left tenderly touched the edges of my spongy wound. *Not for a lack of trying.* I glanced to the corpse of a fat man at my feet. *Better off than you lot, though.*

Something young and pink inside me squirmed, not at the carnage, but at the fact that I could look upon it without feeling ill, or sad, or anything at all. A hundred men had crashed against each other and exploded into a field of gore, yet I felt nothing. My gut was uneasy, but only when I moved too fast. Even now I was forced to stare at the human wreckage just to make sure of my footing and I looked directly at an empty head whose brains had been removed by hammer or mace —

And how did I know that? Had I killed him?

I KNOW NOT

And I did not flinch at the gore. I didn't even bat an eye. Hundreds of men lay butchered as thoroughly as if they had been forced through a sieve and turned into sausages. I could not remember ever seeing such a horrific scene before, but here I was, every internal weathervane saying I was intimately familiar with the like.

Then, just for a second, I caught sight of a young boy. Nowhere near adulthood, he lay lifeless and still, his torso ending just below his ribcage. He was so small, so lost, his face so surprised in death. I could not see his legs and suddenly nothing was as important as finding them. Something stirred finally, a tightness in my heart, a shadowy reflex of loss. I smelled burning and there were no fires. I heard screaming but I was totally alone.

It was at that moment the dark, sharp thing at the back of my head snapped an arm out of the Fog and crumpled thoughts of the murdered child before my mind's eye. The great emptiness swallowed the bile and sorrow and left a vaulted, hollow cavern inside my chest. The emotion disappeared into the Fog so fast, I wondered if it ever had been. I forced myself to look again.

To say I was aghast would have been a normal reaction. It would also be a lie. I was not happy, or sad, or disgusted. I was not even afraid of who I was to see such a scene of valiant defeat and be unmoved. I simply was. I existed, a perfect tool without emotion, obligation, or a hand in sight. It was a long time before I moved.

In the center of the courtyard was a man in his enameled plate armor. From the ornate battle gear he wore, he had obviously been a nobleman and probably the master of this castle. Now the only vassals he would feed would be the flies, the defense he would lend would be to the maggots crawling over his corpse. He sprawled across a man outfitted in metal plate armor that looked like the scales of a serpent. The nobleman on top had lost his head at the instant he had plunged a dagger in the eye of the bearded barbarian beneath. Something called me to them. The Fog, I think, murmuring to me in voices never fully heard. My feet squelched in the bloody soil as I moved him aside to finally reveal a familiar sight.

Its design ambushed me, fitting into a hole in the Fog where it once belonged. The elegant blade was a touch too long for inexpert use by one hand, and it flared three quarters up the length to provide extra heft for the strike. The weapon was more black than blue, as if corroded or stained by soot, but it terminated in a beautifully ornate handle. It was an angelic, silver-plated, ghostly figure, ominously hooded with gold-plated wings that were spread to make the crosspiece. The feet were lost in the robe that blended into the worn ebon-wood that sandwiched the ten inch hilt. Set into the Phantom Angel, over the chest and in pommel, were heart-cut cats eye gemstones. They were from the far west, deep in the barbarian lands. I could tell because they were blue, not amber. Within a second I had determined the exact price such a stone would fetch.

Who would know that? I shook my head again and nearly passed out...again.

I thought we agreed you'd stop doing that? I swallowed more bile.

So we did.

A grave silence settled inside me as I contemplated perhaps I had been an attacker here, not one of the defenders. I felt my face, which was just beginning to show growth; I normally eschewed a beard. That weighed the odds in the direction of me as an Easterner, a Kingsman. My head, however, was more inhuman than civilized or barbaric. The left side of my skull was hugely out of proportion. It felt spongy, springy, as if my scalp had been cut open and a half-full leather bag of water slipped between skull and skin. Of course touching it made the world decide to swirl as if The Mad Painter of the Universe had just dipped his canvas in solvent, making the colors run into a kaleidoscope of insane visions.

I could say I sat down and waited for the visions to pass, but then you'd have to believe that I sit on my back, involuntarily, very fast, and completely unconscious, but that would also be a lie...or four.

I opened my eyes again to dusk. Wasn't it just noon? My skin was crawling with sand. I moved to brush it off and the sky above me disappeared in a pestilent cloud full of thousands of tiny wings and sharp feet. The flies flew to join their comrades that had come to feast, carpeting the dead like a living funeral shroud, covering bodies like dead petals shed by a field of corrupted flowers.

It was painfully obvious, perhaps agonizingly obvious, that my deformation was due to a severe head injury. I had survived the onslaught, but my continued state of living was by no means certain. Clumsily, vaguely, I gathered the black-bladed bastard sword to my breast like a sleepy child with a favored toy and crawled across the rotting bodies to the keep. Flies erupted on all sides of me and horrible, smelling fluids covered my entire front as I made progress as I could, on my belly one hand length at a time. I struggled up each stair in turn, and almost passed out as I had to throw a bruised shoulder against the door.

I don't remember much except a great table set for a banquet, with most of the food tossed on the floor. Someone had made off with the cutlery. I grasped a full clay flagon of warm, watered wine. I downed it, feeling drunken, and drowned flies slipped down my gullet. The world blurred again and I felt like I was looking at the table through a long tunnel, with swirling darkness and stars on all sides. Gravity shifted and I sprawled backward on the cold stones, sword clattering with an obscenely musical tune. My head grew, or maybe the skin compressed, pressure building in waves that punished me. Right Hand cast out, and found a thin bed of straw held together by a coarse, thin blanket.

The Fog whispered that I have slept in worse places, though I don't remember. Then a mocking voice jeered, *Not a few minutes ago you were sleeping in a field of corpses!*

My last thought was that I must be a mighty hero to have survived so far. I had enough strength to crawl fully onto the pallet of straw before the pain became all encompassing. That's when the Fog gave up a chuckle and a dark memory of a bent, toothless man. He was saying in a uniquely carcinogenic voice: "Fate cares not if you be a hero, or a fool. She is cruel, or kind, all the same."

When I awoke, my head hurt less; the rest of me hurt more. It gave me the feeling that whatever my name was, it should end in "The Walking Bruise". I was once again in the company of the dead, but at least here they were orderly dead. The empty space I had found was flanked by others like it, hastily constructed beds of blankets over straw beneath dead soldiers.

They had probably been wounded in the assault and brought into the keep for medical treatment. It had proved to be an optimistically futile gesture. The attackers had swept through here while I lay unconscious outside and dispatched the wounded with typical, barbaric zeal. A woman in the robes of a healer was pinned to a wooden ceiling beam by a rusty spear. She hung, a tortured doll, face contorted in a never ending scream. Like a grisly fountain, her blood had coursed down the shaft to pool onto the floor. Whatever peace and mercy she had aspired to in life; she had been denied in death. I dissected the strike, saw where she was wounded, and knew in my heart that she had not died quickly. I wonder if she knew it could have been worse, much worse.

Maybe it had been.

With that cheerful thought, I picked myself up off the pallet when something struck me. *What am I wearing?* Pasted to my body with old sweat was a scarred, boiled leather breastplate with matching vambracers and shoulder cops. All of them were edged in iron and drenched in dried, stinking bodily fluids. Light, fast, enough to turn aside a glancing blow, it was armor made for speed.

Light or not, it was no wonder I felt like I had run naked in a hailstorm. Sleeping in armor was like fornicating with sheep. Right Hand was thinking independently again, grabbing the short fighting knife it knew I had strapped to one of my soft leather boots. To be honest it surprised the hell out of me as Left and Right cut free the rancid mass of hard leather. I was going to have to scold them if they kept doing things without orders. In seconds I felt free, light, like I could breathe for the first time since...

The Fog was silent.

Damn it! What I did get was the dead-eyed hungry thing that lurked just inside the Void. It glared at me impatiently.

Whoever I was, whatever had happened here, I needed to get moving before more barbarians or scavengers took hold of the courtyard and made escape impossible. I knew pestilence would soon take residence and kill me as sure as a dagger thrust, if slower. I needed food and equipment if I was going to survive. Unfortunately, everything of significant and obvious value had already been raided. However, something inside of me said that men raiding silver would often eschew apples, and apples were worth more to me at this moment than silver.

I levered myself to my feet. I limped through the keep, favoring bruised muscles and strained tendons, but I found it all the same– Death and the Dead. There must be a line a parish long to get into hell just from the number of bodies that littered this home turned to tomb. The noble lady, the stable boy, the servants, the cooks– no one had been spared. Men, women, and children had been crushed, hacked, throttled, or stabbed. One thing became clear; the attack had come without warning, and had probably swept through the gate before the defenders were roused.

Perhaps a guard had been asleep? Treachery from within?

Something inside me began calculating odds.

There was no way to tell, but when I found a body-length mirror in the noble lady's quarters I was sure this was just the spearhead of a deeper raid into the Kingdom. This one thing of vanity was easily the most valuable object in the castle, but they had left it behind, meaning speed was more important than gold. I paced around the lady's room, ignoring the fact that her remains lay in all four corners at the same time. I caught a glimpse of myself in the mirror, and went in for a good long look at the stranger's face inside.

I am a man, a human. When not filled with clotted blood, my hair is thick, wavy, and black, and it travels past my shoulders. That says nobleman.

Who else has time to care and clean long hair but a nobleman?

I nodded at my image. I fought the urge to cut it off and instead found a leather thong and tied it out of the way.

I'm Norian, I think. Way too much parentage had been passed back and forth between the countries during times of strife to be completely certain, but I was dressed as a Kingsman. My eyes are naturally blue, but at that moment, the whites were stained red with blood. The swelling of my skull was going down, at least it looked smaller than it felt yesterday, this morning, or whenever, and I know that is a good sign.

Some may call me handsome someday, though, with a head like an overstuffed sack, that's not likely at the moment.

I'm perhaps late twenties, early thirties, and my jaw blurred by at least a week's worth of flaxen beard growth. My build is muscular, but not an axe man's girth; a swordsman's. My form was pliant yet tough, fast and durable. My arms, chest, and back are like stone, likely from years swinging pieces of tempered steel.

So where is your tempered steel now, hero? A shiver danced up and down my spine like a shaving razor carved of ice. I glanced back at the mirror. A short haired man stared back. Dressed in gray rags, his hands dripped with blood as his eyes burned over an insane rictus grin.

I bolted backwards, over the corpse of the recumbent princess, and toppled over onto the floor. My heart thumped in my ears so fast it seemed only one continuous beat, but as I climbed to my feet, his image had fled from the silvery surface. I bounded down the stairs like a man possessed, my heart crashing in my chest like constant thunder. An inescapable dread filled me as I felt my clothes peeled away to expose me completely to whatever dangers still lurked in this house of flies. My feet hammered the stones like a hailstorm.

I sprang upon the pallet and the Phantom Angel sword was still there, clutching its glittering blue heart. I snatched it up and swung it around in an arc, looking, almost expecting, an attack. But as my hand felt the wire wrapped leather of the hilt, the panic faded and the pain returned. The headache felled me down like a club to the temple. My eyes trailed over the blackened blade in my crimson flecked hands, and it blurred into a moment perfect clarity. As the world strained to fit inside the confines of my broken skull, I saw clearly that the greatest reaction I had gotten from myself was a bottomless pit of dread over my own well being.

This does not speak well of my humanity. And there he was again, sharp and hateful, inside my head. He sneered at me.

Even if a man wishes to lift himself up a sheer cliff face, he can only do it so many times before tumbling back into the abyss. I had to leave this nightmare, and soon, or else the scenes of violence and death would slowly erode my mental walls and I would go mad. As soon as the agony abated, I set to work.

Like a mouse in a tomb, I took from the dead so that I might live. I gathered preserved foodstuffs and basic equipment: blankets, lamp and fuel, tinder, flint, and hatchet. I nearly balked at collecting the clothes of the dead, but the murderer inside me ordered me to be practical. I did manage to find a slight purse of silver coins in the guardhouse. The main vault had been sacked, though, and it would appear that the great evil that had been done here was due to greed and not some darker malice.

There were no horses in the stables, no living ones let me say, but there was a set of saddlebags in which I could store my valuables. I also found ten full barrels of siege-oil in the gatehouse. Apparently the attack had come so fast that it had never been used to pour through the murder-holes and onto the incoming horde. I stared at the abandoned, thigh-sized barrels for long moments.

I have a use for you.

I was generous with it in the main hall, where people getting ready to eat had been summoned to fight for their lives. I bathed the bodies and parts of men alike in the courtyard. Forgotten friend and unknown foe, I made no distinction. When I left, lit torch in hand, I turned once more on the scene of my recent birth. I was made new, without knowledge of myself or the world beyond. I had no choice but to venture forth and begin again until the Fog lifted and let me know what life was truly mine. Not many men get the chance to do what I was about to– start life over. Though, as wombs go, it had a lot of room for improvement. I tossed the torch into the courtyard.

The flames caught cleanly and burned hot, dancing over the bodies like demons devouring their get. But that was unfair; in truth this was a band of warriors getting their well deserved funeral pyre. Once again, the small voice in the back of my head spoke. It said that it really did not matter that they had lost. They had died fighting because they had to. In so doing, they had lessened the burden on the rest of mankind by removing some small part of the evil in it. Then, the sharp, dark stranger swept the voice away with a stroke of his arm. He sat behind my eyes, tapping his foot and waiting for me to get going.

Still not sure what part I had played in this lightning siege, I watched the flames leap into the nameless keep and greedily lick at the lumber of its supports and blacken its stone with greasy soot. I offered a clumsy prayer to both the Gods of War and Death, that the defenders be welcomed. I was frightened that I could not even fool myself into believing it was any more than just another empty gesture.

I knew then that I was a practical man, for I turned from the fires and began along the road. From where, to where, I knew not.

The comforting weight of my weapon pressed on my back where I had tied it with cord, lacking a proper sheath. I tried to remain positive and took stock in my situation. I had food, a little water, a spear to use as a staff, a fine weapon, and sturdy boots. As I cleared the gates I gazed on the mountain range that spread outward in all directions, all directions except ahead. *Well, at least I'm walking downhill.*

The Fog murmured a town should be to the north and west. I would soon need more food and, more urgently, well water not tainted by a soldier's corpse. The Fog assured I could find it. I knew I needed the attentions of an herbalist for my wounds and a bath to stop smelling like a rotting kill. I also knew I would soon have need of a name; men do not trust a wanderer without a name.

Again the Fog lapsed into silence.

…The damned bastard.

Two

The Walk

I GOT my bath in a hot, spring-fed pond only a few hours walk down the dusty road. I had followed a deer in the hopes of getting fresh meat, the thoughts of venison moistening my mouth. Yes, I had preserved meat and hard bread, but eating it is like sleeping in armor, and you know how I feel about sleeping in armor already. Then, as it lined up for a perfect shot, the world shifted behind my eyes and I missed badly with my scavenged spear. The weakened tip shattered against the bole of a tree four full paces from the buck. The deer simply looked at me as calmly as a dwarven lord gazing on a rat and bounded into the brush.

It is safe to say, a master hunter I am not.

There are times where a man can do nothing but laugh at himself, so I did. I sat on the ground, unable to stand as I held my head together with my bare hands, and the pure, joyous sound washed over me and filtered through the trees. I felt small fissures in my fragile self closing. I was vaguely disappointed in myself for having missed, but I comforted myself with the thought that I had recently come close to losing my head.

I don't know who did it, but I hope, at least, that I had returned the favor.

I was to find, however, that my hunt was not altogether unsuccessful.

On the way back to the road, I came upon a deep, secluded pool not thirty paces from my way. Screened by the massive fir trees that populated this area, it was a bastion of comfort and safety. I scooped the steaming water into my mouth, mindless of the slight metallic tint, and gulping until my thirst was slaked. I then filled my canteen. Lastly, giggling like a child, I stripped down to my bare flesh and lowered myself in slowly as men have throughout time, sparing the more sensitive parts of my anatomy as the steaming water seeped into my bones.

My internal calendar was guessing it was early autumn; but the splashes of color that would normally adorn the boughs above were instead a deep, royal green. The floor of this wood was carpeted by rich pine needles that were kind to my feet and had graciously impacted into the mud, creating a soft pillow where I could rest my tender head as the water leeched the gore from my pores. For a few minutes, I could truly let go of everything.

I watched the branches above weave about each other, seeming to cast some ancient faerie spell. My eyes followed them back and forth, up and down, circles within circles, dancing together like the skeletal hands of old lovers...

The world was in color, bolder and richer than I had ever seen. The fir greens reached into me and pulled at me. The sparse clouds above were no mere white, but a brilliant mother of pearl. The water was warm, silken and wet like a virgin's womb. I lifted my head from the coal-black loam to stare at a cloaked angel across from me standing chest deep in the pond.

I had always known he was there.

Something began to scrape my heart with veins of frost as the figure raised his arms. Two hands, carved of aged alabaster, emerged from within the robe woven of webs and night. He held a regal raven in his right hand, carved of ebon wood so pitted and worm-eaten it seemed to wither and crumble in his grasp. His left held the finest sculpture I had ever beheld. Easily ransomed for a king's crown, the gold and ruby blazed in the shape of a lidless eye. Sparkling facets caught fire in the too bright sun, lighting an unending fury within it. He seemed to be offering the statuettes to me, waiting with the patience of one who has no life left to trickle through the hourglass. Power. Secrets. Wealth. I reached for the eye—

I awoke with the night. The water, still steaming, seemed to reach at me with glacier-forged talons. I knew then that I was no soothsayer nor priest, for dreams of this intensity are their stock in trade. I knew, in the deepness of my soul, that I was not the receiver of Great Things. Lastly, I knew that I was determined to leave the dreaming pond many leagues behind me before another hour of the night was upon me.

I exited the water and began pulling on some dead man's clothes. I had left the curiboli armor behind at the keep, all of it a total loss. It had absorbed the worst of the wear and gore, never to be rid of the smells of the death and terror. In my weakened state I should be mourning the loss, but in reality I felt like a rabbit exposed in a wide open field with the shadows of hawks passing overhead. All I wanted was speed.

It took me less time than it took to say it to throw on the heavy breeches and thick linen shirt. I grabbed everything else without packing and took off down the road. Half an hour had gone before I stopped to finish dressing, even with the dark thing in the back of my head haranguing me as a fool. I paused in the shadow of an old evergreen tree and shook off the last of the dream, but I could not escape the feeling that my problems were just beginning.

This was the dress of a servant, a peasant, at odds with my sword and the expensive, rugged boots. It would become a problem when I hit civilization. Someone was going to look at me and figure I was a nobleman in disguise and consider kidnapping me for ransom, or a peasant who had stolen from a noble and stretch my neck. I needed a convincing story to keep myself alive. Again, I probed the Void, the mocking Fog that held me as its hostage.

I cursed as my feet angled down the mountain, trying in vain to put the vision behind me.

I should be happy that the bath had washed away a number of aches and pains, allowing me to move more or less normally. The day was bright and relatively quiet, allowing me to hear any quiet conversation, drawn weapon, or clink of armor. The carpet of needles would disguise any escape I might have to make. I should be buoyant. After all, things were looking up. At least they were looking up in comparison to those I had left behind. After a while, though, the Phantom Angel sword became heavy in my hands and I slung it over my shoulder on the stout leather thong. Then I readjusted it by a fraction.

I stopped, all wraiths and dreams forgotten.

I shifted the sword back to where it originally lay. There, it sat like a nettle on my skin. I shifted it back and indescribably, it was right. I moved it again and it gnawed at my hindbrain. It was like my skin knew where it was supposed to be. I moved it back into its rut. Without looking I sent my hand behind me at its greatest speed, soul screaming at sinew…

…My hand closed about the hilt as if born there.

I again took off the aged sword, its carved angel of death staring eyelessly at me from underneath a metallic cowl just like it did when standing in the pool. The hilt was well worn and the lower folds of the blue-hearted priest almost gone.

Who would not wear such an impressive weapon, given a chance? Perhaps I am a mercenary, but what mercenary carries their sword on their back, where it is too slow to draw?

The spongy bruise that made up the side of my head began to throb as the Fog protested my constant probing. I once again decided that sitting befitted me more than falling, and I breathed deeply as the stabbing, searing hurt made my hands shake and my eyes blur.

I do not know how long I sat there, caught in the hands of some pitiless phantasm. I can say it did ebb, and I cursed the pond as a blighted place. I staggered off into the unknown forest, the quickly lightening saddlebag of supplies bouncing on my chest and back. I crested a hill and my feet stuttered into silence.

Trees carpeted the ground as it echoed down and away into valleys. To the north and south the mountains pushed the clouds out over the hills, into the plains, and across the rest of the world. To the north, a storm brewed in the caldron of the sky. I could see the angry angels of light and sound beginning their symphony inside the black, cottony masses. The setting sun painted the sky in a riot of color, but the encroaching dark came in columns that were legion. The storm crushed the color and light, cutting off the sun from all love and support, forcing it back over the horizon. It was a moment of truth, of beauty, of terrible honesty. I could only watch in wonder at the greatness that made me infinitesimal by comparison, a small light against the black sky.

And then the Dark Thing reached out and snuffed the candle flame with a wave of his hand. Instantly the obvious splendor became banal, drained of color and mass. I stood there for a few heartbeats more, a child with a broken toy, before the Dark Thing motioned for me to get going.

The dead light left an echo of numb cold inside me, and the whole world lost its naked brilliance. A fresh wave of bone crushing force erupted behind my eyes. I blinked away tears, disturbed by their alien feel. I put aside the horrible pounding inside my head and began trundling down the mountain road.

Little did I know my fate was rushing toward me much faster than I could stagger toward it. The storm that night was a city full of wrath and clamor, and a village worth of rain. I was able to weather the short downpour underneath the boughs of a tightly packed family of firs and sleep the night without waking completely soaked. After a sketchy breakfast I set out.

The miles began to blend past me in tones of green accompanied by the hypnotizing scent of pinesap. I imagine that there are those of the bored petty nobles who would have loved to have joined me on my grand, epic quest, whatever that was. The woods were becoming friendlier, the light winning against the darkness the further east I traveled. I couldn't help but feel better the more miles I placed between my arse and the keep. Excepting, of course, at certain times where the Fog twisted and turned inside me, threatening to shatter my skull. Oh, yes, other than the skull-shattering thing, the trip was quite pleasant.

The dirt path I followed joined a well traveled route, large enough to pass two carts abreast. I stopped to probe the earth with my fingers, relishing the ruts, hard packed even after the slight shower. The menace in my mind allowed me a smile. Roads this size, this well traveled, lead only into major cities and this heartened me. The ruts were dug deep, but unused for many weeks. The last of the harvests must have come to market a month or two ago. That would make what I had taken to be the early fall, in reality, a mild early winter.

It did not strike me to wonder how I knew these things after a long, measured look, the knowledge was so easy and certain I never pondered upon it. It wasn't that I supposed that everyone would see what I did; it was that I did it without thinking. I was too busy hoping for a warm bath, a hot meal, and a night with a healer. Should I have pondered it more, I could have saved myself grief later.

There should really be a god of hindsight. Of course, if an inquisitor ever confronts me with these words, I hope he will take into account my grievous head wound. Small chance of that.

In any case, I was an unknown distance from a city that owed it to me and my pouch of coin to be right here, right now. I continued pondering the inadequacies of the unfair and uncaring universe when the ringing clangor of battle rudely interrupted me.

Right Hand snatched the Phantom from my back, the cord looped about the blade parting with minimal effort. It felt warm, good in my hands, like an eager dog looking to hunt. Instantly, fresh winds flew through my head pushing back at the opaque walls. The Fog did not retreat far, just enough to reveal a growling, snarling Animal stalking out of the Void and grabbing hold of the reins.

My heart thumped into my ears, the sword sang against the palms of my hands, and my nostrils flared at the faint reek of blood and bowels. The Thing inside hungered and it heard the sounds of a feast. I flew down the road, booted feet finding every patch of bare dirt, skipping past branches and leaves. Indistinct voices became patterns of words; clanging metal became rapid peals of steel on steel. The Beast reined me in, moving my body from pursuit to a cautious stalk. My eyes caught a trace of movement and I plunged into the brush, slipping past gossiping bushes and into the safety of the wood itself.

Of course I didn't notice any of this either; there were other things on my mind, such as it was.

My progress slowed to a crawl, the sounds of rage and death ahead pulling me on like a current. The Beast chuckled evilly and padded my steps. I was already wounded, no need to rush headlong into 'dead'. Roots reached to trip me as branches clawed at my eyes, but I was a wraith in their midst, untouchable. I reveled in the exultation that came with action. The pain and the uncertainty, the rush swept them up and then began to blaze. It was a furnace, burning away the chaff to leave only behind a red hot Beast inside of me. I reached the edge of the brush and used the tip of my blackened sword to push a branch aside. It was the eyes of an animal that peered from the shadowed bosom of the wild.

Fifteen men were assaulting a coach. Surprisingly, the raiders were not Westerners, though you could never tell the way they butchered their prey. They had swathed their faces in cloths, and fought under no heraldry or banner, but their weapons and voices were definitely Eastern. Three of the ten defenders were already dead, their entrails, brains and other vital internals conspicuously external. My heart turned to steel as a defender was held by two attackers and savagely worried at by a third wielding a short, spiked club. Blood and gore flew in thick gobs as they had at him. The rest were merely being kept at bay by the remaining bandits so no one attacker would have to fight alone.

The Beast approved. The bandits would soon have the defenders picked apart and ravage the coach for anything of value. It was also a little jealous, and it weighed the odds of waiting until the end of the battle and picking off the survivors to keep the carriage for itself. It said, while this plan may have worked while I was healthy, it was a bad gamble with my wounds.

I recognized no one here: not the defending guards in their white and silver, not the pretty noble woman being dragged from the carriage in her silks and velvet, and not the bandits in their varied greens and browns. My heart was not moved by the carnage before me. My soul did not cry out for justice. In fact, the word never occurred to me. The Beast scanned back and forth, and as much as it wanted some action, it saw nothing but great risk against the reward. I turned away. The forest enveloped me with protective arms as I crept off...

A crystal scream, pure and resonant, called out. It slammed into me, billowing the Void and obscuring the Animal within. It caught in my mind and funneled into my chest where it built up power, echo after echo, a crescendo that shattered the hardened fortresses of ice within me.

My soul emerged red and raw, bleeding and screaming like a newborn babe. I trembled and fell, random shocks running through me. A stabbing pain thundered from between my shoulder blades and I fell to my knees, retching bitter bile and half digested cheese. My stomach convulsed and sent a torrent onto the forest turf. My head erupted in blinding misery before a cool rain washed it from behind my eyes. It felt like something inside me had been freed from a prison. It was dark, and it was dangerous, but it was controlled. Were I thrown from a cliff face over the pitiful massacre, I could not have been directed there more quickly, or more inevitably. I was allowed only three breaths to take stock as five defenders fought ten masked men.

My hand tightened upon my sword, then loosened as I took a deep breath.

I knew then that I wasn't a hero because a hero steps forth, challenging all comers with sword in hand. He howls the name of his family, or his lady, or his god. Of course the next thing he does is die messily; but at least he will be forever remembered in song and stage as the man who played his part to type. I, on the other hand, struck from behind, and without warning. My flared blade took the Coward, the one hanging back letting everyone else do the work while avoiding possibility of injury, in the leg. It sheared muscle from its moorings and I felt the grinding slide of the steel across bone seep up my weapon and into my arm. It was a very familiar sensation. He fell backward, mute with shock and instantly pale with blood loss.

Then it was my time to kill again, and my body did it as easily as breathing. The next was sent sprawling as quickly, my sword entering his side just below his ribcage. The blade was held correctly, parallel to the ground, so when he turned in surprise to face me, he neatly slit his own stomach from back to navel. A vicious kick to his chest dislodged the Phantom Angel and sent him sprawling into a pile of his own entrails.

It's always comforting when a partner knows the steps to your favorite dance. This one, however, let loose a scream that would give a moral man nightmares. Two men dead in four heartbeats, but now the rest were aware of me and they turned.

Time seemed to expand like a confectioner's ribbon. I had time to see the woman in the rich, blue dress being released and the bandit that had been holding her come at me on my right side. I had time to see that even the five guards knew– when seven dung-headed murderers turn their back on you, even if it is to face the long-haired wild man who bursts from the bush, YOU KILL THEM. You kill them by striking at their backs, fronts or whatever side he presents to you. You kill them and you do it without flinching. That is how you will live, and they will not.

I could say I valiantly battled all eight to the death (hopefully theirs) but that would be a lie. I backpedaled, putting space in between them and me as the five carriage guards struck, killing three and heavily wounding two. The other three came at me. Then I knew from the whispering of the Fog that there is a special tactic for fighting three armed men– don't, you will die.

I ran at the one who had been dragging the woman from the carriage by her hair, a few paces away from the others. Just a few paces turned three-on-one into one-on-one, for just a single second. As long as a second is all you need, this plan works.

It is a well known fact that once a sword is in motion, it will continue in motion with very little effort lest it meet an obstacle. So as I bolted, I set mine to spinning, my wrist twirling it with minute corrections as I sought a proper strike. It is not a well known fact that idiots who watch stage performers parrying every strike believe every strike should be parried, even those that would never have hit. It was a simple trick to swing far to his right. He was inexperienced enough to try to parry it, and even simpler, to triple the force behind the handle and spin the sword in a screaming vertical arc to take his over-extended sword arm from his body.

That's the nice thing about the arm. There are dozens of nasty creatures of the night that will fight on, mangled and mutilated. But humans, they tend to stop and scream. He did, and thus lost any interest in harming me.

I heard the thump of booted feet behind me and I spun, dropping into a crouch and swinging my weapon low. The Spiked Club bandit had been aiming for my head. Never aim for the head. Aim for the groin. Heads duck, but groins don't usually go anywhere until the very last moment. I was a little high, unable to get the blade to bite into his legs. The shock of the Phantom crashing through his ribs like matchsticks and collapsing his lung removed the embarrassment of my slight misstep. Dead, after all, is dead. The sword slid from his vitals as if oiled, and I was back to en garde before the shock of his instant death had lifted.

Three, as I had dubbed him, was more cautious. He slowed, having seen his two mates felled in seconds, but still confident he could take me while his comrades watched his rear. His comrades happened to be the ones screaming and dying behind him, but I was too busy killing him to tell him that.

The guardsmen held back, making them smarter than the hoods they had just watched me dispatch. Entering a fight was always risky because a back swing aimed at an enemy in front can kill a friend behind just as easily. Unfortunately, that meant I would have to kill him alone.

Great Western sagas tell about warriors trading blow after blow, never slacking in their will to win. I know different, thankfully so did my arms. Real men parry because blows that kiss flesh hurt; my only complaint was someone had obviously told him as well. Our blades having met and shaken hands, we circled around to begin our personal war in earnest.

He felt me out, and I him. Cuts and stabs were sidestepped and dodged. He was the inferior with steel. He was the more tired. He had a shorter reach and less powerful weapon with no shield to make up the loss. All the coins tallied in my favor, and staring into my eyes, he saw that I knew it, too. Had he come in quickly like his partner, it would have been quick. Now he would have to wait for me to kill him slowly and safely. He knew his business, attacking quickly and cleanly, not like Mr. Spike Club– too eager to kill to live. I could not count the number of inbred bastards who had rushed in to end their life on my blade, too dumb to realize—

WHAT?

His steel slid into my vitals like a firebrand pushed into my belly. I felt wet things once attached slide away from one another in ways that cannot be described. The Fog had betrayed me, letting an image flit past when most I needed clarity. He began to retreat, whirling his blade in a flourish, savoring a victory that was not won.

"I'm still alive, you dog fondler." I lashed out, again and again, a hail of blows like the rumbles of distant thunder.

"Thomorgon take you," he spat, invoking the name of the god of Death to draw his attention to me.

I growled a far more vile curse, calling upon a God far darker, "Isahd devour you first."

He parried and dodged, but found there was nowhere to go. My life was pouring out of me and I knew it. There is nothing more dangerous than a man who thinks you have just killed him, because he has nothing left to look forward to except having company on the trip to hell.

My blade batted his aside, sending it arcing into the bush, then swept back to his crown, smashing through the thinking part of the bandit until it rang against his bottom jaw. The Phantom stuck, and when he fell backward, I followed. I was mildly embarrassed again to realize I could not find the strength to stand.

I heard the guardsmen surround me and the woman whimpering. I smelled her perfume, a scent of vanilla and lace. I felt the pain become very far away, as if racing off on a fast horse. I heard a clear voice that my mind couldn't be bothered to translate into words. I felt my breath leaving me, bubbling up from within to scrape past the bile in my throat.

"I'm not dead," I said. Then I passed beyond pain.

The Fog was still with me, though. A great bear of a man reached out of it and grabbed a younger me, shaking him like a dog with a rat. " 'Eros die, boy! You've got ta be betta!"

Then, even that was swept away by the sound of beating wings.

THREE

SUPERSTITIONS

I AWOKE, again.

I should have been grateful, really, but I was still "The Walking Bruise". My head felt as if it had been split open several times by a particularly agitated woodcutter, my back ached between the shoulders as if someone had placed a live coal there, and finally there was a little ball of fangs and claws tearing at my insides that virtually guaranteed that I was going to die.

So, no, I was not that grateful.

In fact, it would have been much more kind should I not have opened my eyes ever again. Belly wounds do that to a man. The stomach fluids begin seeping into less resilient organs and dissolve them into pudding and it is neither a quick, nor painless death. Lastly, no chiurgeon in the world can save you.

I felt an intense desire to open my eyes and savor my last few hours of life, though something in the Fog told me to wait. People will speak the truth when they think you can't hear. Then something alive shifted on my chest and my eyes clicked open like a pair of shutters.

He was large and black, his glossy wings folded behind him like a gentleman's cloak. His head turned to spear me with one, bottomless ebony eye. He was a raven.

I heard a cat voice his distress. With a titanic act of will I shifted my head, bringing new heights to the ringing inside my skull, and saw a gray cat with a golden collar cowering in the corner. He watched the raven with eyes that were wide, a tail flared to the width of his own body curled in front like a hedgerow. His head twitched left and right, fruitlessly seeking a more secure hiding place, but always returned to watch the black bird perched on my chest.

Peasants believe that Death itself watches the world though his princes, the ravens. He tallies all the good and evils of life and renders judgment in the end. Then the birds come and eat the sins left behind in the body. If there is only corruption in a man, the ravens will devour him all. Of course the legends are silent on how he favors rooks or crows. Perhaps they are simply vassals, or even milkmaids. Or perhaps it is just a worthless superstition of the gullible created to explain why it's useless to throw rocks at carrion birds. I moved my hand up weakly to shoo the bird away.

Death's Messenger shifted to look at me with his left eye, freezing me in mid motion. True and honest fear reached inside of me with calm, marble hands and plucked from me my pride and disbelief. In its depthless black orb I saw myself captured, twisted and distorted by the curvature of the reflection. Or maybe it was myself that was twisted. I saw him reflected in my eyes, and myself reflected in his, and him reflected in mine, an infinite number of bent simulacrums spiraling into infinity. That is when the tent flap opened.

I had not mentioned the tent?

Well if you had been grievously wounded, then woken with the living symbol of Death itself on your chest, I daresay you would be distracted as well. At this point I could not tell you what was in the tent, other than myself, a cat, and the bird of Death. I could not tear my eyes away even to look at the newcomer that stood, gasping, at the entrance. It seemed like days before a pair of heavily wrinkled hands gently moved the scavenger onto an offered arm.

A voice, soft, and yet rough like a summer rain sifting through sand, spoke. "Great Lord of the Dead, if it is your intention to take this one, please do; I know I could not stop you. My Patron, however, bids that I help this man. I seek not to defy You, only to do as my Mistress commands."

The tent flap opened, spilling undiffused light across the floor. The raven seemed to consider her words, studying her with his far eye while his near one was still stapling me to my cot. Then, entirely without preamble or glorious miracle, he took wing out of the tent and out of my life.

The old woman left behind was wrinkled and plump, her pear shape accentuating her grandmotherly bearing. Her face, staring out after our visitor, was fixed in such a state of rapture I dared not speak. Truth be told, though, I was becoming less impressed with the raven the further away he went. The cat howled again.

The old woman, cowled in a habit of white, turned to expose a red circle inset with a golden flame picked out in thread on her right breast. Against all odds, I had found a healer in the middle of the forest. Far better than any chiurgeon with his scalpels and books, their gifts were near miraculous in making broken men whole. I pasted a charming smile beneath my nose and tuned the perfect level of weakened gratitude into the chords of my voice, "My thanks for my care reverend sister…"

I simply trailed off. Her eyes had latched on to me and her face had gone from rapture to disgust. I had imagined I would have to be a corpse, maggot ridden and cold, before eliciting such a response from a woman, any woman. I tried to smile ingratiatingly, but I don't think I quite succeeded as her countenance only deepened in its righteous fury. The cleric of life and mercy stalked (Stalked!) across the tent to hover far above me like a statue of cold, uncaring Amsar over a gallows.

She knelt down, craning a finger into my face and whispering in a rage-bathed hiss. "Now you listen, blood-shedder! I only care for your body because both my oath to the Goddess Ethryal," like most clerics she spoke the name of a Goddess boldly, "and my oath to my mistress calls me to. The thought sickens me, but I am trapped in between letting Death take you and letting the Justice of Amsar send you to him! Do not take too much comfort; I know your secret, and if you make any move to harm that girl, I will let the guards at you like a pack of wolves!"

As you might have noticed, my friends, I am prodigious in my verbosity. However, this time my mouth failed me. I simply gaped like an air-drowning fish as she rose and turned to the entrance.

I glanced about and saw the Phantom Angel leaning in the southwest corner, near the tent flap and far away from my bed in the north east portion. I knew why too. It would have been an unconscionable insult to deprive a soldier of the weapon he had used to save your life. However, I know the cleric had moved it from my grasp. If it had been in reach this very moment, I would have slain her from behind as I had the brigands.

I didn't know why, but more importantly, she did.

I guess I was still looking like a plate of raw meat that had been dipped in the midden when the princess came in. She stopped in the entry, gazing at my bandage-clothed chest with some amount of flush in her cheeks, as the priestess of peered in over her shoulder like a demon of retribution. I decided to pull the sheets up to cover my partial nakedness. If there was anything I did not need, it was more complications.

"You are well, sir?" Her voice was like crystal, beautiful but fragile. Apparently, being dragged from the coach by her ladyship's hair did not agree with her– and where in the hell did that come from? The venom and callousness simply seethed inside me from some polluted spring.

Silence reigned.

"Sir?"

I had not answered her. That same mental closet filled with almost similar copies of me yawned wide at the edge of the Fog and I desperately shoved an imaginary hand inside. I came out with something that felt gallant, polite, and servile. I put the mental clothes on like a thief donning a dark cloak and spoke, "My apologies Milady, I am still addled. Some dreadful creature took umbrage at the shape of my head and sought to remedy it with a blunt instrument."

A small smile cracked her brittle exterior. At about seventeen years, her hair was long, held up in a beautiful, complex design that almost matched the knot-work patterns of her dress. She had probably never been party to violence or death until now, and the experience did not sit well upon her. "It would seem your blade work was not affected."

"Not to be contrary, Milady, but I would say it suffered immeasurably. I am now dying." My voice cracked because of a jolt of pain from my belly, ruining the carefree tone of my words. It was for the best, though, as the princess was now really concerned. Four princesses beats four clerics in any card game in the Kingdom.

She turned to her cleric, "Nana?"

The old woman's demeanor smoothed to the placid calm of a still pool before the girl had turned to see. No one gets that good at holding back their emotions from their face unless they have to– a lot.

"His condition is severe. His head has been broken along its left side; this is the reason it swells so. The belly wound has pierced his vitals and they are now leaking foul humors into his body to poison him. He has a remarkable strength, but it will not save him. If his wounds were not so severe, I might be able to help, but alas, my talents are not up to this level of mutilation."

Maybe it was just me, friends, but she didn't sound as if it was too grievous a loss for her.

The princess turned to me, almost catching my questing eyes. I could tell you I was questing her body in search of an appropriate cave to place my dragon, but it would be a lie. As much as I hate to admit it, I was marking the position of guards outside from the sound of their talking and judging the chances of my escape. The pavilion was expansive enough to fit a knight and his page, and it was furnished much better. The candelabra next to me would fetch enough to by some health from a local healer, if one could be found, but the Fog did not give me good odds.

"Then I shall help him."

"Your father purchased that potion at a dear cost for your use, not to be wasted on some drifter!"

Her highness was properly scandalized, "Nana! How could you, of all people, deny this man, who has saved me, anything to insure his life?" A silence that weighed tons settled in until the cleric bowed her head, as if in shame. I saw only frustration there instead.

The auburn-haired girl came forward and knelt beside me, her red dress spreading about her like a crimson halo. Dipping two fingers deep into her cleavage, she retrieved a silver vial that was carved in swirling patterns, stoppered, and sealed. She broke the red wax using one manicured nail and uncorked it with the smell of foreign lands, exotic spices, and blood. She leaned in, exposing a valley of pale flesh between her firm breasts as the vial clinked against my teeth. The bottle itself smelled strongly of woman and I felt my blood beginning to stir, but I could not watch her. I could not take my eyes off the cleric, who saw me and feared me.

She could not be as afraid of me as I was.

Lethargy stole over me, seeping in to mix with the Fog, seeming to make it bloom and envelop me whole. I'm not against sleep, in fact I quite enjoy it, but enough was enough. When I wake up, I'm not sleeping for a week.

And as if no time at all had passed, I awoke.

This time there were no birds and no hurting. I was grateful, honestly. The only problem, if it could be said I only had one problem, was that Gelia, priestess of Ethryal, hated me with a passion reserved for blood enemies, rapists, and tax collectors. She would not speak to me when alone, and was cool, unhelpful, yet professional to me when the others happened in. She had sewn the rent in my shirt and tossed it in my face like it was the shroud of a leper. Most of the Ethryalite clerics I have met have been much nicer.

That wasn't strictly true, I can't *actually* remember, but I'm fairly certain. One does not usually get to be a servant of love, life, and healing by threatening the lives of patients.

I donned the shirt and stretched to test my wounds. My balance was perfect, my belly tender but serviceable. Apparently whatever eldritch concoction the Lady had bestowed upon me, it was enough to bring my battered body back into working order. As soon as I was fully clothed, I exited the ivory colored pavilion and found the early morning sun was much weaker than it had been in living memory, which granted for me was two days. Its rays warmed my face, but not enough to take the sting of frost out of the air. My breath made tiny clouds and my cheeks ached as if being stretched too taut.

The oldest living member of the princess' retinue, no great distinction, they were all barely men, was apparently in charge. He was supervising three of the others manhandling a large chest made of oak and iron. It clanked as they jiggled it, making me salivate with thoughts of piles of golden coins. The eldest boy turned to me and I quickly blanked my expression and focused my eyes elsewhere.

He was just shy of twenty years, his face unlined and unscarred. That was one new thing I had discovered about myself was the huge amount of scarring present on my body. Thankfully, that was at least one mystery solved to a near certainly: the scars, combined with my obvious talent to making armed men into corpses, made me a career mercenary, and a very successful one at that from my ornate weapon. Perhaps not all the corpses I left behind belonged to the keep. Perhaps some were my own mercenary company, joining the defenders in a desperate attempt to hold the lost fort. Mercenaries are often bloodless men, bitter realists who murder for pay. Soldiers get cushy jobs. Mercenaries are too poor to be sentimental, at least that's what they'll tell you. That would go far and explain much– like my lack of reaction at the horror in the courtyard. I had probably seen such many times before, and just not remembered that I had. Those exposed to violence and death eventually become inured to it. All a nice, clean package, eh? A nice, logical train of thought. I couldn't have been more wrong. Well, I supposed I could; I have a significant talent for being wrong.

"Ho, Friend! I am Theodemar, guardian of the lady Aelia. I would know the name of our savior." Theodemar's beardless cheeks were as red as mine as they stretched into a guileless grin.

I quickly donned the friendly mental costume.

"So would I, Theodemar." I flashed a smile, a hollow one carefully crafted to betray both embarrassment and a sociable demeanor, neither of which I was feeling. In fact I was feeling...

Nothing. Not a thing.

A thrill ran down my spine as I looked at the guardsmen gathering around the dying fire from their appointed tasks of breaking camp. They were just empty bags of blood and muscle, some rated as higher threats than others, but none seemed like people. None were quite real to me. Opportunities and threats–that was all.

Thomorgon's Gates, what kind of man am I? Theodemar chuckled and was about to speak when out of the pavilion to my left exited the noble lady. The guardsmen bowed, as did I, though a moment late and much more uncomfortably. I hoped she would take my stiffness as a result of the now healed belly wound, but I knew it was because the Fog rankled and made the motion jerky.

A slight smile graced her heart-shaped face. That could be very good, or very bad. "My dear savior, I expect that your tale would be some entertainment while we prepare to move on to Carolaughan."

The guardsmen-as-servants took the hint and scrambled back to their work, though none found anything out of earshot that required their attention. Gelia exited the tent in which I had rested and entered the princesses own, exiting a moment later with a folding chair. "I am Aelia, daughter of Duke Robert Llewellyn. It would seem," her smile took on a cleaner edge, "I am in your debt Master...?"

The priestess put the chair down behind the princess, who sat upon it without looking. The display of noble efficiency made my teeth itch, though to say I knew why would be a lie. I cleared my throat, "I am truly not sure, milady. I..."

Her eyes were the color of fresh heather, like a tranquil river for they too ran with a hidden strength. My mouth was open, and the truth began to emerge. She leaned forward, her slightly-too-big nose melding with the rest of her face's perfection to put me at ease. She was not an elf, seemingly carved from marble by expert hands, and was all the more human for it. As I felt the story spill from me, her eyes twinkled knowingly. I suddenly felt exposed, like a man who stops with one foot carelessly hovering over a previously unseen abyss.

Without causing a single eye to bat or muscle in my face to ripple, walls of steel and stone slammed shut within me. Immediately I began sifting the story, leaving out my dream at the pond, the Animal that had overtaken me in the woods, the way I almost did not help her, how her cleric had treated me, and my odd detachment from other people. Once again, she was a threat– and I had to grudgingly admit an opportunity.

Her body was sheathed in silver velvet, trimmed in white rabbit fur. A cloak of heavy black wool with a rich platinum trim further armored her from the cold. Her jade earrings were simple and understated but worth more than their weight in gold. Only a yellowed cameo hung between the curvature of her thickly covered breasts, winking in a silver setting that subtly whispered of lineage and money. At last, I finished and my eyes rose to meet hers. "It was then I heard your scream, and was compelled to help."

She raised a dark brow. "You are mistaken my dear man; I would not scream and give the ruffians such satisfaction." Her spine stiffened and her face bore a certain resolution reserved for the rich and ignorant. "It was Gelia who screamed in fear of my safety."

The cleric met my gaze, and her stern face clouded for a moment. Her pride was not injured by the revelation, but something about the account reached into her and twisted. She dismissed my story as a complete fabrication in mere seconds and her face became placid once again. Her mistress continued. "It is grave news you bring. The man you described could only be Sir Walden, Marshal of the Northern Ridge. He was adept at holding back the barbarians within the dark pines of those mountains. His death and the loss of his stronghold may prove disastrous. We must make haste to Carolaughan so the King and the surrounding nobles might be alerted."

I had time to be properly shocked. *I've been wandering around alone on the Northern Ridge? I'm lucky to be alive!* Every society has outcasts, even barbarians. The cruel, heartless men of the north and the bloodthirsty, vicious men of the west tended to force their incorrigibles into the Northern Ridge mountains in the same way a man may place a bloody axe in a closet against a future need. The peaceful journey had been a masquerade; I was safer now than I had been since I had first awakened in the keep.

Her face made it clear she was worrying at the problem in her mind, and seemed genuinely concerned. So, the almost-beauty was not only a woman of breeding, but practical, "I can say that Walden was known for hiring mercenaries and scouts of the finest quality. He had a great treasury in the castle to pay them and always hired the best for high wages. You, it would seem, would fit his qualifications as a master-at-arms." She turned to her nanny. "Gelia, would a head injury such as his have caused such a loss of memory even after his healing?"

Gelia's eyes pierced me, tried to read me even through my Fog to see my innermost being. *Good luck, Grandma.* Her face screwed up as an inner battle against some conflicting judgments warred. I was startled to find my hand creeping toward the hilt of my sword; I had not even realized I had brought it with me from the tent. *Apparently the Fog knows me better than I do, no surprise there.*

"Yes, if he is speaking the truth, he may never retrieve his recollections in any sensible manner."

I felt like cursing and cheering at the same time. She could have poisoned my relationship with the Lady, but did not by opting for the truth. Then again, if she spoke honestly, I might never fully realize who I am. My face, of its own accord, portrayed picture-perfect resigned determination. Theodemar came forward from helping harness the horses to the carriage and the Lady nodded for him to speak. "Mistress, at our present strength, perhaps an extra sword would not go unneeded if Walden and his fortress have indeed fallen."

She set those sparkling green eyes upon me, "Well, swordsman?"

"What waits for you in Carolaughan?" I asked.

"My father has sent me to barter with a Dwarvish mining clan for iron." The shock must have been readily apparent on my face, for she laughed at me. My estimation of her had already been thrown heavier into both the threat and opportunity scales. Sending a girl to barter in a far town spoke volumes of her talents in statecraft. This woman would not be easy to...

What? What was I planning to do?

"Of course milady, I would be honored to ensure the safety of such a remarkable woman as yourself." Well, I am apparently planning to protect a very intelligent and resourceful young woman with a gaggle of beardless youths in tow.

I knew I was heading for trouble because she smiled warmly at me. It was an honest smile, one that comes from the deepest part of the soul and could make any face shine like a heavenly figure. Somehow, that alone was worth it, and that fleeting second of sentimentalism felt alien. The warmth dissolved under the withering gaze from Gelia's pale, gray eyes, rekindled when Her Ladyship paid me a fist full of gold crowns, up front, for my work.

History has shown that money is a salve unto itself for any malady of the troubled mind.

FOUR

VULNERABILITY

WELL, my string of good luck was holding; the Lady Aelia was quite taken with me now that my head did not look like it was distended by generations of diligent inbreeding. I was quickly being looked to as her personal guard, something between a swordsman and a whirlwind composed of razors. I just had to ignore the glowering old woman over her shoulder.

Perhaps it was as simple as that. I did slay several men before Gelia's eyes with almost festive zeal and no compunctions. Such a man as that may not win any smiles from a Cleric of Love and Mercy, even if hers were the goiter pulled away from the knife. Within the depths of the Fog, mocking voices told me it wasn't that I had done it, but that I enjoyed it, that bothered the nanny nun. In seconds of solitude I turned over those joyously brutal moments of mayhem, trying to dismiss the disturbing feelings of exultation, but such doubts were easy to push back with Aelia and the boys hailing me as a hero.

The rest of the camp was broken down easily and packed efficiently, making it obvious that the soldiers were much better servants than swordsmen. Sad for me, because it soon became clear that my job was not merely ornamental. While I didn't have to help them dig the graves for Aelia's fallen guardians or string up the bandit corpses to act as a warning to others, I did have to walk alongside the carriage with the other guardsmen. It was so laden with camp gear that, even though pulled by a pair of magnificent geldings, it could only crawl on its round, wooden legs. Massive and obedient, their burden rattled down the heavily rutted road mile after mile until about an hour after midday.

We had left behind the high pine road and come down into the lower slopes of the Northern Ridge Mountains, into the forested northern bosom of the Kingdom. The trees here were exploding in cold flames, leaves of orange, yellow, and red shushing the wind dryly. It was peaceful like old age, life winding down as the growing season breathed its last.

I caught the shadow of a tall building thorough the trees and I waved the boys back as I readied the Phantom Angel. I crept forward alone, but my caution seemed unnecessary. A charming spring spouted from the native rock of the hillside, and at some elder time had been walled up into a beautiful, flowering pool. What interested me, however, was the blackened skeleton of a large building.

It had been sizable, with the shadows of burns along the ground marking the graves of a wooden defensive wall and stable. What was most telling were not the piles of charcoal or shards of burnt wood, but the green plants that grew through the carnage. I stood up and waved the entourage forward. I idly climbed over the cracked pile of stones that once made the foundation and lower wall to the building and poked at the dirt.

Something was speaking to me here, amidst the fledgling saplings and resurrecting ground cover. Despite the certainty of renewed life, the echoes of devastation stripped away layers of calluses from my soul. I smelled the sour ghost of old smoke. I heard a child crying.

I dipped my hands into the water to splash the strange ghosts from my head, but the face in the water was not mine. Short bristles of hair sprouted from his head. His eyes perched on hollow cheeks like monuments to madness. His smile was not that of a lover or a friend, he was an animal baring his teeth in preparation for battle. He reached for me. I recoiled, feet churning the earth.

"Is it recent?"

I looked back at the water, but the short haired man was not there. I shook off the feeling of being hunted and focused on what I knew was real. I want to say I heard the boy coming, chinking in his chainmail like an elephant made of links, but it would be a lie. Uncertain emotions wilted inside of me, frozen and shattered by the dark thing in the Fog. I clenched my fist, but squeezed the resentment out of my voice as I stood and turned, "No, Theodemar."

The guardsman's eager young face peered past the fallen forest of black beams, "From the Reunification War, then?"

"No, Theodemar." I could not stifle a sigh as I picked my way out of the wreckage, "This happened only two years ago, four at most."

I pointed my boots back toward the pool when Theodemar caught up with me, jingling discordantly, "How can you tell?"

I worked the knots out of my jaw, desperately trying to keep my voice light and easy going, "The plants were growing through the ash. There were a few saplings, less than an inch wide and hip height."

Theodemar the walking chime came to a complete stop, turned back to look backwards, and then caught up to me as I palmed water out of the pool to my mouth. "Sir, sir? How did you know... I mean, I understand how you know, but how did you see...? What I mean to say is, why did you notice that?"

I stubbornly brought another clear handful of water to my face, but inside I saw a tadpole trying to find a way out. I dropped the water as my stomach turned. "I don't know."

Gelia walked up to the well, a silver decanter held in her wrinkled fists like a weapon. Her face was set in an expression of cold stone, "The mistress commands a word."

Commands? I swallowed a growl and folded my grimace into a smile, "Of course, good priestess."

Of course she commands a word; she can theoretically command anything she wants. I comforted myself with the idea that other than the few boys, she was in charge of a nun, two horses and a cat. Any noble could command the wind, but unless they parted their legs and made it themselves, it did them little good. Those thoughts sustained my temper as I made my way to the carriage window. My only source of annoyance now was that Theodemar decided to follow at my side like a puppy in chain armor.

"Sir?" Lady Aelia pushed back the curtains, lips pursed in mid thought. "You know, you are going to have to come up with something to call you except for 'swordsman', 'sir', or 'you, there'."

I bowed slightly, "I will endeavor to pick out something appropriate, Lady."

"Very good." Her eyes probed my cherubic features, having caught a whiff of sarcasm and seeking out the source, proving again she was more perceptive than I would have guessed. "I watched you range bravely ahead approaching the ruin. It seems to me a fine idea. You should take one of the guards and keep watch ahead in case of more banditry."

I smiled sweetly, "Of course, good Lady."

She matched my expression, and I wondered if there was also a mirrored hostility beneath it. "Carry on, then."

I bowed and backed off from the carriage, feeling my insides twist a bit. I walked out back to the road and looked down the curving expanse, cursing my bad luck. It was one thing to walk while others got to ride, it was another to be forced to walk twice the distance, ranging back and forth to sweep for trouble. Not to mention winding up the first one into the bear trap if there was an ambush. I considered just going off into the woods and leaving them completely. To my north and west were the Ridge Mountains. To the east was Sorrow Woods, a place not named because of the light and airy denizens of the dark hollows and swampy valleys. The only convenient way was southward. In that case, I might as well tag along.

Again, within seconds there was the telltale sound of a thousand fat coin purses jingling an invitation to robbery and murder.. I took a deep breath to steady myself. Theodemar was the nearest thing the Lady Aelia had to a guard captain, or a lieutenant, or a sergeant. Considering their ages, they were barely footmen. He was the first to enter Aelia's service amongst his peers, and so now leadership fell to him. At least it should have.

"Are we ready to forge ahead, Hero?"

Heat pulsed behind my eyes, and I could not completely remove the wasps from my voice, "First, never call me that again, second, we are not ready, third, we are not going; I am going. You stay with the carriage."

Theodemar set his face into a picture perfect expression of young,(read: ignorant) determination. "Pardon, Sir, but I am commanded to come with you. The Lady believes that four eyes will see more than two."

I turned to face the boy, and it struck me that his cheeks were flushed, the rest of his face pale, and it was nowhere near cold enough for his hands to be trembling so much. The kid didn't want to do this any more than I did, but for different reasons. Despite my best efforts, I softened to him, shaking my head in resignation. "Very well. Go and rid yourself of that chainmail, the shield, and spear. If you have some bows, we should take them."

He nodded and headed off like a good little soldier. I sighed again. I appreciated his ability to snap to orders without complaint, but it just didn't seem right. My only qualification for giving out orders to Aelia's guards was appearing from nowhere and swinging a sword with just enough skill to outlive my opponents. He should be questioning me, pushing me, requiring more from me than simply an order. Then again, the kid was a guard. I get the vague certainty at the base of my skull that all nobles have a skeleton or two in the closet. Or in the dungeon. Occasionally one or two in a tower somewhere. And there's always a legion or three more buried all over the countryside. He was probably discouraged from asking too many questions lest he become one of them.

I busied myself tying the Phantom Angel to my back with a thong, cursing the lack of a proper sheath, but it wasn't discomfort or inconvenience that was fouling my mood. The man from the spring had been the same lunatic in the mirror in the keep. He was following me, or at least the delusion was.

Theo trotted back without his armor or livery. I swear, inside his gear he looked like a guard; out of it he was an off duty guard. He couldn't have been on the job for longer than a year, but it had already worked itself into his very bones.

"We are in luck. We brought these," He handed over a crossbow and a bundle of quarrels, "for foraging."

And he was right. A war grade crossbow could put a quarrel half through a horse or a tree, and could core an unarmored man without slowing down. Even the heaviest of plate armor would become an expensive tomb as the iron head crumpled in the breastplate, slowly suffocating the knight while pinning his lungs to his backbone. What I had in my hands was no toy, but it wouldn't do if we came up against...

Why is he staring at me? I opened my mouth and the words popped out, "Why are you staring at me?"

Theo jumped, and then smiled self-consciously, "You really look like you know what you are doing."

I grunted and went back to the bow, testing the strength of the catch on the trigger bar, examining the twist on the string for fraying, and giving the groove an eye for straightness.

"Can you teach me what you are doing?"

I stopped, staring at him as dozens of replies flicked behind my eyes, each one of varying levels of nasty. I was going through them the way a lover picks rare flowers out of rich soil, the only question was how much scorn I could get away with, and how badly I needed his help in the future. My stomach fell as some part of me took a step back and judged myself the way I was now judging him.

The boy's brow wrinkled and his smile became frightened and fragile as he retreated a bit. "Is it something I said?"

And that was when I realized I was still staring at him like he was a roach beneath my falling foot. Seventeen excuses fluttered inside my head, and I settled on the simplest. I faked a gargantuan sneeze, sniffled a bit and blinked my eyes furiously, smiling like a man caught behind a bush with his trousers down. "My apologies. That one was building for a whole day."

His expression said, *Oh!*, and he bobbed his head knowingly. I turned toward the road and waved him on, a smile of friendly sincerity hurriedly slapped on my face. I hooked the quiver of bolts onto my belt, sneering inside that it did not have a ring to be tied down to my thigh. If I had to run it would flop all over the place.

"I might be able to show you a few things, but since I'm not sure what I know, it's going to be a little unwieldy. I suppose you could ask questions and I'll answer what I can."

The young guard watched me cock the bow, fit a bolt into the center groove, and set the light steel spring arm that kept the stubby arrow from falling off. He began to do the same, grunting with surprise at how difficult it was. "What's it like to live without your memory?"

It's like stumbling through a dark room that is carpeted in broken glass and furnished in whetted daggers I chuckled falsely. "I don't remember normal, so I couldn't say."

"Oh, well..." Theodemar blushed, feeling as stupid as he should. "So what were you looking at the crossbow for?"

I stifled an angry retort, "I'm not sure what you mean. What's wrong with your crossbow?"

He glanced at the weapon in his hands before looking at me askance. "Nothing."

"How do you know that if you don't examine it?" I shrugged and pointed down the road, reminding him to keep his eyes in a useful direction. "List all the things that can go wrong with a crossbow." I didn't bother to take the sting out of my voice. "No! Keep your eyes cast outward. We are out here looking out for an ambush, so keep looking for an ambush. While you do that, tell me what can break on a crossbow."

Theodemar flushed again, breathing heavily as he swallowed apologies and protests, "The...the...the string could break," He glanced at me and saw me scanning the forest on either side and made like to do the same. "The limbs could be cracked. The string could be frayed. The stock could be chipped..."

I let him wallow in silence for a minute before continuing for him. "The trigger could be bent, or broken inside, or the stay-clip could be loose. Anything wooden can be warped, the sight could be bent, anything metal could have rusted, the whole thing could have been made by a drunkard. Any part of the bow, sword, shield, suit of armor could be broken and cost you your life in the heat of battle."

He nodded and smiled, saying somewhat dismissively, "They have us maintain the equipment."

My eyes, armed with daggers, slid across his throat as he was looking the other way. By the time he felt the cold steel of my irises, I was back to scanning. "And what if the guy you trust to maintain the shared equipment is hung over? What if he's lazy? What if he's been paid off by the other side? Whoever you fight with, or for, you are alone behind your blade. Ultimately, you are responsible for your own survival. Think of anything that can go wrong with every bit of your equipment and check for it."

"And what do I do if it needs replacing?"

"If it can be replaced, replace it. If it can be repaired, repair it. If you have no other choice..." I shrugged and while my brain was complaining that I should getting paid for teaching children, another shard of honesty snuck between my teeth, "...swap it with the equipment of someone you don't like."

Theodemar laughed, a little too loudly, but at least honestly. Then his face fell fast and hard like nighttime in the mountains. "You sound like the Captain."

I doubt that. We walked in silence for another few minutes; even with a casual pace we outdistanced the carriage. Again my mouth worked without me, "What kind of man was he?"

Theodemar's face aged, dark emotion fighting a war on his youth, "He was a decent man, a good and loyal soldier."

I nodded, bringing up a dozen unspoken phrases to lasso the young man and bring him closer to me. Loyalty is a vulnerability. Actually, emotional investment is vulnerability, but loyalty is a vulnerability that is especially easy to exploit. The first step was to make sure he was loyal to me. It would take subtle abuse to break down his self esteem, flattery to forge his new self image out of materials I would provide, shared knowledge to cement a bond and begin to unveil his secrets. I would dissect his personality and build my golem from its remnants. Soon, when push came to shove, he would back me instead of...

Is this the kind of man I am?

Then a crashing, cold wave collided with the Fog inside my head and shattered it into a billion crystal knives. They coalesced into a barbed dagger buried between my shoulder blades. The crossbow flew from my hands and went off harmlessly as it slapped into the dirt, approximately half a second before I joined it.

Theodemar was there. I barely heard him over the roaring of my own blood. "Sir? Sir? Sir?"

It took several minutes before I could breathe, and longer before I could answer. "I don't know. Hurts. Maybe an old wound." I rolled onto my back as the searing, stabbing agony pulsed into weaker and weaker echoes. "Help me up."

Theo did it, but I must have looked like a maggot ridden piece of meat because he screwed up enough courage to ask, "Are you certain?"

"We have a job to do," I said. But those last, handful of seconds had turned bravery into bravado. As I straightened, the last of the pain evaporated into just a horrible memory. Nothing was more important than refusing to look vulnerable. "Besides, I'm feeling better." I picked up the crossbow and scanned the forest, "How long have we been here?"

"About a quarter of an hour."

I would have loved to try to understand what was going on inside my own body, but the only person who could probably tell me was a cleric who would like nothing more than to excommunicate me off the edge of a cliff if she could do it without sin, guilt, or whatever it is religious people fear living with. In any case, sitting here in the middle of the road was helping nothing.

"Then we had better go."

The rest of the afternoon was taken up with creeping ahead, finding a likely ambush site, circling each and every damn one and making sure nobody was planning a party there later, and then rushing back out to get ahead of the caravan again. It was boring, because nothing happened. It was stressful, since at any time something could happen. It was strenuous, because if we weren't sneaking, we were climbing, searching, or running. It was just short of hell. I was dripping in sweat by the time we made it to the crossroads and the typical sign, but Theodemar was completely wrecked.

I hooked a thumb up at the sign, its arms pointing down different roads, "River's Bend or Cornhall?"

"River's Bend is a more direct way to Carolaughan." He nodded at the sign. "You can read?"

I glanced back at the crudely carved out letters, filled with aged and chipped paint. To me it was as plain as day, but until tapped to become an officer, nobody was likely to bother to invest in a footman's education. No point in lying now. "Looks like it."

Theo smiled wryly. "I knew you were an officer."

I faked tired indignation. "Let's hope not. Officers are a pain in the ass."

For just a few moments it was just Theo and I, and while Theo was always Theo, I was feeling like I was being me. My knees felt a little weak. My heart was beating fast. I was forgetting to manipulate him. My hands were moist and shook as I put the bolt back into the slot on cocked bow. I knew I wasn't in love, but the feeling of being exposed and defenseless remained. Can't say I liked it much.

But I did like it a little.

FIVE

BLOOD MERCHANT

THINGS had become a lot easier the closer we got to River's Bend as the natural progression of human settlements has a tendency to demolish handy ambush sites. Constant foraging for building materials and fuel for fires clears out the underbrush and flattens hills. The roads become better maintained and more often traveled. Even this close to Sorrow Wood, the atmosphere was changing from the oppressive throne of the wild to the yoked domestication of arable lands. What sealed the deal was the appearance of rank upon rank of winter rye that marched right up to the edge of the trees. They waved like a sea toward the clumps of buildings that made up the village of River's Bend.

People who grow up in cities believe that all poor families live in squat, thatched roof structures walled in wattle, what everyone else calls woven sticks, and daub, what everyone else calls excrement. It will collapse under the brutal force of an old woman waving a cane and it bursts into flame whenever anyone coughs, but at least it's cheap. The reason people can live in something like this within a few days ride of a city is simple; in case of trouble, they run behind the big, stone walls their liege lord provides. Stone walls are cane-proof and cough-resistant, but they are grossly expensive.

Out in the country, especially in that lovely area between the Northern Ridge Mountains and Sorrow Wood, people are responsible for their own survival. The farmers out here build clan houses, tall, rambling structures that grow bit by bit as children marry and have children of their own. Each clan works wide swaths of land taxed by the lord but defended by the family. The walls are heavy wooden logs, meaning they can still burn, but while they are easier to knock down than stone, they   do provide cover from axes, blades, and arrows.

Only one thing could drive a man to risk his family so far from civilization like this; the law says that the family that etches the farm out of the forest owns it. Landowners, just like nobles, they can pass it on to their children and hire workers. While they are taxed for the privilege, they are relatively free of royal excesses and city blight, at least until a rival family, bandit group, barbarian tribe, or marauding soldiers come along and wipe them out. Then, in exchange for all those years of taxes, the lord moves a family of serfs into the cleared and freshly turned arable land. If the new tenants are lucky, the houses are still standing when they begin slaving away for the distant lord. It's a pretty awful deal all around. Welcome to being a peasant.

From this distance, River's Bend looked like one of the few success stories. Several families had built six three-story farmhouses, equal parts home, barn, and wood stockade. The country folk build their homes like their women: big and blocky. Generations worth of one family name might occupy one of these ugly, square...

My hand arced out and slapped into Theo's chest, stopping him in his tracks and nearly setting off his crossbow. His mouth made a little 'o' and his wide eyes flicked across the irregular rows of rye. He managed to hold off his questions for two whole breaths. At last he whispered, "What? What?"

The trouble was, I didn't know 'what'. I crouched down and he followed suit. We crept forward. Every single second, my eyes flicked left, right, up, and down. There was something... something... We advanced cautiously, but even with our view completely blocked, it was sinking in that we weren't about to stumble in on a harvest celebration.

All these small communities have dogs. They catch rats, they warn of intruders, and in a pinch they even fight in your battles. Mostly they run around like idiots and bark at birds, trees, and passing clouds– except now when they had all decided to stop barking. Even more obvious was the lack of children. Country women are either nursing, pregnant, about to become pregnant, or some combination of the three. Older children work the fields. Younger children work around the house. Infants yell and play. All of them make a great deal of racket, except now when they decided to be quiet little darlings all at once.

I felt like standing up in front of a crowd and announcing my brand new motto: 'If I ever approach a village and I hear no children and no dogs, I will not go in.'

I moved to the side of the road, almost into the field of winter rye, and slowly, raised my hand. Theodemar followed the line made by my outstretched finger. There, far down the road near the gate in the village stockade, the grain was disturbed. Well, I say disturbed, but that is a lie. I mean it was flattened, churned like a few dozen energetic people had burst through there and stormed inside.

That's when I discovered an addendum: 'If I ever approach a village and I hear no children and no dogs, AND there is evidence of an armed attack, then I will not go in under any circumstances.'

I waved Theodemar over and leaned in so close my breath bounced off of his ear. "Just back off slowly. We'll head back down to the crossroads and meet the carriage. We will take the other track."

Theo shook his head and whispered back, far too loudly, "That will take us around the Sorrow Wood. We don't have time before the bidding starts."

Bidding? The lady is supposed to be negotiating a trade deal. Bidding suggests more than just a negotiation. I glanced back down and up the road. "Do you think we can skirt the village?"

As the words cartwheeled past my teeth, Theo looked askance at me and I realized the answer just as he whispered, "The village is called River's Bend. There's only one bridge across and it's in the middle of town."

"Of course." *Stupid, stupid, stupid.*

Of course there would be an unhappy corollary to my motto: 'If I ever approach a village and I hear no children and no dogs, and there is evidence of an armed attack, AND I have some kind of motto that says I should make my way anywhere else, then it is an absolute certainty that I'll have to go inside.'

I shook my head, wondering at what god in heaven or devil in hell was enjoying watching my misery. I quickly came to the decision that one of each were in a tavern called Limbo, having a friendly drink, and laughing at me. "Looks like Barbarians. Hang back ten paces. If you see something, shoot it and then draw your sword. If I run; don't ask, don't yell, just try to keep up."

Theo nodded and rubbed his chest, obviously missing the weight of his chainmail hauberk. I clapped him on the shoulder and screwed my courage to the sticking point.

No, that is a lie.

It would be normal to say I was afraid, but not accurate. I was cautious. I was even apprehensive. I was blindingly aware of every detail, but I was not afraid. I was pretending to be for the sake of Theo, but it was not in me. The Dark Thing, half-hidden by the Fog, was muttering that this was a waste of my time and provided no reward for moderate risk. At least the way in would be easy; I knew the gates would be thrown open for the morning chores in the field. Harvest of this late growing crop would be chilly, it would be quick, and it would involve everybody. We passed the agitated winter rye and I could look down the corridor of trampled plants that led all the way back to the skirts of the forest. The slightly soft soil was torn up by hard boots.

We made the gate without alarm or challenge, but then the smell of rotting meat and pierced bowel wafted across our position. Theo retched far too loudly. Inside me, icy cold walls sprang up, transparently separating me from the rest of the world. I was certain that I could tell you everything we would find long before I placed one foot past the gate doors. I wasn't disappointed.

Historic homes became places of ambush, cover, and possible wealth. Rotting animal carcasses were only sources for disease. Bodies of the young, old, and everyone in between were little more than cause for caution lest I slip in a fluid or trip on a limb. None of it mattered to me, personally, which meant none of it mattered at all.

Theo tried to shuffle his features into unmoved professionalism, but his young eyes failed him. "They are all dead."

I shot him a cold glance, but he didn't notice. It was for the best, because to my eyes he was transformed into an expendable resource. In fact, the emotional color was drained from everything in the village and I don't know how my face would have read.

I waved the boy guardsman to a stop in the middle of the compound, unmindful of the decapitated old woman next to a spilled wicker basket of half shelled beans. I hissed at Theo, reminding him to quit staring at the body and keep his eyes cast outward. I carefully set the loaded crossbow down in the pile of beans to keep it from going off, and then unlimbered the Phantom Angel. A quick tug parted the thong and I moved across the path carved from the gate, along the front of the houses, and over to the stone bridge.

I set foot on the span. It was wide enough to pass a carriage, made of stones twice the height and width of a man. The blackened cracks and crevices were so tightly fit, not even a razor could be slipped between them. Idly, the back of my head whispered, *Dwarves built this.* I reached the apex, twenty paces from either bank. I could clearly see the cold fire pit that had been dug in the center of the far square. Some kind of beast of burden had been slaughtered and roasted here for the barbarian celebration. Only the Gods knew how many survivors there had been to act as entertainment. All I could see was even the fire was not smoking, which put us over a day behind. The cold would keep the insects away, but there should definitely be scavengers here by now.

Then the wind shifted.

Out here, just away from the bodies, I could smell something that clawed at the back of my mind. It was oily, mossy, and rotten, like a body buried inside the hollow corpse of an old oak tree. The claws grew in size, scraping down my spine as fear, real fear, reached out of the Fog and filled me. Everything inside of me was screaming for me to run, to hide, but the friction of it ignited a raw, rude flame inside my chest. The terror was funneled into hate, a consuming abhorrence of all things.

I heard a stifled yelp and spun around. Theo raised his crossbow at the hint of movement and fired. Even hurried, the boy's aim was true and I heard the bolt slap into meat. A pig, until now spared from the slaughter, staggered drunkenly out into the road. It seemed to breathe heavily for a minute, unsure of what was happening, bolt sticking out of it and jittering in the air.

Then it started screaming.

The sound filled up the village, echoing from wall to wall as a traitorous tattletale. Theodemar turned his guilt stricken face toward me but before he said a word his eyes flew wide. Without hesitation, I jumped towards him and spun around, the Phantom Angel singing in a deadly arc. With a forge of fury exploding in every muscle I swung and hit a weapon, in reality little more than a sharpened rusty bar of metal. Using both hands, I circled my blade over my head and hit it again, and again, each hit moving it further and further from in front of the owner. Finally, the rusty bar jerked just enough out of the way and the Angel bit flesh deeply, blood fountaining out in a black fan from an ugly gray throat.

The thing that collapsed at my feet could only be mistaken for human in a pitch black room. Three more had gained the far side of the bridge and clawed feet were pounding onto the stone with fierce anticipation. Their skin was gray and knobby, and it was draped in loose folds despite the obvious power inside of their thick, stunted limbs. Their faces were things of horror, heads melding almost completely into their chests, joined at a massive jaw line that even now opened to expose numerous rows of razor sharp teeth. They yawned wider and wider, spittle flying in gobbets as they gave inhuman voice to alien battle cries. Their mouths were toothed pits large enough to swallow a thigh whole. Their massive manes of white hair were slicked back and stained black with old blood. It dripped down onto crude white leather clothing. They were things of nightmare, and men tried to tame them by giving them names: goblins, orcs, or redcaps, but nothing could capture the truly inhuman nature of these scavengers. Now they had come for me. Deep inside I always knew they would.

Everything became crystal clear as fear continued to fuel my rage. Their cries were cobbled together of the death rattles of a hundred corpses, backed by the screams of a thousand mourning women. My answer was a roar of all life and the living screaming at death itself. My scalp suddenly felt too tight for my skull. I cradled the Angel in my hands, letting the cold metal of the Phantom's robes flow into me as they came closer. The Fog released images, smells, thoughts and impressions. In a strange way, I remembered their kind, but I remembered them much taller, much bigger. As I glanced down to their brother, who even now was gurgling messily at my feet, the specter in my brain whispered that they can die, and death was my one, true calling.

I leapt back and then planted my feet in preparation. Redcaps are powerful, far stronger than a man though shorter. Inside my head a foreign flavored voice whispered tantalizingly: *Be the wind, untouchable and supple. Power is only good if you bring it to a target, strength is only worthwhile if it is concentrated.* My hand tightened upon my sword, then loosened as I took a deep breath. Between one heartbeat and the next, I plotted a bladed course through the three of them.

That's when the Beast erupted inside my chest and began the butchery.

The one on my left came straight on as the one to the right moved behind him to avoid the thrashing redcap. The last came more slowly, allowing the others first crack at the dirty work of murdering me. It turned three into one for a brief instant. The first pulled back his heavy sharpened bar in a blow that could cleave me in half from shoulder to hip if I let it.

I did not.

It cocked its cleaver in a four fingered hand, but I sprang forward, diving under the swing even before it was made, slapping the sharp edge of the Angel against the redcap's spine. The thing recoiled as the blade slid along its shoulder, severing vessels and unleashing a torrent of black blood, leaving it dying quickly behind me. No time for congratulations, because my second attacker was already before me and my sword tip was pointing directly away from the thing's heart.

The next foul faerie thing was already starting a double handed overhead chop of his own, but I sprang at it, grappling desperately. Well, to tell the truth, Left grabbed at his wrist, but that nasty bastard Right slammed the pommel of the Angel into the pouchy throat of the second redcap with the full force of our bodies meeting. Though shorter by a head, the redcap's dense weight brought me to a dead stop, but not before I felt the grinding, popping vibrations of its throat muscles collapsing. Its crude weapon slid from nerveless fingers as it tore hard nails into its own throat, fighting for air. I had to gasp myself, but with more success as I brought the beast in a harsh embrace, and moved my sword to its chin. I gripped the damnable thing under the arm and heaved it right, allowing the creature's weight against the blade of the Phantom Angel to sever its own throat.

Yes, it was cold blooded. Yes, it was an act that would horrify anyone looking upon me. At that moment, however, it was just a way to get the corpse out of my way as the last redcap came within striking distance. As the second slumped into a shower of its own juices, I yanked at the Angel and brought it up, ready to impale.

The redcap slung its sword in a circle, leaving me no choice but to lunge forward, mating our chests and making sure the only part of his swing that connected was his arm. The Phantom Angel took the thing low, in the gut, and pierced the faerie effortlessly from front to back. The thing howled, but it did not slow in the slightest.

Remember when I said there were things out in the world that would fight on, even when mutilated and dying? Redcaps are like that, and this is why things stopped going according to plan.

We went down in a tangle of limbs, my sword lodged in the redcap's entrails and his too long to bring to bear while we embraced like lovers. It abandoned its sword and locked both hands on my shoulders, seeking to swallow my face. There seemed to be no neck, and no place safe to jam an arm while it tried to bite whatever part of me it could reach. I heard Theo shout, but the horrible rotting-meat smell of the redcap's open maw enveloped my entire world.

It bit once, twice, again, and again, catching nothing but air but nearing frenzy with the anticipation of fresh blood. Left continued to hold him barely at bay using the hilt of the Angel while Right continued to play the heavy offstage. The cap dug its claws in and yanked me closer as Right came back into the light with my boot knife.

I plunged it into the thick mass of arteries I hoped the redcap had hidden in its armpit, took it out with a twist. Hot, sticky blood burned over my fist. Four rows of teeth snapped shut next to my face. I stabbed again. The teeth came even closer, rubbery lips brushing my throat apple as I removed the blade with a twist, aimed the tip of my weapon for the ball joint in the shoulder, and rammed it to the hilt. The thing screamed. The hands loosened. The arms slackened. The mouth snapped again...and again...slower and slower.

I heaved, throwing the creature from me as it trailed thick ribbons of black blood that streamed from a dozen wounds. My boot knife trembled in my hand as I lunged at the redcap. It began to roar, straining not just against me, but the sword buried in its chest and the host of dagger wounds I had bestowed. It was a matter of only a second to guess at the right spot, drive the dagger in deeply into the back of the skull, and remove it with a twist of grinding bone. I smiled obscenely as it died.

Then the moment was stolen from me as Theo yelped again, accompanied by the fading sounds of a dying pig and the distinctive ring of shattering steel. Momentarily I considered letting him die. I had a dozen aching muscle groups, stinging scratches across my back, and a strained finger that was starting to throb insistently. He cried out again and something whispered that it would be a shame to waste all that effort I had spent getting him to worship me. I hawked a gobbet of phlegm on the head of one of the bleeding bodies, scooped up the Phantom Angel and ran to his rescue.

Theo stood on the north bank of the village, his sword

truncated by the strike of a redcap's weapon. The creature pressed its advantage, swinging a stolen axe wildly. The boy dodged back and forth as his enemy cleft posts, sliced through a tree limb, shattered a sapling, and threw clods of soil into the air. Every strike seemed to shake the entire world, and splinters of wood, blades of grass, and specks of dirt hung suspended by fear and adrenaline in the air.

Veiny, powerful muscles even made the air cry as the dull wood axe split it into invisible pieces. The boy ducked and weaved between the paths of the steel death warrant, but he wasn't looking into the future, simply captured in every second for fear it was his last. It would be his undoing.

The 'cap backed him to the log palisade of River's Bend and struck to his left, burying the axe deeply in the wood. Theo stared at the dull metal head, pondering his near death for a second too long, and the redcap gathered the boy into its disgustingly strong grip. One hand on either one of his upper arms, the faerie drew him forward and roared like a lion into his face, then leaned back with opened mouth preparing to bite. The thing leaned back, back, back…

It would be his undoing, *but not today*.

A flash of blackened steel severed one of the redcap's wart strewn arms.

Theo scrambled on his rear along the fence away from the thing trying to eat him. His wide eyes took in my merciless hand twirled into the redcap's bloody mane, pulling back with all my might. I doubt he noticed the equally important knee planted in the small of the redcap's back, which goes to show my genius largely goes unappreciated except by my victims. And who cares about impressing them? Who are they going to tell?

He watched as the Phantom Angel rose and fell again as the other arm came up to strike at me. Another flood of black blood, another meaty thump as the limb struck the ground. Theo screamed as the fairy-thing continued to thrash and bite at every bit of nothing it could reach. I brought it around and kicked it to the side, sending it sprawling onto a chopping block. It flailed momentarily, trying to find purchase with the stumps of arms, before there was another dark flash and I used the Phantom to pin it, face down, to the wood. Still it raved, still it screamed, as I moved heavily away and sat down on the grass, back against a nude apple tree.

I flexed my aching hands and arms, wiped off a thread of black blood that had splashed across my face, and sighed. I heard Theodemar's rapid breathing to my right, and a quick glance told me he was close to fainting.

I had to yell to be heard, "Are you hurt?"

"Aren't you going to finish it?"

My head turned left and right, but I honestly couldn't tell what the hell he was talking about. "I said, are you hurt?"

"No!" But I didn't think he was answering my question. He pressed both palms against his ears and sought to squeeze the unearthly screams of the dark fey I had unceremoniously stapled to the axe-scarred block. "Can't you make it stop?"

There was something desperate, pleading in his voice, and it moved a rare iota of pity inside of me. This poor boy was a month's travel from home, further than he had ever been from the only place he had ever felt safe. Wherever the Lady Aelia's domain lay, it was painfully obvious he had never so much as touched a riot, uprising, or battle. It must be a very boring place for a castle guard. *Lucky boy.*

I felt an echo from inside when I gazed at the terror evident in his eyes. It took a full minute to yank the axe from the wall, but only a second to turn the bent, nicked head to a more deadly purpose. The axe came to a halt midway through the beast's skull, but it was enough for it to die. The rest of its last scream came out between dead lips like a bladder being squeezed. After two more strikes I was confident enough to yank the Angel from its torso and sit back down. I sat there breathing for what seemed like a long time, just letting the rush of the Beast go, burying the relish with which I had done my business.

Like a wounded animal, Theo crept forward toward the gray lump that used to be his enemy. He touched it, twice, and each time yanked back his hand as if burned. "Wh...what is it?"

"A faerie. A redcap. Battlefield scavenger," I said, levering myself to my feet and heading for the corpse of the beheaded old woman. I tore off part of her dress and used it to clean the ichor from the Angel and my hands before realizing I was covered in the stuff and it had the consistency of snot. I was going to need another bath. "The Barbarians raided this village, killed some people, took some supplies and moved on. The redcaps smelled the carnage and showed up later, looking for food and clothing."

"Food and clothing? They aren't wearing..."

"Theo, don't!" But, of course I wasn't quite fast enough.

He had gotten a good look at the crude, white leather garments. He saw the raw, pink edges, the splotchy patches of blue, and the unmistakable hints of stitched shut eyes, noses, and mouths. He spent several seconds vomiting, and then several more minutes heaving. I grabbed him by the scruff of his neck and dragged him back into the center of the square where the air was marginally clearer. He regained control of his stomach and I sent him back down the road to the carriage, carrying a message urging the Lady to make her way here with all haste.

An hour later the whole group arrived. I already had a pyre started.

The boys again showed their skill as porters, piling the villagers in a large stack spread with kindling while I hung the dead bodies of the fairies over the wall. I hoped the smell of their own dead would ward off any other fell scavengers. To be sure, as the night went on and they seemed to dissolve into bundles of sticks and piles of white curds, no fly, bird, or furred creature took even remote interest in consuming any part of them.

In any case, we could go no further today, and I was eager to have the protection of the palisade. Aelia flat refused to sleep in any of the houses and instead had the boys pitch her tent. Her cat had no such trouble, and wandered into one and came out with a fat mouse. If danger showed up in the night I would have rather had her behind wooden walls than pegged curtains of silk, and I would have argued that point if I thought there was some use.

Worse, the boys had the enraging habit of unpacking the oak and iron treasure chest from the top of the carriage and setting it down in an out of the way spot of the camp. Surely it would take four burly men to make off with it, but I assumed all of the funds for Aelia's mission were inside, and if we lost that, we lost everything. Unfortunately, nobody was asking me what I wanted right now. Instead I made sure the watches were set for the night, and that the pig Theo had shot was well cooked and portioned out. *Shame to waste fresh meat, after all.*

Theo did not eat with us, but instead kept himself away from me for several hours, only joining the campfire after I had eaten and moved on. At least he gave a full report to her Ladyship, and allowed me to get on with more important things, like sneaking into a home to procure a tub so I could wash my body, my clothing, and my hair. I don't remember hair being able to hold so much blood, but there you go. In fact, anything I could find to keep away from her, and the feelings she brought up inside me...

The dark thing within flung handfuls of broken glass into my mind's eye, and the sounds of screaming inside my skull drove all the softer thoughts away. Long after dark had vanquished any trace of the sun, I took a seat on the apex of the bridge, watching the whole of the village from this one central location. I just stared into the night, drawing cold curtains inside myself.

Theo came to me carrying a bundle. He stopped just out of sword's reach, face pale and eyes wandering. I squelched all thought toward words and just let him sit, second upon second of sand weighing down his mind until he was ready to speak. He was normally a friendly boy with such an easy laugh, and even the horrors of the day had not erased that from him. It was still there, buried under the shock of River's Bend, but not gone. I found myself respecting him for that, and not a little jealous. I would be a liar if I said that the hollow shell that represented him inside of my mind was not being filled with more vibrant colors. He was becoming a person to me. Not a friend, not yet, but now much more than a simple, expendable thing. Something within me rejoiced while another something growled in anger. No, it was *fear*.

The least I can be is honest to myself, whoever I am.

"How did...I mean, why did you fight them?" The boy chewed on some bile and silently called himself a host of horrible names. "No, I mean, I was sure we were going to die. No! I mean..." Theo squared his shoulders, "You took on four of those things. How did you do it? I saw part of it, but I still can't tell you how you killed them. How do you know how to move, how to dodge? How do you fight like that?"

Ah. "Theodemar, I can tell you this: if they bleed, if they die, then they can be killed and everything else is a matter of speed, will, and timing."

Theo stared at me, trying to decide if what I had just said was very profound, or a cartload of crap. He shook out the bundle in his arms, revealing a beautiful, heavy traveling cloak. "The cleric says there is a frost coming tonight, so I spoke to the men. This belonged to the Captain, and we know he would have wanted you to have it."

The chestnut fabric was hardy to the touch, and the copper colored fox fur lining promised to fend off even the worst winter winds. I could not stop smiling as I put it on, the rugged iron broaches fixing it perfectly in place. I walked back down to the fire with Theo, thanked the guards there, and waved to the one on duty at the gate.

The spotty kid, *Jonathan?*, came back to the fire and raised his ration of wine toward me in salute. "We all thought after the day you had, you deserved some kind of reward."

The entire group chuckled, but not as loudly as I. "Really? Yesterday seemed to me to be far worse."

They looked amongst themselves for a moment, nonplussed. "What happened yesterday?"

"I woke up with a fractured skull and a damn black bird on my chest waiting for me to die!"

They sat in stunned silence for a few uncomfortable seconds until the weight of the idea hit them. Then, as one, they roared with laughter and slapped their thighs. Theo reached out and plucked at the lining of my new cloak. "Surely, my friend, you are as much a fox as he who wore that trimming before you! Even Death can't land his crows on you for long!"

Another boy, *Miller?*, waved his eating knife in the air at me. "Fox! You are a magician with a blade. Where did you study?"

I shrugged, "I don't know."

A boy with a face of angry red acne spit tidbits of pork into the fire. "Don't call him that, he's much more crow!"

"But you must know something! How long have you been at it, then?" A gawky lad with a prominent throat bulge on a near nonexistent neck swallowed hard as he repeated, "I mean, how long? Don't you remember?"

I shook my head, tagging him as the slow one of the group. "I don't know."

Theo leaned forward, betraying his desire far too clearly. "But could you teach it?"

I looked at all the eager faces, sensing the serious question buried in the mirth. I took a deep breath and fought against every instinct in my body. "That depends. Who else feels like getting up early tomorrow?"

The boys cheered, and chanted, "Fox! Crow! Fox! Crow! Fox! Crow!" until Gelia came out of the pavilion to express her mistress's displeasure at such revelry in this mournful place. She scolded us thoroughly and retired, but she was too late.

63

I Know Not

I had earned my name, bestowed by the boys with whom I would face death– Fox Crow.

Six

Withershins

IN a perfect world, the rest of our trip would have been swift and neat. I would have made love to the Lady and scampered on my way with my memory fully restored and a hat full of gold. Of course, if you remember, life is neither perfect, nor even fair. That's probably why we were standing in the center of the road, screaming at one another. Well, to be fair, one does not scream at a noble lady. That is why, when history books look back on this moment, I am sure it will say that I was screaming irrationally in a calm, collected tone, while she was making salient points at the top of her lungs.

"You can't have understood.: We are catching up to them! If we continue going forward, eventually we are going to run into the back end of the Barbarian raiders. Then this trip of yours will be well and truly over!"

"The future of my father's territory rides on this trade deal." Tears welled up in her eyes and part of me instinctively rejected them as a negotiating ploy beneath her. As she spoke, however, I became less sure, "I have no intention of going home and telling him I turned back when I was almost there. It is this discussion that is over, Crow."

And that was that. I nodded, bowed, collected my gear, and then lied like a bastard. "Theo, stay and get the boys to break camp. I'm going to scout ahead."

The boy-guards were moving a little stiffly, and their faces were pictures of misery. That was to be expected. They wanted to learn how to fight, and that always starts with exercises. The one who talks with his mouth full (*Miller*, my hindbrain whispered) was still massaging his wrists and waddling on burning thighs. I chuckled as I hitched up my pack and shook my head. *The kid was an eager student, no doubt about it.*

Then I realized that I would never see them again. There was an echoing, hungry hole, too high in my chest to be my stomach. A claw swept out of the Fog in my skull and murdered the mournful feeling. Aelia's life wasn't worth the pouch of silver she had given me, and mine was worth more than a mountain of it. If she chose to march her serfs into a trap, so be it. I was not going to follow along to my death like an obedient beagle. I took to the road.

Every few minutes, I attempted to lengthen my stride. I pulled my new cloak tighter against the chill that had settled in overnight. The day was clear, and it seemed that every sound would carry for miles. Even the soft chink, chink, chink of coins in my pouch echoed back from everywhere. At that moment it crystallized that I had left the carriage party behind and I had no intention of ever going back.

After a few miles the road began to shoot out more spurs. They were not large or well traveled, leading doubtlessly to lone farmsteads, charcoal burners, or grazing lands, but it was still further evidence of civilization. The wind brought a burning, greasy smell to my nostrils, and the Beast took hold of me so seamlessly I did not even notice. I found a path heading upward and raced along it, hoping to get to a hillock so I could see any trace of another blasted settlement.

I did even better than I could have hoped because I found a cliff face. It wasn't completely sheer but dramatically steep all the same, with trees cleared by a helpful storm that raged years previous. The exposed brink was like a massive panorama painted in a king's palace. Green had exploded into autumn colors that were rich and vibrant in coming death. The sky was wind-tossed and splashed carelessly with cotton combed into horse-tails. Still, what demanded the focus of my gaze was the exposed field of harvested corn where two armies clashed.

Around six hundred men desperately struggled for the right to draw in air. The Kingsmen army, resplendent in reds and yellows, struggled against a barbarian horde, in furs and raw wool. Only the shadowy echoes of sounds reached me, the clang of sword on armor, the cry of a life stolen, the screams of fallen horses.

Suddenly, the battle was on all sides, with the screeches of steel and strained creaking of leather. The brown ground was being churned into a bloody froth, looking to the sky as a red sea slowly clotted into black clay. I blinked as my eyes stung viciously, pressure building behind them as carrion birds swarmed like flies. Armor shrieked as it peeled away from ruined flesh. The smell of bowels thrown into sunlight mingled with freshly spilled blood. The distinctive grinding, tearing sounds of sharpened steel slicing through flesh shot through me as I collapsed.

The world was in color, bolder and richer than I had ever seen. Even the honest hand worked wood and peeling paint of River's Bend held a poignant, simple beauty uncomplicated by shadows or judgments. All around, the inhabitants of this village went about their business on either side of the river. I was standing on the apex of the bridge, but I could still hear the winter rye rustling, whispering secrets to me beyond the wall. I turned...

Wings cast outward like gates; an angelic priest barred my path, shining blue heart bleeding light.

I had always known he was there.

My stomach flipped inside my belly as the figure raised his arms. Two hands, carved of aged alabaster, emerged from within the robe woven of webs and night. He held a regal raven in his right hand, carved of ebon wood so pitted and worm-eaten it seemed to wither and crumble in his grasp. His left held the finest sculpture I had ever beheld. Easily ransomed for a king's crown, the gold and ruby blazed in the shape of a lidless eye. Sparkling facets caught fire in the too bright sun, lighting an unending fury within it. He seemed to be offering the statuettes to me, waiting with the patience of one who has no life left to trickle through the hourglass. Power. Knowledge. Wealth. I reached for the eye.

All around, I heard the shuffling feet of the villagers as they came close. I turned and saw those coming up behind me still bore the horrible wounds inflicted by the barbarian raiders. Close, too close, was the decapitated old woman from the bean pile. She reached for me, bloody neck hole whistling with a mouthless scream—

I woke up face down in the dirt, choking myself. I heaved myself onto my back and panted at the clear, blue sky. Uncounted minutes slipped by as I lay there, a confused jumble of thoughts invading the space between my eyes and the miserly Fog. There were impressions of people I know I should remember, and bloody corpses I knew I had some connection to. I shook my head and for once tried to shove it all back into oblivion, but I might as well have been bailing out a boat with a bread knife.

My stomach convulsed, streams of half digested food splashing against dead leaves and steaming even before it finished moving.

To my skin the winter frost turned hot, sweltering, and sweat began to pour down my back and face. The crackling, empty melon sound of a skull collapsing drowned out my coughing inside my own mind. I vomited again and rolled away from the fresh puddle before concentrating on breathing.

In a flash, the Thing in the back of my head made up of Claws and Night swooped forward and gathered up all the smells, sensations, and sounds, shoving it back into the Fog with ruthless efficiency. Again, a voice that was not mine echoed inside of my head, *Are you going to get up, or am I going to kill you here?*

The agony across my back once again dried like sweat, leaving discomfort but no real damage. I gingerly rubbed against a tree, but I couldn't detect anything but skin back there, and thankfully I did not set off another attack. Nonplussed, I leaned against the tree to consider my options, of which there were none.

Ahead there were two armies. If the barbarians won there would be no safe passage whatsoever. If the Kingsmen prevailed, then I would be a nameless vagabond with a very expensive and confiscatable sword in the vicinity of a major battle. It would be hard to guess a time measurement short enough for them to finger me as a spy and hang me.

In the middle of the empty forest, under the cover of the dying and damned, I screamed at the sky, cursing all the gods, devils, angels, demons, and pretty much everyone alive in alphabetical order. Behind me was a stubborn noble; ahead was a barbarian horde. I needed the princess to survive on one hand, and I could always ditch them again on the other. I dreaded going back to being under that woman's thumb, and at the same time wanted to slice out the part of me that rejoiced at the same thought.

I turned over every possibility in the back of my head, sifting through plans and discarding the dross. I had to make up time. I had to find the carriage party. It was what would happen next that I didn't know. There are times in life where suspense is preferable to the alternative.

I sprang unsteadily to my feet as if I had been branded. Unsure hands grasped clumsily at a tree trunk for support. A clear, long note echoed across the treetops. My eyes snapped open and focused on the battlefield below. The Kingsmen troops were rallying, and giving chase. I blew out the acidic dregs of puke that had packed into my nose and then spit viciously. Somewhere nearby a small forest animal blinked and I was gone. Soon my breath came in harder and harder, but still my feet flew like the spirit of retribution. A stitch collected on my side, and I cursed every spare waterweight of gear on my back, but my boots still slapped the hard dirt.

I heard them long before I saw them. I skidded around a corner and there they were down the road. Everything looked normal, with one carriage, two horses, and five boys. Still I ran to within a few paces before slowing to a jog, then a walk. The carriage rattled to a halt and the curtain moved angrily aside. Aelia fixed me with a dire gaze as I moved toward the cabin. "What now? Why have we stopped?"

"Kingsmen... and Westerners... ahead." As I gasped I motioned to the stinky boy (Wesker... no, Ryan... Daniel? My mind searched uselessly), handed him my pack, and motioned for him to stow it with the rest of the baggage, "Kingsmen... won... remnants of... barbarians... retreating... this way... We have to..."

Her eyes flew open wide, "We have to get off the road!" I gulped air and tried to say something, but she was already giving orders. "Turn us around!"

But I reached up and took hold of the reins from the stunned boy (Godwin) that sat there. "There's a spur closer up ahead... have to hurry." Behind her frightened eyes, a thousand questions danced. The one that pressed most obviously against the front of her head was, *Can I trust you?* Whether she decided she could, or that she had no other choice, I do not know. What she said was, "Onward! Quickly!"

I yanked the traces, and Godwin snapped the reins. The huge horses strained to move the overladen carriage fast enough that we had to jog to keep up. I sent the boys ahead to pull from the ruts any branches, rocks, and anything that might suck the speed from our wheels. We reached the side track and we yanked the foaming horses into the darker shade of the smaller road, the rest of the boys using fallen branches to obliterate any tracks.

We brought the carriage a few hundred paces down the road before I waved it to a stop. The horses were wheezing, trembling, and perilously close to permanent damage, but to say I was worried for their health would be a lie. If I thought running them any further would make us any safer, I would not have hesitated to kill them in their traces. If my desperate calculations were correct, however, the sounds of rattling wheels would soon be heard by fleeing Westerners on the road behind us. We could only go around the corner, let the carriage rattle to a stop, and pray neither of the chargers made a sound.

Minutes refused to drag themselves by; they just staggered down the road like bleeding survivors of the conflict. The Lady and the Priestess descended from the carriage and meandered back and forth without any real purpose. The rest of us waited tensely, listening to the fleeting sounds of battle near the road behind us as Kingsmen soldiers caught up with wounded invaders. I walked amongst the boys, abused legs tightening at every moment of rest.

"I'm worried about the horses. They need water." (That one's Godwin, I needed reminding) He whispered, "They're thirsty, and I'm anxious that they might be hurt."

I patted Godwin on the shoulder as I moved past him, rubbing my thighs hard enough my hands began to ache. Aelia turned an eye to me. She meant to be frosty, but was thawing in a way that exposed her fear. She faked a cough to collect herself, but failed. She leaned close and hissed, "We must continue."

I nodded, pitching my voice just as softly, "I appreciate your concern, Lady. Gather whatever you absolutely need. I'll tell the boys we are moving out light. We'll grab food and..."

The Lady looked as if I had slapped her, "No! We must keep the carriage."

I stuttered to a stop for a moment. Gelia had no problem with summoning winter from within her, and from over the Lady's shoulder the old woman's eyes flayed me alive. I ignored her and tried sanity again. "I advise against it, but we can take the time to have the boys pack up heavy packs from the luggage, and we will continue on foot with whatever we can carry. We will make the oak chest a priority but..."

The Lady had recovered her dignity, but none of her intelligence. "No! We must keep the carriage."

Something bitter cackled from inside the Fog. When given the choice between a good idea and a bad idea, a noble infallibly reached over your shoulder to find the catastrophically worse idea. I stared at her, catching glimpses of secrets flitting behind her eyes, but I swallowed my arguments, "I will..."

"You will what, Crow?" the Lady asked, turning the boys' name for me into an insult.

"I will range ahead to find the horses water," I said, picture perfect but wholly affected indignation drawing me up straight, "lest they die in their harnesses."

She flushed, eyes tracking over my face for any trace of duplicity. I simply brushed past her, and motioned Theo over. I put my palm against the back of his neck and pulled his head close to mine. I whispered orders to him that he probably didn't need: be alert, protect the Lady, be prepared to fight or run. Then Gelia approached me and handed me two folded leather buckets. I accepted them and licked my lips, "Thank you Reverend Sister."

She did not sneer, her words did it for her, "How wise is it to have the Lady's most skilled defender leave her?"

I took a deep breath, swallowing the bile that I yearned to spit into her face. When I spoke, I was amazed how calm and level my voice was, "If thirty barbarians come up this road, my blade will make no difference to the outcome. On the other hand, out in the woods, I'm the only one that can disappear if I wander into a knot of Westerners." I fixed her with a deadly serious stare. "But if you swear before your God that you want me to stay, I will stay."

Gelia's jaw locked in place, and she shook her head sharply before blessing me angrily and stalking away. Theo, bobbing in the storm swept surface of our conversation, looked back and forth between the priestess and me. I smiled at him and shrugged. Minutes later, I was back into the comforting silence of a forest that smelled of distant, but fresh, blood. I could say it spooked me, but that would be a lie. My only thoughts were not for myself, but stray ones that kept slipping back to the carriage party. The dark thing at the back of my mind swatted at these worries, but they continued to buzz between my ears.

I walked for half an hour, but once the road passed a series of hilly meadows, grasses sheared short by the teeth of herds, the flow of dirt became a stream, than a path-like trickle. There was no escape this way, and no water, either. Without thinking it through, and without knowing why, I turned around and walked back. Despite the hollow hurt in my legs, the release of tension created a definite ache in my shoulders. I felt old doors inside creep open and flush the musty halls of my soul.

I reached the carriage party, but they were not alone. Fifteen Kingsmen soldiers and what was obviously a noble of some kind surrounded them, but the scene was distorted, tense, and paranoid. Instantly the Beast caught scent of impending murder and snuck out of the Fog. I felt my skin go cold as I scanned the forest on every side, picking out many places where a man could secret himself. The Beast chose one at random, and I disappeared into the tree line.

Even off the path, my boots made only the softest of coughs on the wilting carpet of limp leaves. The silence of hiding birds and cowering mammals utterly refused to mask any movement around me, but the Kingsmen appeared to be more interested in the boys than the woods. The noble was faced away, and I could not understand his softly pitched words. I got closer and closer, melding with the trunks of trees and shadows of thick branches. Ahead, the boys gave up their weapons, and I wanted to scream inside.

During the commotion, I darted forward within a handful of paces from the back of the noble's soft, unprotected skull. Then, Aelia's eyes caught mine. She inclined her head sharply, once. Telling me it was over, telling me to run.

I kicked the Beast screaming into the Fog, and reached deeply into the mental closet filled with masks. I screwed a stupid looking smile onto my face and wandered down into the midst of the group. The noble jumped, several soldiers cursed and drew weapons, so I held the buckets up high and ratcheted my voice up a few octaves, and took on a lilting, poncy tone, "I apologize, Milady! There is no water to be had for your noble beasts. But I see we have been saved!"

The noble, at least the man in the best armor and wearing the stupidest expression, sneered and hit me hard on the jaw. It took everything I had to let the blow land, but at least collapsing into a heap was easy. I tried to ignore how close his dagger was to my hand. I tried to ignore how exposed his neck was. I tried to ignore his horrible breath as he leaned close and said, "My name is Captain Andrew O'Conner, Scion of the Imbel line. Do not speak in my presence again."

After being struck by Captain O'Conner, the boys and I were disarmed. I clamped down on the Beast as O'Conner himself took the Phantom from me, his eyes already claiming it as a prize for himself. Her Ladyship and the Nanny were bundled back into the carriage with the Captain, and we were turned around to head back to the battlefield. The low-born amongst us were discouraged from speaking, as being clubbed across the face is a great discouragement. Soon, corpses hanged from the trees said that we were approaching the decided battlefield.

We were stopped before we ever reached open ground, and only the smell on the wind, increased presence of blood spatters, and macabre tree ornaments told of how close we were. One of the fifteen guards left with O'Conner.

The world has a lot of injustices. Nobles love to pretend they do not exist, but usually only for themselves. Any poor sod who gets caught on the battlefield can look to a short hard life inside of a mine, or perhaps a quick hanging, or a knife across the throat. Nobles, on the other hand, are whisked from the battlefield and treated as, well... nobles. I would have a note of genuine disgust at that, but I think it might be hypocritical since that self delusion is the reason I'm not being hanged, stabbed, or enslaved. It was especially useful, since winter came down upon us with the subtlety and kindness of a hurled anvil.

If only the sequence of events made sense.

Hour after hour passed, and though discipline became more lax, there wasn't any kind of opportunity at escape that included the Lady and her carriage. The runner returned with food, bread for the boys and I as well as a cold repast of roasted fowl and fruit for her nobleness. We were all watered, and to Godwin's relief (did I mention relief?) the horses were included and began to recover.

It was near night by the time O'Conner returned, a self satisfied grin firmly in place. I weighed his traits and decided that if I did anything next it would be met with violence. I took a guess at how much.

I stood up and put myself between him and Aelia, voice lilting, "Captain—"

I forced my hands to stay at my sides, I locked my legs to keep from moving, but I couldn't stop myself from leaning away from the blow as he hit me again, this time across the cheek with a riding crop. The blazing column of pain caused the entire world to dissolve into bright white. I had planned to fall down, and it was a good thing too. I missed what he said to Aelia, but there was some shouting. Inside of my ringing ears, everything was confused.

At least I was able to get up by the time we were being collected to move on. O'Conner walked back by me, tantalizingly within reach when he paused.

"The next time you sully the memory of my noble lineage with words directed at me, fool," O'Conner smiled grimly as he made what he thought of as a joke, "one of us is going to die."

I Know Not

I bowed my head, meekly, but inside the Beast roared a promise loud enough to shatter mountains. There was no doubt that we were prisoners, but there was no explanation yet as to why. We had a cell large enough for thirty more people, and it was even out of the wind, though only through a quirk of history, and not due to any kindness of our captors. The King came to power twenty years ago in The Reunification War between the Grand Dukes and Duchesses of the Kingdom. The civil war had raged for fifty years, enough for the Kingdom to be well on its way to considering itself a series of separate fiefdoms. That's when the last of the great raids of Western Barbarians flooded over the Northern Ridge Mountains. They made it half way through our nation, laying waste to whole regions and demanding tribute from everyone else before they were stopped.

A simple knight from an ancient family rode into the conquered territories and began organizing the people. Defeated knights, bow carrying woodsmen, and footmen wielding hastily forged spears became a tide behind him. He resurrected a tradition of our ancient fathers: the castra. It is a military discipline wherein, every night, soldiers cut down trees, raise a palisade, dig a dual-purpose trench and latrine around the walls, and fill the trench with sharpened stakes. Where there are no trees they use dirt, or snow, or even stacked rocks. Within these impromptu walls they are allowed to pitch their tents. It slows down the progress of an army by as much as a quarter, but it always means they have a place to retreat to, or to fight off a midnight assault by barbarians.

For three years he waged war from his home near The Gray Forest all the way back to The Northern Ridge Mountains, crashing through the barbarians, traitors, and even the warring nobles ensconced in their private lands. He was brilliant, ambitious, and ruthless. Thus being the biggest bastard with the greatest talent for making living men dead men, he became King Ryan the First, sovereign of Noria. Eventually he lost his interest in the welfare of his people behind mountains of tax money, but the resurrected tradition of the castra lived on.

That's where we were. Inside one of the most settled-in castra I had ever seen. Apparently, someone knew the barbarians were coming and had mobilized almost three hundred troops to meet the raiding army. I was willing to bet they had begun construction on this wooden fort weeks ago, waiting here as the mountain keep and the people of River's Bend died. It was good ground to meet a barbarian assault, even if it cost hundreds of innocent people their lives. At least they had time to complete some rough log-construction barracks. The Barbarian horde had crashed against the walls and their fists had broken. Now the army had left for home, with only our fifteen jailers left behind.

Thankfully, we were inside one of the officers' quarters, and I was enjoying just being alive and indoors as the sky spilled sleet from angry clouds. The boys and I were still living on bread and water, and the fire pit in the center of the room could use a few more logs before our breath stopped fogging in the air. There was no latrine for our use in here, and the doors had been hammered shut so there were no opportunities at escape. My sword was at least fifty paces away, but you can't have everything.

I watched the smoke from the fire pit lurch up against the wind and slip out of the hole in the center of the ceiling.

Not yet, anyway.

SEVEN

A SHARD OF NIGHT, ALIVE AND HUNGRY

AELIA sat in the corner, somewhat walled off from the rest of us by a few of her trunks brought from the carriage. One would think that by allowing myself to be captured and struck on behalf of on my employer, her crew of beardless youths and her damn cat would bring some amount of praise. One would be dead wrong.

I lay on a pallet rolled out on the hard, cold dirt floor, Aelia casting me glances that had been stropped to an edge that could shave rain out of the clouds. Godwin and Jonathan were sleeping. Miller and (I can never remember his name) the stinky kid were talking furtively next to the fire. Theo had come over to ask me a barrage of questions I could not answer until I sent him across the room to sulk. Now was not the time for teaching a boy about getting into the head of an opponent. Now was for the three most tactical events in a fight: eating, and napping.

I leaned back and closed my eyes when the rustling of silk, fine linen, and whalebone raced at me like a dog attacking. There was another flurry of activity, and the other conversation in the room ground to a halt. I ignored the implication of floral perfume and the alluring scent of a woman who has gotten slightly sweaty. I ignored it because there wasn't much to talk about, not to mention there was a second odor there and it was as alluring as a steel gray hair in a severe bun and romantically caustic holy robes.

Then I heard what I had been dreading, "Crow? Crow?"

One eye snapped open and swiveled across the room. Next to me, Gelia's wrinkled hands lay primly on her knees. Just beyond, Aelia's hands twisted themselves on an expensive expanse of silken clad lap.

My eye slammed shut and I attempted to ignore her, a plan that only worked for about as long as it took to exhale before she hissed again, "Crow!"

I huffed and sat up, resentment moving from my stomach to

just behind my eyes. I turned to speak with the Lady, but she resolutely faced forward. I immediately thought I was lost in a badly written comedy, Aelia speaking to me covertly across the stiff shoulders of her chaperone. This was another example of noble in-breedery, since even now it was just as important that she not be seen being too friendly with a commoner (who was in a bed of sorts– for shame!) with whom escape was being discussed. "Crow, speak to me, damn you!"

I took a deep breath and felt out the thousands of conversations just beyond our tongues. I saw all the deviations and switchbacks, and sought to chart a course to the end I desired. Like a crown–princess picking through gowns before a ball, I decided on just the right amount of hoarfrost to edge my words, "Yes, Lady?"

Three sharp breaths of increasing indignation preceded her next. "By what right do you address me so?"

"You must excuse me, for I am greatly perturbed, Lady." I turned away from her, lying on my side and casting my face in shadow. "A noble lady is found by a small group of Kingsmen. Instead of giving her safe conduct through an area rent by strife, they virtually guarantee their execution by taking her into custody and holding her. Stranger yet, not only is she not ravaged, but no word is made of ransom for her safety. I am quite certain that the only people that shun from spilling royal blood are royal themselves." I measured the pressure between us, waiting until I heard her draw breath to speak and then said, "It is a riddle, Lady."

"Crow..." I turned back around to face her, and saw the fear there. "Captain O'Conner recognized my family's crest and knew who I was. He knows of the bidding, and knows if he holds me here a few days it will make things easier for his kinsmen to compete."

I felt truths lingering like shadows behind her words, "Tell me of the bidding, Lady."

Her voice was tinged with panic now, "My father has sent me to stand against many noble families and merchantmen. Any one of them would pay well to keep me from the table."

I closed my eyes, desperately recalculating the odds of reaching Carolaughan alive. At the edge of my mind, I heard the beating of wings. In the corner Leoncur, Aelia's cat, yowled.

She broke my concentration, "We must flee."

I glanced back and forth and saw no trace of the oak and iron chest from the top of the carriage.

"Your moneys are still hidden on the cart, are they not?" She nodded stiffly, and so I shook my head. "We will never make it out of the castra with that cart."

Aelia stared at me with all the self importance she could muster. "We must have it."

"You may be safe, good Lady, but such an action may provoke them to kill one or more of us in retribution."

She thought for only a second before setting her jaw and thrusting it out, "Death is not the worst of evils."

I almost said something biting and snide about her risking death before making that determination, but the look in her eyes stopped me. There was so much life inside them, so much strength, that I was stunned into silence. She was beautiful beyond any words. I glanced at Gelia, but she was looking at her Lady, face as awed as mine. Rage beyond measure welled up inside me, focused inward as a pillar of fire, yet I still gathered myself to my feet and stretched out muscles still tight by the day's exertions. I brusquely walked to her dinner plate and liberated the small knife from the remains of some cold roast. Even now she couldn't trust me to work unmolested. "Crow, what are you doing?"

I crossed to the wall and set the knife blade between the rough logs. With a few sharp taps, I had a chink in the mud, and then in the snow beyond, too, showing a world of black night and white ice.

I am letting you win, I thought, anger from my own personal forge licking at my face in punishment. Instead I said, "I am getting ready."

"Getting ready for what?"

"I'm going to kill them all." I turned from the wall and glanced at her luggage. "Do you have a white cloak?"

The answer was as I feared, "No, but Gelia does."

The old woman looked horrified, but still she stood and took off her cloak and thrust it at me in one, swift motion. A quick examination saw that the back was decorated with the holy symbol of her order, but the lining was untouched, though slightly dirty, white. It was perfect. I took a deep breath, reversed it, and slung it over my shoulders. My skin crawled to be so near anything having to do with her, but it was wholly necessary to have any chance whatsoever.

It was time to go.

I Know Not

I turned to stare meaningfully at the fire as my plan coalesced in my head. Then I looked upward to the hole in the ceiling where the smoke escaped. Of course there was a hole in the ceiling. Where else would the smoke escape? At the same time, the Lady was the important member of the party, and she was dwindlingly unlikely to climb out of a hole and then race across a frozen landscape without supplies. Still, there would likely be a guard nearby. I closed my eyes and ran the odds again, and again, liking the answer I got less and less each time.

The worst thing was how hard O'Conner's bastards were trying to make this. If some syphilitic bard were telling you about this, I could have pled sickness to the guard, or screamed of fire, or needing to make water. Unfortunately the doors were nailed shut and there were no guards to beguile. I guess, as a hero, I could have crashed through the barracks' rough-hewn door with a sword in one hand, an axe in another, screaming a challenge for all to hear. Unfortunately, no sword, no axe, and no way my shoulder would make it through a door that was at least four fingers thick. I could have climbed out of the flue with a rope and grapnel, but of course O'Conner had not left me such heroic implements.

Instead I kicked the sleepers awake. We stacked Aelia's trunks end on end, then I had the boys hold them steady. Without pause I clambered onto the top of one, then managed onto the top of the second. The chests jostled unsteadily as I straightened, extending desperate fingers that fell short of the hole in the logs above.

I jumped.

In stories the hero does not miss the edge of the opening, fall to the side, barely miss the coals of the fire, and slam shoulder first into the hard packed floor. I, on the other hand, bit back a cry, shoved the tears into the deepest part of my soul, shook off helping hands, and gave it another try. The sensation of my palms clapping onto the edge of the rough hewn frame of the crassly primitive chimney would have been more satisfying if it wasn't accompanied by a wrenching pain that traveled down my left side. The pain only intensified as I pulled myself up until my eyes were able to scan left and right. There was no crackling of ice beneath boots, no challenge, no axe cleft my skull, and that meant so far my plan was working (shoulder tackle of the dirt below notwithstanding).

The world was obfuscated by gauze curtains of blue and white, water and ice, tumbling through the air in a lovers embrace until they shattered on the hard ground, freezing together into a singular sheet. It would be beautiful if it weren't so cold, and trust me, I would complain about it a lot more if it weren't so necessary to my survival.

As would be expected, the army of three hundred built this place to house three hundred soldiers. O'Conner and his bastards had a unique problem: leave the fortress and have no secure place to keep Aelia, or stay inside the fortress and be unable to man the walls fully. Luckily, the Barbarian horde that had made it necessary to build the castra largely resided beneath two full strides of earth, or swung from trees encased in coffins of ice. So looking outward was not as much a problem. Add to that O'Conner's brilliant idea of nailing the doors shut and leaving us no guard to bribe, fool, or coax and he had neatly turned the castra into our jail.

Still, chances of an organized force attacking were small, but O'Conner was a military man— walls were to be manned. It was a sure bet that somewhere it was written that soldiers on walls need light sources, and so it was. The chances were so small, however, that rather than lethal pairs, or difficult roving groups, they stood as exposed singles. So I marked four, miserable men meandering on the walls near shuttered lanterns that did nothing to illuminate the world beyond and made them easy to see. The closest was a mere twenty paces away. The path from the top of the barracks to the adjoining wall was clear. That was the end of the good news.

I stifled a groan and heaved myself up onto the sheet of ice that entombed the barracks. It didn't crack, or crackle or creak. All heat was instantly sucked from my hands and the cloak became links of lead that almost toppled me back into the officers' barracks. I got a foothold and climbed out onto the quickly building glacier, making sure the hood was up and staying flat. In seconds, my whole front was soaked through with freezing water. Spreading the cloak out like the skirts of a warhorse, I began to more forward, finger-lengths at a time.

Whether you are striking a man down in the heat of combat, shooting him from a distance, spicing his favorite wine with belladonna, or knifing him in the spleen, it is all the same. Murder is a matter of being prepared. That is all. You must be prepared to use every bit of equipment with no thought to its cost. You must be prepared to seize an opportunity with no warning. You must be prepared to strike with no mercy. When given no equipment or opportunities, you have to be willing to make do with a white cloak, a sharp knife, five boys, and two pieces of luggage. Normally it takes hours, sometimes days, to commit murder. Many times it only feels like it. But finally, finally when you get into position... even when the target turns at just the wrong time... even when he squints into the gloom, trying to figure out what he saw, or smelled, or heard... even as he steps out of the protective circle of light and stands within arm's reach and waits and waits and waits, especially when he looks too long and the breath you've been holding begins to poison your blood, and bright stars flash before your eyes– even when he starts to look away and you exhale, making a cloud perfectly illuminated by the dregs of the lantern pointed away from you...

Even then you must be prepared to leap to your feet, ignoring the protesting of muscles that have been crawling, you must leap forward, even as the ice weighted cloak pulls at your throat, you must bat his panicked hand away as he instinctively raises his spear. Even with all the darkness and sleet and pain and confusion you must bury your knife in his throat to cut his cry in half before it can gain more than a second's worth of volume. You must do it, and do it quickly, but your job is not over.

Knifing a man just below the throat apple is certainly fatal. It's just not quick. Until he finally dies from suffocating on his own blood he's going to be fighting unless he's lost his mind from fear, and then he'll still be thrashing uselessly. If you are a particularly cold hearted rogue, you might rip his cloak from him and knock off his helmet. A really nasty customer would lever him over the wall, perhaps killing him with the fall, but definitely muffling the sounds of his gurgling fits as he bled to death in the cold and dark outside. But you'd have to be a special kind of bastard to relieve him of his dagger as you did it.

His body hit the hard packed ice as if it was stone, and the muffled crunch barely broke the silence. I flung the guard's cloak over my shoulders, popped the helmet on my head, and sniffed as I tested the edge of his dagger with a thumb.

Then, heart pounding, I retraced the soldier's four fatal steps back into the ring of light as if nothing at all had happened. I glanced back and forth, but it was too far to see faces, too far to do much more than read body language, and if any of the other guards were interested in me, they hid it well. I moved the lantern to a hook closer to the outside of the wall and set the shutters to project the light fully outwards. Then I moved out into the darkness, ditched the helmet and extra cloak (minus a thick strip) out over the wall and began creeping to the next island of light.

Three more on the walls. Fourteen more to go.

Out across the grounds there was a stable, and three barracks. One was where the carriage party now waited. One of the others contained the grunts. The last would doubtlessly have O'Conner and maybe a lieutenant or assistant. *Which was which?* That was a problem for later.

Stupid soldiers brag that they can sleep standing up. They just borrow two or more cloaks, bury themselves deeply into the folds, lean on a spear, and doze. I bet it makes getting up for inspection much easier. *If you wake up.*

Yes, I still crept up on my stomach. Yes, I moved like a star stuck in the heavens. Yes, I only took short breaths through a muffler made from a torn strip of cloak to diffuse vapor from my lungs. From the Fog, chilly words whispered in my ear, *The moment you cut a corner, it will leave an edge sharp enough to slit your throat.* I shuddered. The unfamiliar voice was colder than all the winters throughout time.

It was almost anticlimactic when I checked that the other two men on watch were faced away, then slapped my hand over his mouth and rammed the thick, dull blade of my stolen dagger deep into the base of his skull.

The blade ground against bone as it went in, and then thumped home against the front of his head. I lowered the body and flipped the shutters on the lantern to cast him in shadow. I left the dagger where it was, since brains have a powerful stink, and replaced it with one from his belt. He also had a sword, which I left as too cumbersome for stealthy work, but I unfastened his belt. It was heavy duty leather strap that could be looped though the metal ring at the end and it was made to hold a sword steady while the soldier was running. It had a thousand uses, so I wound it around my forearm.

The next man turned his head at just the wrong moment, so instead of cold steel into the base of his brain, it skittered off his skull. He screamed once before I shoved the dagger into his eye. It barely paused as it broke through the thin bone behind the gelatin orb and entered his brain, but he didn't stop fighting until I twisted it once. I heard a cry, looked up, and saw the guard thirty paces away on the last wall running along the crude parapet.

I took a chance, and left the dagger to plug the hole in the corpses' skull and dumped him into the parade grounds. I faded back under cover of the white cloak, flat against the ivory ice as I unwrapped the belt from my forearm. The soldier's boots thumped against the frozen carpet as he flew through the pool of light thrown by the lantern. He blinked, slightly dazzled as his eyes flew straight over me. He finally glanced over the edge of the parapet at the dark corpse of his comrade highlighted on the snow below.

The quick look became long as he leaned over and peered out at the body spread eagle on the ice sheet. His lips quirked up in a smile for a heartbeat as his mind worked out the chances that the guard had gotten sleepy and simply slipped off of the edge. About the time his eyes adjusted so that he could see the halo of blood staining the snow and the dagger protruding from his eye, a thick leather belt looped over his head. He jerked back, dropping his spear and clutching at his sword when I went right past him over the edge.

It was only two manheights to the ground, hardly dangerous at all. I landed easily, absorbing the shock with my legs, fate and chance kindly bypassing the opportunity to twist my ankle or break my shin. My next victim, however was pulled by his neck, and he absorbed the shock of the fall with his face. There was a sound like the first bite of a crisp apple, and then his head flopped bonelessly.

Eleven. I had murdered well, and my reward was a little bit of time. I stripped off Gelia's cloak, and took the cloak, mail, sword, shield and helmet from the broken-necked soldier. *Advantages of a bloodless kill.*

Something inside the Fog sneered at the loud, snickering mail as I pulled it on, but older, wiser memories nodded sagely. The Fog parted for a moment, and a man built like a razor blade, with a face ravaged by pox leaned to me over a forgotten fire. *"Not all stealth is quiet. The ears hear danger in the unfamiliar, boy. If an ear is used to a creaking mill, no creaking will disturb the sleeper. If a delicate lady is used to hearing boots tromp past her door every hour, boots are a sound of comfort. Stealth is about learning to blend in, to be the color of the world around you, about making the sounds of safety and you will..."*

The memory faded into a shadow with no beginning and no

end.

I walked calmly, slowly, like a man almost rendered witless by monotony. I made it to the stables, and opened the gates. It was abandoned except for Aelia's chargers, her carriage, a pair of unremarkable workhorses, a wagon piled with military supplies, and O'Conner's horse. I quickly found two wood axes, three large jugs of lamp oil, and the pegs from Aelia's pavilion. I exited the stables, walked the walls to collect the lanterns, and made for the barracks.

Of the three buildings, Aelia's let out only a trickle of smoke out of the top. The second on the opposite wall vented a great deal of smoke, but the one in the center looked like a volcano. I was willing to bet that the center, the most protected, the seat of power, was where O'Conner was staying. It had probably been inhabited quite recently by a general, and that, most of all, would appeal to him. So, I headed to the western barracks building, carefully set down my burdens outside, and took out twelve wooden pegs.

Then I walked in like I owned the place.

Inside, everything was as expected. My thick boots and jingling mail blended in with the sound of men snoring loudly on too-thin military pallets and under too-few military blankets, snide voice quoting sagely, *The reason the military want you to be able to sleep under the worst conditions is they expect you to.* In the center the fire pit burned low. My eyes swept over the men, marking half the beds filled; ten men total. I walked right through the center of them, right to the door on the other side. I stopped by a small wooden box in the corner and flipped open the lid. As expected, there were handfuls of twigs, shaved wood, tinder of all types.

A voice came from the blankets to my left, "Whatyoudoin'?"

I coughed twice and pitched my voice low and gravelly like a man with a cold, "Lamp's out."

But the blankets were already snoring again.

I made a basket of the stolen cloak and filled it with all the tinder. Hands sweaty, heart racing, I exited the barracks quickly, to hold in the heat, keep them comfortable. Outside, I began sticking the wooden stakes into the cracks at the edge of the door. I could not risk hammering them in, so instead I gripped the edges and pushed as hard as I could. Desperate men have desperate strength, so I used many more than were probably necessary. Then I went to the bundle and carried most of it, with the lanterns and shield, to the roof, leaving only the two wood axes and four stakes behind. Once I was back to the ground. I picked up the first axe, set a stake in the door jam, turned the axe around, then quickly and gently hammered the stake home. I got the second one done. At the start of the third, an irritated voice whipped through the wood. "What the hell is that banging!"

With one stroke I drove the third one home, then followed with the fourth.

"Thomorgon take you and Amsar judge you himself! If you don't stop that I'm going to come out there an' arrange it personally!" I reversed the axe again, drew back, and planted it with both hands, clefting the lintel and door and wedging them together. A body slammed against the door. It held. "What the hell?"

I ran to the other side. I drove the pegs on that side, the very first just as a body slammed into the door. As they pounded on the door, I finished the others off and planted the second axe.

An argument started inside the barracks as I ran to the roof. Bodies began shouldering into the spiked door as I carefully edged out onto the ice and threw the bundle of tinder down onto the fire. It flared menacingly and shouts turned into yells and less manly sounds. Next, I ripped the tops off of three of the lanterns. I dumped them unceremoniously down the hole onto the fire, which flared higher. I heard someone trying to beat the fires out with a blanket, so I began dumping the jugs in next, eliciting screams from everyone inside. Bodies threw themselves even harder against the doors. The light and noises from inside the building brought to mind a pit of hell even before I slammed a dead soldier's shield down over the flue and staked it in place with a dagger.

Remember this: while all people talk about is the bright murder of the fire, it is the creeping black smoke that is the real assassin.

I grabbed the last lantern and carefully slid from the roof. One of the doors of the center barracks slammed open, exposing a half dressed O'Conner to the wicked winter's teeth. He spun in a circle, confused as he hefted the Phantom Angel as a shield against his fears of attack.

"What is this? Barbarians?" Behind me the blackness of death coughed and seeped from holes in the building, but no ruddy glow yet, so when I threw open the lantern shutters facing O'Conner, he squinted in pain.

When in doubt, soldiers shout, so I did, "The barracks are on fire, sir!"

Galvanized into action, O'Conner brushed past me shouting orders, "Assemble the men! Start a bucket line! Use your helmets if you have... to...?"

The blade had not been especially sharp. Pity, because it seemed to have torn as much as it cut. Still, the overall effect was the same as O'Conner's intestines spilled onto the ice. He staggered and reached for me. I put out my hand, but only snatched the Angel from his grasp as he tumbled, half dressed, to the funeral slab the sky had provided him.

I discarded the dead soldier's sword and marveled at the perfect edge, the excellent balance, and wondrous grace of the Angel. *How many have owned it? How many have been killed to possess it?* One more, to be certain. I flipped it high into the air, watching it spin as it tumbled end over end. The handle smacked into my hand as if placed there by a God. Then the smell of bowel hit me and ruined the moment.

O'Conner was shaking violently, though from cold, pain, or blood loss I did not know and guessed it didn't matter. I settled onto my haunches next to him, grabbed his chin cruelly in my hand, and forced him to face me. I tipped the helmet off of my head and saw recognition flitter behind his eyes. His mouth worked uselessly but I saved him the trouble. "Captain O'Conner, I have come to tell you that you were right! I am once more sullying the memory of your noble lineage by speaking to you, and now one of us is going to die."

And I left him there. I don't know exactly when it happened, but by the time we left the castra, O'Conner was dead. He had managed to make it three paces toward his barracks, a feat of endurance. His noble ancestors should be proud, really. The soldiers had managed to knock loose several of the pegs on the door on this side, but all that escaped was thick, black smoke. The hammering had stopped. I had a flash of another place, burned to the ground, but the Dark Thing swept it away like a gambler seizes a pot. I shook my head.

When I removed the nails from the door and released the carriage party, they cast me looks that could only be described as awed. They moved out into the open air and saw the burning building, the bodies of the watchmen, and the disemboweled corpse of the Captain, their expressions changed into something far different. For my part I claimed some of O'Conner's more rugged clothes and tossed his quarters for anything valuable. I secreted another bag of coins on my person, and was pleased to find O'Conner had gone to the trouble of scavenging a barbarian's crude scabbard for the Angel. It was two hands too short, but its iron throat made it a perfect stopgap measure. I slid the Angel home, wincing when it bottomed out. Then I filled my time alone, strolling around the perimeter of the castra as the Lady packed, and the boys prepared the carriage.

Finally, it was too cold to delay any longer. I returned to our prison, a wet bundle of white in my hands. Aelia started when she saw me, and Gelia spun and placed herself between us. I could not suppress a scowl as I crossed to my fox cloak and collected it from the floor. It was then the Lady's voice, so strong but brittle, set a hand on my shoulder, "Crow. Where did you...? How did you...?"

I cast her a barbed glance over my shoulder, "If you did not think I would succeed, or if you were afraid I could, perhaps you should not have sent me at all, Lady."

She accepted the rebuke head-on, taking it into her heart and secreting it there as holy writ. She drew herself up as full understanding came to her. She nodded, and said something unexpected, "Accept my apologies."

Unexpected, because she truly meant it. I nodded in lieu of a bow and began to walk out as she turned back to her packing. I paused by the door only long enough to shove the Priestesses' white cloak into her wrinkled hands. "My thanks, Holy Sister."

I did not make another step before she whispered, "Oh, Dear Merciful Lady."

I turned to see her holding the cloak by the shoulders, spreading the sides out for inspection. I looked at the back of it, slightly sooty but otherwise unharmed, and wondered if she was just complaining about my smell. Then she turned it round.

I could see the outer surface, the one that I had worn closest to my skin, was stained so badly it had obliterated the holy symbol of her order. It was not with dirt or blood, but with a dark foulness that had no name. It twisted in spikes and whirls that tempted the eye to follow them into madness, whereupon it formed two symbols superimposed upon on one another as they were on my very soul. The spread wings of a raven, and piercing it in the heart was the all seeing eye.

The Priestess looked at it, and then at me, terror etched in every crease of her skin.

"Gelia?" Quickly but subtly, the old woman bundled the stain to the inside of the cloak and turned from me, a slightly worried but loving look chiseled onto her features. I retreated, my head swimming with unknowns so deep and dangerous my eyes hurt just from the pressure of them. I ran to a hidden corner of the castra like an animal, throwing myself into a dark niche as the pressure built and built, longingly tonguing up and down my back and giggling as I shuddered at what was to come.

And then it hit, brutal and wild, a pain that erased the ground, the cold, and even the sky above. There was only agony from the center of my back, echoing into the eternity of a few minutes. And then, like magic, it was gone. If there was a dream, I didn't remember it. Still the vague unease of undeserved punishment remained.

Without further order, consensus, or even a single word, we left the castra. I am certain Godwin was the one who had re-rigged the traces and decided to hook up the two extra workhorses to the carriage. It gave us more speed and that much more chance to reach Carolaughan alive.

Had I been less tired, I would have remembered to question why the road so perilous, why the princess so insistent, why the noble O'Conner so familiar with her. But I was tired and drained by the merciless pains along my spine. The others were no better off. As we left the place though the gates, there was a pall on the party. Before it had been bandits, fae, and possibly barbarians, but now we had killed Norians like ourselves: more daring, more dangerous, the King's soldiers. Someone would come looking for them, and would find only bodies.

The true measure of our peril had never been made so real.

EIGHT

A BLACK
WINTER WIND

THE winner will declare the bloodiest of battlefields a honorable victory. King Ryan was said to be a vicious tactician without a shred of mercy, but the songs of his battles are full of honor and glory. The reason is that it is hard to begrudge breath. By midday, the shocked disgust at the means of their escape had faded. Miller even asked for a blow by blow account until Gelia came by and whipped him in the back of his neck with a leather thong as if he were a schoolboy. He howled like a scalded cat, but nobody dared laugh because of the look on her face. When we continued, I could feel two pair of eyes on me from the carriage, one warm and one cold.

By my reckoning it was five more days 'till Carolaughan. Aelia made comfortable conversation with me while Gelia made uncomfortable silence. Theo kept up a fine banter but for the times when it was my turn to tell a story, for I had none to give, that space still held by the miserly Fog. Winter had shaken the sleep from his eyes to descend upon the lands of Men, seeking to make up for lost time with very real hostility. The world sparkled almost painfully, with every trunk, branch, twig, leaf, or needle encased in thick globs of cold glass. Our steps crunched and the carriage wheels set up a dull roar that threatened to hide the approach of anything smaller than a rampaging wyvern.

I had not slept all night, and the strain of escape, murder, and revenge had drained me. I began sending the boys ahead, one at a time on O'Conner's horse, finally letting them take the lead. They were so eager, so desperate for approval, that they never seemed to realize I was doing them no favors. If someone was going to die, it would certainly be them first. My heart started to paint in the lead frames of these hollow youths with hopes and dreams, bad breath and dirty jokes, quirks and foibles. Still I had to risk them, because I was becoming fatigued to the point of uselessness. Worse, the weaker my mental state, the more I began to walk through imaginary murders of my companions. I would shake myself after each ersatz killing, so sure that I could shut my eyes hard enough to banish the demons, only for them to creep back and paint the world around me in dreamt violence and blood.

Before noon, I found my boots wanted to slip more often. The light stabbed more cruelly at my eyes. I began to swim in the Fog at the back of my mind, sliding from second to second on pure inertia. Aelia made plain she wished to stop for a long lunch, and wished us to find a respectable spot.

Spoiled brat– first she says hurry and then... My hackles froze, half-raised.

The Lady was staring at me with soft eyes, gaze lingering on me too long. Her true intent dawned upon me and I felt shame for the first time I could remember, not that it was a long time, but still I felt it was significant. I nodded thanks to her and was rewarded with a smile that could coax flowers to bloom from beneath the ice. Inside me something, long unused and mostly forgotten, stirred. A cold wind blew out of the Fog and the alien warmth fluttered deeper inside me, hiding.

I slept as others ate, and a long time besides. Still, our mission was urgent and the next morning I was shaken awake before I was completely ready. The boys would not give up another day lost with no practice, and so I trained them before they packed up the camp. The road, however, would soon show hostile intentions again.

We, and by we, I mean I, found disturbingly fresh signs that lots of men wearing hard traveling boots had been by. I was grateful to Aelia when she gave permission to take a smaller side road. It was longer, less civilized, but it would greatly cut the chances of meeting an ambush. It was likely that the extra horses would make up the time, but there was a bigger chance of a felled tree that would take hours to clear before we could move on. We continued apace until nearing the next day's dark, and then it became necessary to look for another place to bed down.

I brought the boys in close so we could stop soon, but nothing convenient appeared. With no springs close to the road, nor signs of habitation, all traffic passed here quickly. The forest began to press in again, thick brush on either side that promised not to hide ambushes, but also provided no place to make camp. We went another mile, and then another. It seemed we had set upon a road that never ends, where every corner looked like the one before, and all the differences just made it seem all the more alike.

I decided at the next clear space big enough to make any kind of camp we were going to stop. Then particles wafted to me on the breeze. They entered my nose, ricocheted inside my sinuses before being thrust into the deepest parts of my brain. It slapped aside the cobwebs in my head and wrenched my guts in a spiked fist. I stumbled, threw out my arm to grab the carriage and stifled a scream. The Angel was in my hand before anyone else had a chance to ask. Theo immediately echoed me, with the other boys following suit. I quietly ordered a pause of our small band and went to the carriage. Aelia was within, calmly stroking Leoncur, while Gelia murmured prayers for mercy and intervention. From her pale face and light sweat, she recognized the smell, too.

There wasn't enough room to turn around, and we weren't going to run away too quickly in any case. What I needed right now was not an argument, and I let it show in my voice, "Stay down. Keep the curtains drawn."

I moved two boys to cover the carriage's rear, two more to walk beside the horses while Theo drove and I walked in front. None of us were trained in mounted combat so O'Conner's horse got tied to the rear of the carriage. We kept our weapons drawn, but held them low (which I've always thought was the absolute friendliest way to show you were ready to kill someone).

I closed my eyes for a moment, summoning up the Beast until it lurked behind a very thin veil in my eyes. My hand tightened upon my sword, then loosened as I took a deep breath. Only then I motioned for us to move out.

There is a special way an animal moves when it is willing to shed blood. If you say any different, you have never seen an animal kill, man nor beast. Showing that you are ready for a fight will drive off all but three groups: the stupid, the desperate, and the skilled. Unfortunately, bandits usually fall into these three categories. Still, there was nothing for it but to continue forward and look as mean as possible.

Around the turn, we found one of those little villages too small to be on any map, further proof that we were making progress into civilized lands. It was not like River's Bend, in fact it wouldn't even fill one rambling clan house in that fort town. It was barely a village square containing ten hovels, one pillar of smoke, fifty hollow-cheeked and tear streaked faces. From the undercurrent of musky odor, they raised some kind of small herd animal. From the threadbare state of everything in sight, they did it badly. In the center there was a well fed man in shining armor astride a massive warhorse. He reined his mount around to face us, exposing the blackened husk tied to the stake at the center of a dying pyre, the source of the smoke and the smell that overpowered almost all others.

Heavily bearded, with hair that exploded from his head in heavy steel colored braids, his face was powerful but wrinkled from decades spent in a suspicious squint. His armor was gold inlayed, no less functional for the ornamentation, but the sheer weight spoke volumes for his physical fitness. This was no doting grandfather, but a crafty warrior cast from an ancient mold. He lifted his helmet, forged into the face of a horrible angel of war, and pulled it on. Despite the shining brass halo carved to wreath his head in sanctimonious flames, I couldn't summon any faith in his righteousness. The other hand balanced a bluntly functional war hammer across his lap. Black iron was consuming the silver plating where it had worn through with age and use, conferring in deadly whispers its master's skill. His destrier was as white as driven snow, saddled in red leather with saddlebags painted with an iron fist crushing a bundle of burning arrows and scrolls.

It was the sign of Amsar, merciless God of Justice. Those in his service simply could not be bargained with, showed little ability to stay out of the affairs of others, and were universally not quite sane.

The Fog surged and vomited forth such raw disdain and hatred it immediately turned my stomach into a cauldron of boiling acid. I reined in the hot words of the Beast and forced my head down. I saw no reason to make an exchange, nor to face so formidable a foe for no profit, so we made to go by. The Knight of Judgment simply stood like a statue, a pose I was pleased to see his mount spoiled by shifting constantly. It was a petty victory to see horses do not like the smell of greasy flesh–fed smoke as much as some masters. For my part, I wouldn't be able to eat pork for weeks.

I hung back and touched... *Damn it, I can never remember his name!* I touched the quiet, smelly kid on the arm. He obediently and quickly switched places with me so I would pass closest to the armored sentinel. The knight's helmeted head shifted to follow us as we passed, the steel mask frozen in an expression of howling indignation. We drew nearly abreast him when I let a small sigh escape. For once, just once, we were going to make it a little closer to Carolaughan without further risk.

Then the voice cracked over us, full of military bearing, "Why do men carry naked blades on the King's road?"

Given the opportunity, I would have put a knife to Theo's back to keep the carriage moving, but he was young, and a soldier, and out of reach of my knife. He was trained to obey orders from voices like that one, especially orders that had not actually been given. He yanked the reigns and the carriage came to a halt. The knight urged his mount into the center of the path to block us.

Shit. I was now able to chalk another tally in the 'wrong' column, bringing my average to 'fairly often'. I kept walking forward, hoping to shunt him aside by force of will as I spoke, "We were attacked a few days ago by brigands. We are low on men and cautious of our charge to protect the Sister of Mercy and the noble Lady riding in the carriage. Stand aside."

My gambit failed, making my new total 'nearly always wrong', but while I stopped well within his ability to strike at me, I also stopped close enough to strike at him. My fingers caressed the robe of the Phantom Angel, memorizing his heft and promising deadly use. I stared at the knight insolently.

He peered left and right, then his voice came forth again like a gape of magma, slow and fiery echoes from the depths of his helm, "The boys hiding behind you are guards, but you, yourself, are not. You wear no livery."

Even after the horror and death of last night, I realized my blood thudded in my ears like war itself, my arms tingling in anticipation of a kill. *Right bloodthirsty bastard, am I not?* "I am Crow, a mercenary hired to ensure a speedy trek to Carolaughan. Now stand aside."

His demeanor changed for the worse. I admit, I was pressing, almost hoping for fight. My eyes saw not the scene before me, but a hundred tactical decisions playing out at the same time. "Have you grievance with the Holy Sword Arm of Amsar?"

Everyone in earshot winced at the naming of a God. Naming Gods called their attention to a place, and such places in scripture usually wound up as battlefields, plague pits, or craters. Their names were used in the vilest of insults and curses. This fool had a dangerous tongue and I needed to stop this, but I also needed to let him an out to back down. "As long as I can walk the King's road," I gestured to the frozen track about us with my sword, for emphasis, "in peace, surely not, Holy Knight."

My brain was trying to smooth over the burrs in the conversation, but the words tasted like offal as I spit them out. I heard the whipping whistle of a switch, a cry, and then echoes of humiliation. Then the Fog billowed, and quite without warning, the pulsing hatred, the bile, the pressure, were gone. I blinked and finally saw the knight clearly for the first time. There was a pause. Silence, like that before the first charge of battle, where men commit themselves to whatever god they think will hear, echoed all around The rider leaned toward me, his voice ringing in his helm. "I recognize your sword, Crow. I do not recognize you." He shifted in the saddle, moving like a predator. "It belonged to one of my brothers, who named it Witch Light. How came you by it?"

In many a bard's raving tale, told with cutouts silhouetted against a lit screen, now would be the part where I explain everything and he joins my quest. Or else perhaps I might challenge him. Or he would call me a liar and attack. None of these happened, because he was already trying to kill me. Apparently he knew that trick, too.

He swung his five-waterweight hammer single-handed, gravity lending strength where muscle could not. Do not sneer, five waterweights was enough to reduce bones to pudding when swung by a skilled man, and he was indeed skilled. At this point his unwieldy two-handed weapon would nearly reach the ground, smashing everything standing alongside his horse. With death approaching like a rockslide, I suppose I could have growled something witty and heroic between clenched teeth, but there simply wasn't time.

Allow me to pause here, a last coherent thought as the Animal inside burst forth from the Fog. On the field of battle, a charging horse will mow down the opposition with ease, but not in a static duel. A horse like this one costs a lot of money, and is a fine weapon in mobile warfare, but right now it was little more than an ungainly and expensive high-chair. So, if you are ever so lucky to be able to hand over the obscenely large amount of gold it takes to buy and train and ride one of these mountains of frothing muscle and iron shod hooves, do not (for the love of all that is pure and holy) ever take one into static close combat. If you do, someone like me will do something like this:

With wild abandon, I dove under the animal's belly between the front and rear legs, removing myself from the Hammer plus Crow equals Corpse formula. I heard the maul displace air behind me and knew he was less than a second from either bringing it down on his left side to smash me, or perhaps rearing his destrier to trample me, or worse, galloping off to turn this into some kind of mobile confrontation I was sure to lose. Instead, I pretended I was a good man and had to quell any qualms about spinning on my heel, Phantom gripped with both hands.

I felt every ounce of muscle from my legs to wrists threaten to tear from their moorings in protest as the blade arced through the air like a siren. I was not aiming at the knight's noble head, for that was too far above. I was not aiming at his well-deserving thigh, because it was plated in steel. Have I mentioned that you should never bring a horse into a static duel?

Packed for a long journey, the war horse was still traveling light without the weight of armor. The Angel moved as a black flash and rang like a bell as it severed the front left foreleg. The mount reared in shock and rage, thick streams of crimson ribbon spurting from a clean stump before it tumbled over backwards with the Knight. So did I, truth be told, unbalanced from the effort of the stroke. In my favor, however, was the fact that I wasn't being laid on by most of a ton of horse.

"Get them back!" The passion of the words burned my throat as the order surged forth like a hungry wolf.

I spared only a moment to make sure the boys were retreating the horses from the melee. I know, you ask why I was crying out when I should have fallen on the armored bastard and finished him as he lay like a tortoise? Fortune has not smiled on me much as of late, and apparently she was still flirting with some noble bastard who was right now discovering a crown shaped birthmark on his buttocks and claiming a kingdom.

For one thing, he was not lying on his back, helpless. Armor's weight is displaced across the whole body. Yes, it is heavy, and impedes split second timing, however it does not make a man as ungainly as some would have you believe. My enemy may have been a zealot, but he was a skilled zealot. Knights are not just men with long spears in tin cans. They train long and they train hard.

Eventually they can leap onto the back of a horse in full armor. Getting up off the ground is no problem. Even worse, they practice so they can ditch a falling horse without having their legs, spine, or head crushed. Which he had just done.

Damn it.

I focused on my opposite as he circled the thrashing body of his dying mount, an inhuman growl forcing from deep in his chest. I unleashed the Beast within and leapt. My blade took a chunk out of the bronze halo of flame on his helm. His black and silver hammer slammed into the frozen field where my foot had just been, sending sharp shards of white rocketing into the air. I rolled away, bounced to my feet, and raised the blade like a sharp wall between us.

This was no bandit. This was no foot soldier. This was a professional warrior, a product of a venerable and refined tradition of mortal combat, and he demanded my respect and caution. A whisper from the Fog echoed down my arm. Left Hand quickly snatched my dagger from my boot and showed it to him.

The trap was set, the spring taut.

He came in slowly, wisely, aware of my dual-weapon stance. He knew, however, if he stayed distant, he would be safe from the dagger. His grip was spread on the war hammer, able to separate further to get speed or close in together for powerful strikes. I waited for him to come, and being no coward, he did not disappoint. His strikes were varied and expert, sometimes fast, sometimes slow, high and low and seeming random. I was having trouble keeping all my precious bits out of the way.

He struck for my center of balance, my torso, knowing any strike with a maul would liquefy anything beneath the hard uncaring end, killing or crippling me instantly. He came in with a flurry of blows that I alternatively met with the Angel or avoided outright. His mattock whooshed in the chilly air and the ragged sounds of our breathing were swallowed by the wail of the mutilated horse. Without parade or show, I reversed the grip on my dagger and laid it flush with my forearm, hiding it from view.

The trap was now baited.

He swung again. I let my blade meet it but be turned aside, giving him the feeling of contact and whetting his appetite for victory. His blows came faster and faster, thirst for blood clouding his judgment. This is a fatal flaw in a soldier. He stepped in, and the trap he had set closed on me.

I swung Phantom with all the power in my right arm to meet his weapon, but the weight of his mattock, powered by a surprisingly mighty blow, cast it aside like a flower caught in an avalanche. The barest echo of the strike slammed into my right collarbone. Nothing broke, but the shoulder blazed and threatened to seize up. If that happened, I was dead. I sunk to one knee, not entirely by design, as the throbbing spread to my lungs and neck. The Holy Knight cocked the hammer behind his head to spatter the thinking part of me across the road—

Not today.

My body was failing; it was only will that drove me on as I sprung forth and trapped the butt of his cocked hammer with the Phantom. He cursed and tried to back up, but I followed him doggedly, keeping his blow blocked as the blade caught between his gauntleted wrists and the butt of the hammer.

Regaled in his armor he must have felt near invulnerable, his whole front presenting a beautifully terrifying façade to the world. I know better, however. Even in the heaviest armor, joints still need to bend, arms need to move, and the armpit is an area near naked for lack of space to place plates or chain.

When he could see it, my dagger had been a cause of caution for him. I had hidden it for mere moments and he had forgotten about it in the rush of the here and now that takes over men in battle. The blade spun from along my arm into an eager and furious fist. Into that chink between the heavy steel is where I inserted the killing edge.

The trap snapped shut.

The studiously honed blade sliced through a thin layer of leather and into the vital artery that lay there. I twisted it, feeling it grind against bone and opening the seeping wound into a torrent that bathed my arm in reeking blood. His strength left at once and he collapsed away, his heart pumping carefully measured amounts at frantic intervals upon the frozen winter sheath. The ice pockmarked as if he leaked acid, or perhaps concentrated hate.

I took a moment to dispatch the screaming horse before coming back and watching the knight from a safe distance, the lights in his shielded eyes slowly going out.

"To all things come the fire eventually. And in the flames there will be an accounting," were his last, angry words, quoting his angrier god.

I Know Not

I waited a few more moments, then I stepped in quickly and put a foot on the haft of his hammer. I lifted the Angel and slid it into the small gap between the bottom of the helmet and the breastplate. I shoved until I hit frozen earth, pulled it part way free, then shoved again hard. He had been my enemy, and I bestowed upon him the greatest respect by showing him the proper amount of caution even in death. Only then did I stiffly retrieve my dagger and wipe it clean on his cloak.

My shoulder started to pulse and quiver angrily as the heat of battle cooled in the nippy breeze. I looked up to the people of this unnamed collection of hovels, and saw only shock there. One may have thought I had just turned aside a vicious storm with harsh language. Well, there was one, teary old woman who glanced at the burnt stake and then nodded to me a grim thanks.

"Clean water," I said softly, and three boys ran off. As long as they came back with water, I didn't much care where they went. I turned back to the carriage party that stared in something of shocked amazement. The women had departed the carriage, against my orders, damn it, and Gelia made a holy sign before her. Maybe it was vanity, but I thought it was against me.

Like a tongue probing a tooth for pain, my mind gingerly explored the inside of my skull, and found the panting, bloody Beast was still at the helm of my battered body. I wrestled it into the Fog, and it responded by removing the bulwarks against the stomach churning waves of agony. I felt the blood drain from my face, and cold needles danced along my skin. The Fog leapt upon my weakness and covered me for a moment, blocking out the world with claws made of spiraling, liquid light.

A wise man, I just can't remember his name just now, once said, "If you faint standing up, you will always, always, always, smack your face on a rock." Just because I didn't doesn't mean it's not true.

My eyes snapped open, and hovering above me was Gelia's lined face.

I'm dying.

I swear, that was my first thought, because the look of utter pity and loss on Gelia's face could not otherwise be directed at me. The tenderness, the determination, was not, had never been, for me. I tried to shift, but instead of slapping me down or growling at me, old, powerful hands gripped me gently and held me still. The words being spoken on all sides made little sense, but her posture, her every glance, told me I was a human being, and I was in trouble.

My inner cynic chuckled and whispered snidely, *That's how clerics are supposed to act!*

She gave me something bitter to drink and I felt wakefulness slipping away. I snatched it back to me, desperate to escape the cloudy hell of dreaming sleep. My hand spasmed, and she took it in her own. Her skin was warm and soft like perfectly clean velvet. She began murmuring prayers, holy words that slipped through the haze of pain and disorientation like moonlight through tight branches. She continued to push and prod, to feed and poultice. She even cut open the skin over my shoulder with a small silver knife, and then used the blade to hold open the wound as she leaked a thick sludge into the skin.

To her credit, she stayed with me every second of the night. To my own, I did not surrender to sleep. I clung to consciousness as a holy writ. Hour after hour passed, but only the most feeble of dawns came upon the sleepy forest village. Gelia cleaned her bloody hands in a bowl of water and then leaned back against a rain barrel. She shut her eyes. The entire village was asleep around me, so I waited until her breath became slow, long, and regular, then I counted to three hundred. Only then did I slowly gather myself and attempt to move.

Miraculously, everything responded. Silk thread held closed the cut in my shoulder, but underneath the slicing pain of a fresh cut the joint was hale and whole. I got to my feet, feeling the icy air slam gloriously into every inch of my naked skin. I stretched silently. Even the black blanket of the forest above could not extinguish the simple wonderment of my body.

Behind me, Gelia's voiced walked quietly and respectfully into my moment alone, "What are you, Crow?"

I took a deep breath, staring into branches that blotted out the sky, "I know not."

She sighed, but only to slow down her breathing. She was frightened. "Are you a hero or a villain, Crow?"

I looked down at the pale, glowing flesh of my open hands, marveling at the power of life inside and wincing at the flecks of blood caught in the tiny hairs and caked under the nails. I glanced at the black patch of ice and snow where the knight had fallen. My eyes fell to the corpse of the horse, hacked open and meat parceled out to the four winds. I winced a bit then. It had been a lovely animal. "I know not."

Somewhere in the village there was movement, and the cleric's voice took on a panicked edge, "Crow, you must cover up."

I ignored her, but I watched the perfectly black sky, feeling subtle movement hidden therein.

"Please, now. Cover up," she insisted.

Uncountable winking stars twinkled to life. I reached down and scooped the Angel into my hands, relishing the weight. Only then I realized that none of my instincts said fight or run. I was at peace, a foreign and frightening thing.

Gelia's voice was a quiet murmur. "So, where did you get that sword?"

I looked up into the black canopy above, drawing the dregs of truth up from my soul. "I know not."

The world exploded into a flurried eruption of ebony feathers and golden beaks. The morning sun blasted my eyes as an uncountable number of crows shattered into action, lifting from every tree on every side, becoming a wall, then a cloud, then a fading black mist that scattered into infinity. The twilight of predawn had been a lie to the crystal clear winter morning hidden by hundreds of thousands of dark wings. Somewhere a cock crowed, confused and late.

I turned to Gelia and accepted the hurt, the uncertainty, and fear I saw there. I took them to me as blades unto my naked skin. I spread my arms, defenseless and helpless. "I don't remember."

I wind up saying that a lot these days.

Then the day crashed in on me with the speed and finality of a scythe. I lay down and fell into a deep, dreamless sleep. Trust me when I say that it sounds more romantic than the reality. I didn't wake for a full day, dragged to my pallet and watched over by the elderly cleric.

When we finally started off again, we reached a clear hilltop that allowed a fine vista. In the distance we could see the snow covered top of Orphan Mountain, at the base of which sat Carolaughan. We were only days away.

NINE

LIES AND GOLD

I WAS drinking in a dive and enjoying myself. Well, I was sipping swill and being eaten alive with worry, I imagine that it's almost the same thing.

I sipped at a beer that tasted as if it had been aged with a drowned cat in the barrel while a storm of eyes rained furtive gazes down upon me. This bar was like most others, crowded and smoky, but I had been careful to pick one in the poor quarter. That was not true, there was across this place as a matter of luck, really. When I had poked my head in and saw a room filled with lowlifes, dirty and violent men who eyed me with suspicion and avarice, I knew it was perfect. nothing careful about it. The moment we had entered Carolaughan, I had marched straight to the slums as if hooked on the end of a line. We came

To be totally honest, it doesn't take a genius to find a place like this. Simply look for a sign that has no words, and is sufficiently vague it could mean any of a dozen things. In this case the weathered board out front showed a crudely carved, naked woman that was either dancing, running, or maybe fleeing. Which was it–dancing, running, or maybe fleeing? Was the woman a human, an elf, or god? How long does it take for all that paint to completely flake off? There was no explanation whatsoever. When you see a sign like this you know it does not matter what the place is called, because the select clientele who know of it do not want outsiders intruding. If you don't know the place, you don't want to know.

I took another sip of the dead-cat-beer, stifled a wince, and spooned through the congealed-stew-of-unknown-meat-type. Automatically my hindbrain marked the place of every person in the bar, everyone who was looking at me, and every weapon that was less than fully and competently concealed. This was a place of predators and prey, of killers and victims. It had rules and I understood them deep in my bones. The promise of my money was balanced by the Phantom I had set in its new sheath across the table. I tallied more in the threat than opportunity column. Balancing on a knife edge is still balance, after all.

I had hustled the disguised Lady and her entourage past the crowd of hidden knives and ensconced them in a room upstairs with the aid of a few foreboding looks at the innkeeper and fewer silver coins. The threat of the unwashed masses kept the Lady and Priestess in their room, and the boys busy playing guard. It finally left me some free time. I used it to explore the streets between this place and our destination. Or should I say our next destination, or perhaps our true destination.

I wondered how it could have happened. *You are a man and she's a woman. That made you stupid.* I rejected the thought with a sneer, but it crept back underneath the table, nipping at my ankles and denying me any chance at relaxation. *Then you wanted to be a hero, idiot.*

As I could have guessed, the road into Carolaughan had gotten no easier. Every day we walked toward our destination, and every night before bed the already exhausted boys learned a little more of the art of killing. Less than three days after burying the Knight of Amsar we were waylaid by another group of 'bandits'.

Winter was upon the land as never before in recorded memory, and it was certain that some men would turn from farming or soldiery to banditry. It was easy to stab a stranger so your children could eat, but the presence of tribes of bandits on every major road and hiding at every major intersection near Carolaughan was beyond belief. There would literally be nobody left to rob, only bands of masked men shrugging at one another as they camped along the otherwise empty roads as their families starved at home.

Besides, a mask does not a bandit make, not when they were wearing the slightly rusty armor and carrying the chipped and dented weapons of professional soldiers. Mercenaries, by the smell of them. I wrestled with one masked man, rolling around on the hard, cold ice as I tried to get his heart and my misericorde to shake hands. Another bandit had shaken off Miller and came at me, prone and occupied. Then there was...

You don't even remember his name.

A ghastly cold hollowness surged inside of me, pushing tears into the back of my eyes. I blinked them back furiously, willing the buildup away. I scowled and put the tankard down with slightly more than necessary force. Many of those who had been looking for a likely pocket to pick went back to their own drinks.

DORIAN!

His name had been Dorian. The triumph was short lived, because the worst kind of lie is to say it was good enough to eventually remember the name of someone who had died to save your life. We killed the bandits and we lived. I lived, but it was only because of Dorian. Gelia and the rest had buried him– no older than seventeen...

Dorian didn't know me well, no one really can without me knowing myself, and he had been a quiet boy. I had taught the boys everything I could during our morning training sessions, but it hadn't been enough. I guess he decided I was more important than he to safeguarding his lady. He matched himself to a man many years his senior and many times the swordsman. He died upholding his oath to her and I decided I had a powerful need to know why.

Out there, covered in blood and under a cold, clear sky, I felt storm clouds eclipse every bright part of my soul. Then, there It was. That Darkly Vicious Thing, always half hidden in the Fog, floated up behind my eyes. It settled in like a comfortingly numb cloak. It whispered in my ear terrible things. Terrible things, terrifying things, but true things. It said that people do not respect someone who loses his head. They can dismiss you, disarm you. They can disassemble your arguments by sliding lies in the gaping cracks of your rage. It said you can distill rage into a compact line and use it as a whispered weapon. You can slip it into their skull and pry out their secrets.

Man, this beer is horrible. I've a mind to not order a third. And I glanced around the bar, but only for a second before the scene of a few days ago continued.

I had stalked across the clearing with the dark cloak of the Thing in my mind flapping around me, invisible in plain sight as I took all light from my eyes. She saw me coming, still off balance from the stress of the attack, and she retreated before me without even a protest. Aelia continued to give ground, managing nothing but clips of words as she stumbled on her dress. She threw out her hands, tripped again, and fell against the bole of an old oak tree encased in a cocoon of blood-spattered ice. Everyone waited, tension sparking in the air as Theo laid his hand on his sword, ready to kill even me to protect his charge.

Even as I made tentative plans to murder him the moment his sword left it's sheath, a small part of my mind whispered to him, *Good boy.*

But I never looked at him, never glanced away from Aelia as my eyes stapled her to the tree with thunderingly silent questions and accusations. Tears welled up in her eyes, and her lips trembled, revealing at last her lack of years. She was only as old as half her guards, and younger than poor Dorian. Under the crushing weight of my silent judgment, cracks began to appear in her mental walls. From inside the carriage Leoncur yowled.

Then her clasped hands found an unobtrusive ring perched ungainly on her thumb. She looked down at that plain, gold band as if she had never seen it before. Her head snapped up and her lost, lonely eyes locked with mine, but then she began to change. It started in her shoulders, which started clenched around her neck and dropped like an executioner's axe. Then her chest swelled, filled from some hidden reservoir inside. Her jaw set. Iron flooded from her heart and straightened her spine. Though more than a head shorter, suddenly we were equals, and her fear fled before her unfathomable strength. One, last deep breath brushed aside her lingering doubts, and her eyes blazed like the noon day sun off the snow.

She mastered herself and in that moment she became more beautiful than any creature of legend. She took the legs out from under the Beast and sent it sprawling in my head. Just gazing into her steady eyes released something fluttering and fragile inside of me. I tried to ignore it, to say I was more than passing successful would be a lie. She gestured to a fallen log on the other side of the road, and even that little motion was enough to push me aside. She walked over, adjusted her skirts primly, and sat on the rotting icy wood as if it were a throne. I took a seat and gazed deep into her eyes. She did not shrink nor flinch.

You are one hell of a woman.

"We are not heading to Carolaughan to trade for iron." Several seconds slipped past, giving the sky precious time to come close over our conversation. The pressure squeezed out white flakes of snow that swirled down on every side as if to curtain off her secrets from the world. "We are going to bid on Red Sky."

This was the point where I was supposed to say something witty, something insightful, or failing all else, something dashing.

What I managed to get past the flying, trembling lump in my chest was a guttural throat noise. Thankfully, she took it as a sound of disbelief instead of an audition for village idiot. She took a deep breath and continued. "I am completely serious, Fox. The dwarves have long been pressed for men. They have finally begun stripping their outlaying forts to strengthen their main towns and city centers. They cannot simply leave these outposts... "

"It would open them to attack without warning," I finished, nodding. The harsh northern mountains were not just dangerous for men, and there were worse things than barbarians and redcaps. The dwarves were a bulwark against the untamed lands beyond, but it was not kind to their population.

She smiled at me. "They have taken to selling these lands to humans who can afford the price. They have traveled to Caro-laughan, the center of the Kingdom, to give all the noble families a fair chance to bid on the land and the fort." *And, incidentally drive up the price with access to more bidders,* I thought as she continued, "They get an infusion of gold and the protection of the fort maintained..."

"And the high bidder gets to tax anything that goes in or out of the pass." I finished. Considering the amount of luxury goods and implements of war that come out the Dwarvish kingdoms, whaever outrageous sum the winning family pays will be made up in less than ten years. Not only that, any enemy buying Dwarvish weapons or armor in bulk, whoever taxes the goods will know of it. These thoughts and their implications propelled me to my feet where I paced the road.

Just as the safety of the Ridge Mountains and the peace of the Sorrow Wood had both been illusions of luck and fate, so now too the path before me was not a wide trek but a thin board over a rushing river. Still, something did not fit into this new scene. My eyes flicked to the boys, and to Gelia, who still watched like wide eyed children, "You are not from the family of Llewellyn."

She lowered her eyes and nodded, but stood to face me with the bearing of a queen, "I am not of the family of Llewellyn, servants to the family of Conaill: I am Aelia of the ancient and revered family of Conaill, Grand Duchess of Conaill, Warden of the Eastern Plains."

I didn't feel any more like bowing to her, but I did feel the river below my pathetic board bridge turn into a lake of fire.

"Ishad's bones!" I screamed at the sky, invoking in my mindless rage the name of the God of Murder. I spun to face Theo and his crew, all of them pale at my blasphemy. "Make camp!"

Four days later, I slammed my hand against the table. People on all sides winced. The bartender shouted something, but one baleful eye wilted his objection on his tongue. Drinkers on all sides decided to make it an early night and filed out meekly. Under the hubbub, I slipped my hand under the table and rubbed it as it wailed like a baby. The pain was good. It focused me. It also opened up the floodgates at the back of my head.

Four days ago, I looked around at the carriage party wondering if my blindness was an effect of the Fog or something softer and far more sinister. It made sense when I thought it through. Having the Church of Ethryal assign one of their number to a noble's daughter took substantial and frequent donations, out of the reach of even some of the most affluent families.

Nana, she called her Nana! I should have seen immediately that the cleric was not related to the Duchess. That meant she was hired help, meaning Gelia had been Aelia's keeper since before she could form full words, and that takes money the likes of which most people could not even conceive.

Have you ever noticed that no matter how many times you tell yourself you should not to trust a pretty woman, you always do? Have you always noticed you always wind up getting kicked where you fork your horse for it? We were on the outskirts of the Sorrow Wood, one of the great bastions of darkness in the Kingdom with a Grand Duchess!

Low Dukes and Duchesses had enough intrigue in an afternoon to cause a hundred deaths, but the little honorific 'Grand' meant she was related to the King. The Grand nobles all like to assassinate other Grand nobles, or capture them for ransom, or to keep them out of the way, or to try the rape-that-turns-to-marriage angle. These are just hobbies they engage in when everything is peaceful! What they would do to one another when there's a crucially important and mind bogglingly lucrative deal on the table can only be guessed at. No matter what, killing the guards, including myself, would be necessary.

Wait a minute. I looked back at her through narrowed eyes, now leery that any disturbance in the conversation was a covered pit, "Conaill has a Grand Duke, not a Duchess."

Again, she fluttered for just a second before she reasserted control and grabbed hold of something inside herself, impressing of me again, "My father took the direct route. He employed a massed caravan guarded by two hundred men in heavy armor. An assassin took his life before the procession had marched its second day." My eyes flicked to the stricken faces of the boys, to the heavy, lined face of Gelia, and back to Aelia who lashed her tears down inside to save her dignity. "As his successor, I decided twenty men, moving swiftly, would have a greater chance. I have spent more time than I would like to remember circling the Sorrow Wood the wrong way around to reach Carolaughan. Many men I have known since I learned to speak have died in front of me." Her voice, on the edge of cracking, gained an underlying plate of rock. She gazed proudly at me and straightened. "In their memory, and that of my father, I will not stop now." She paused, gathering words against me. "I will pay you ten times what I said to see me to Carolaughan—"

I stilled her with an upraised palm, my face a hard mask, but the words popped from between my lips with a life of their own, "I have taken a contract. I will complete it as I have sworn."

The words were familiar in my mouth, running along a deep rut in my tongue. They were also the truth. I am only vaguely sure of what kind of a man I am, but I know that had it been me, I would have lied too. I don't have to like it, but I also don't have to be a hypocrite. I looked amongst the carriage party, and was frightened at the respect I saw there. The enormity of my words was finally driven home by Gelia, who turned away as she blinked back tears of relief.

I had just committed myself to guarding the whelps that mindlessly worshipped me, the holy woman that hated me, and a lovely lady who lied to me at every turn. And a cat.

What have I done? Self-loathing bubbled up from deep inside the Fog, a poison that dribbled down my spine. *What you have done is put yourself between countless swords and their target. Idiot.*

The point was driven home by the carriage itself. An anchor around our necks this entire trip, now it was almost beyond hope. It had dozens of arrows and bolts prickling from its side, not to mention out of one of the chargers as well as one of the workhorses. The workhorse had already laid down and been silenced, and it looked like the warhorse would be next. We could have lost both the stolen army horses with no trouble, but the heavily muscled chargers were vital to keeping the heavy wagon moving. Instead of saying anything twice, Godwin just patted the shivering, arrow-freckled side of the left charger. Even hooking up the officer's horse would not make up the loss in strength. To top it all off, one of the carriage wheels was canted slightly and would surely shatter at the very next bump.

I shook my head, "There is no way this thing is going to make it much further."

"We cannot leave the carriage, Crow."

The words ignited the poison of my own recriminations, burning down into my belly and exploding into my arms. I ran the last few yards to the door to the carriage, cocking back a fist meant to break the wooden coat of arms that hung there. I grabbed the door with the opposite hand and the curled fingers trembled by my ear. Forgotten disciplines tied down the temper seeking to command my body and, after long seconds, the arm dropped. I swallowed mindless screams of rage, doubtlessly turning an interesting shade of red. Hot breath whooshed out of me with all the pent up energy rage had lent me.

I just stood there and considered our next move. Well, I stood there and made the boys really nervous as they unhitched the horses, and that's almost the same thing. Miller and Theo stumbled unloading the money chest from the top of the carriage, it scraped and tumbled, missing Theodemar by less than a fingerlength. It crashed against a jagged stone sticking up out of the frozen soil and a dozen rivets snapped like whips, disgorging the entire contents of the chest out through the broken side. Instead of wealth beyond imagining, it contained only three chainmail hauberks, a few small bags of coins, and some plain goblets and platters and a man weight worth of bricks. This entire time, hauling this thing from place to place, always placing it at the edge of camp, and the damn thing was filled with dregs and dross.

A light dawned behind my eyes. She had left it at the edge of camp, hoping it would be taken, hoping that our pursuers would waste time trying to escape with it and waste more opening it as we escaped with the real fortune. It was a plan so cunning that I would have been proud to think of it myself. Now I just had to figure out how to convince her that I had known all along. Then I remembered that Aelia was heading to a bidding war, and there had to be wealth, somewhere.

Suddenly I had to lean forward and steady myself. That's when I noticed the unnatural cold of the flourishes carved upon the door. It sucked the warmth from my grasping hand faster than any painted wood ever could. I gripped it harder, twisting nastily and marveling as it deformed under my rough ministrations. The chunk came free of the nails that sought to keep it in place and lay fully in my hand; cold, harsh, and heavy. I comforted myself with the thought that nobles paint everything within reach gold, as everybody knew, and would make the same assumption I had. There was no doubt this was not a painted gold design, but the real thing.

With the amount I held in my hand, I could have purchased River's Bend and all the lands surrounding. My eyes jumped from one golden carving to another, adding to the grotesque weight of the carriage, the most obviously camouflaged fortune in the kingdom. Suddenly I wanted it, wanted it all more than anything. I closed my eyes and marked every one of the boys in the clearing by sound alone. I plotted a deadly dance that would kill each and every one of them with a single cut, swipe, or thrust. The Lady would be last, least dangerous and easiest to dispatch. The Fog swirled forward inside of my head obliterating the deep seated starvation of wealth and washing it away just like the loathing for the holy knight. I looked back across my thoughts and felt a cold rush at how deadly, how emotionless, how serious the urge to murder had been.

I hefted the twisted golden chunk twice and smirked hollowly at the noble lady. "Aelia the ruse worked for as long as could be expected. You set some bait, you changed your name, you disguised your treasure. You did well, but now the carriage is broken, your enemies know your true identity, and your bait is now exposed. It is time to change the plan."

The nanny came to Aelia's side as if to lend her charge confidence. She needn't have bothered; the young lady faced me like an equal though her irises were still stricken by dredged up memories of loss. Gelia's face lifted to me and our eyes locked. Again, I felt she knew more of me than any other living soul. It made my palm itch for the Angel. She set her jaw against me and asked, "What do you propose, Crow?"

"They are looking for a noble Lady traveling with a wagon, Priestess, so we must find a way to be as little like that as possible." I smiled and tossed the lump of metal into the carriage. "You brought hunting bows, did you bring hunting clothes as well?"

Neither of them smiled back.

Days later, I emptied the bitter dregs from my cup and slapped two slivers of cut copper coin onto the table. *In a bard's tale, there'd be a pretty and particularly wonton busty barmaid.* As if by magic they disappeared and the fat, sweaty barkeep replaced them with a foaming mug. *And of course he's busty, but in a bad way.*

I escaped that disturbing thought by focusing on the dull moaning pain in my back. I had not mentioned it, had not rubbed at it, had not even acknowledged it for four whole days. I was betting as long as I didn't complain about it, nobody else would either. I took another drink, and couldn't stop from making a face. *I need to start drinking something less corpse flavored.* I glanced at the bar, wondering if such a thing existed here.

On the road, we had been a very conspicuous, slow, and under-defended target. We had to change as much of that as possible. We worked like the fevered, throwing ourselves into the tasks needed to change us from a royal carriage party into a family of wood carvers. The boys alternately cursed me behind my back and marveled at my energy as we stripped the bandits and used what clothing of theirs we could. Next we used hammers to remove all family crests from weapon scabbards and burned every scrap of Aelia's heraldry as well as the boy's shields.

No, I don't have the right to call them boys any more. They have fought and died beside me. They were men, and I let them know it. Even as they smiled proudly at me, a dark voice snickered in the back of my head. *Outrunning the thoughts of all that gold?*

We unhitched the horses and took axes to the carriage, prying off chunks of gold moldings and hewing thick oak beams with endless strikes. I soon buried worries about my darker desires in a shower of sweat. By that time the last few bits had been rendered down into thick planks. We set the least luxuriously carved pieces aside for our costumes, and then placed the barely recognizable broken skeleton of the carriage on the bonfire. At least we were warm for the night.

There was no way to hide most of the wreckage, so we made it completely obvious and patently faked. The bandits provided mutilated bodies. The dead horses provided massive amounts of blood. The chest we left in the middle of the road, empty and broken open. The entire scene, broken wheel, corpses, and empty chest, would allow anyone who came by to draw precisely the wrong conclusion.

Aelia came forward, smiling resignedly at the ruined coach and then proudly at me. At least it was proud until I handed to her the roughest, poorest dress she owned. They were not hunting, but plain riding clothes. They were of far higher quality than any peasant would own, but they were in muted colors and of simple cut. She made a face, but she dressed in them, but even there it took some careful fraying with the razor edge of a knife and a few handfuls of dirt to make her a convincing peasant. The cleric was easier, owing to her owning poorer clothes to start, and the men easiest of all. *Now if I can just get them to stop walking like guards, we might survive.* But, once again, they were not the ones giving me the most headaches.

"It will cost me money I severely need to replace those goods in order to be presentable for the Dwarves," Aelia groused, again.

I gazed along her form, now only covered in a simple brown and tan dress and stained, dull red cloak. The perfect kind of thing to wear if you were going to be playing in a place with a lot of horse manure, dirt, and sweat. "Your enemy will have spent more still."

"How do you know?"

I turned to her slowly. "Because they have failed with thugs and they have failed with mercenaries." I let all mirth leave my voice, "The assassin guild's talent is not cheaply bought."

Those words lay in the center of the group like a sputtering bomb, quelling further discussion. Now, with Gelia and Aelia dressed simply, I had the men load the horses with the gold plaques ripped from the carriage and weapons, disguised underneath the beautifully carved wooden beams. Once the horses began to protest at the weight, I doled out packs and sling bags, similarly laden, to the men. I took one myself onto my shoulders, but there were still two packs worth of gold left to carry.

Gelia started to ask an indignant question, but Aelia waved her to silence and bent to pick one up. She stifled a grimace at how the pack cut into her shoulders. I smiled at her, an expression that came from the deepest parts of myself. Gelia stiffly took the last of them, wincing at the cold heaviness.

It could have been worse. We had only our clothes, our weapons, and three days of food each, very little horse feed and a few skins of water besides. We were now under deadline cast harder than any iron forged by any dwarf. In three days we would be out of our sparse supplies of food and water. More than two days after that and we would begin losing gold as we slaughtered the horses to eat. Even with all of that, Aelia decided that Leoncur shouldn't have to walk, she carried her pet in her arms as we set off.

I will never understand nobles, but to her credit, she never complained about the weight. Not once. We left the road, paralleling it a mile off. It took four cold, hungry days to reach Carolaughan instead of two, but we arrived unmolested.

Like a dark festival day, fifteen small armies of fifty to a hundred men sat outside the walls, courtesy of the other Dukes and Duchesses in residence. These groups had not built castras but were spaced far from one another to avoid accidental conflict. These were highly motivated, antagonistic, violent men, and having them anywhere near one another was a colossally bad idea. But the Grand nobility were here to bid, some against mortal enemies, and too many dealings amongst my 'betters' have turned to bloodshed in the past to ignore that a war might start here. I was utterly certain every camp kept wartime watches, and they were fully manned. I did not see the King's banner and cursed. No one would start a war if the King were here, but he was conspicuously absent.

Above it all, Orphan Mountain stood alone. White topped even in summer and always wreathed in clouds, it sullenly stared at the awaiting carnage.

We entered Carolaughan as peasants, discovered the bidding would not begin for a few days yet, and made it to this bar. While the men quietly ferried the gold to the room, I had all day to rest and recover from my exertions on the road. It was late, and any assassin would surely be waiting for us on the few roads leading to the more affluent areas of town. He may be out there right now, waiting patiently, but I was damned if his job was going to be easy. The beds here were infested, the tankards were dirty, and for dinner I think I ate the cat that had been drowned in the beer I was drinking. It was also the safest (read: least likely) place in town for a noble and her retinue, for now.

I had determined that I was not going to order a fifth rancid beer when a purse fell onto my table. The dull sound from inside was not from coin. I looked up at the owner, an old man with a mouth full of blackened and rotten stumps. His breath was decay itself as he sat and smiled across the table at me.

"Well, 'tis a fine night." His voice was rattish, lazy. He scratched at an old scar beneath his sparse white beard. He looked as if something unwholesome had burrowed in and sucked all the spare flesh and color from him– from his white hair, pale eyes and jaundiced skin, to his yellowed nails. I simply leveled the practiced, steady gaze of a killer at him. He waited, sipping at a mug grasped like life itself to his breast. He cleared his throat and hawked a gobbet upon the floor.

"'Tis a fine night..." *Apparently, his parents were not only inbred, but had dropped him repeatedly as an infant.* I reached across the table and grasped Phantom's sheath. His eyes widened, and sweat beaded his brow. "'Tis a fine night...?" he again, almost desperately as I stood, looming over him like a gallows.

He finally got the message and hissed, "Fine, just take it! I never liked you. Ragmen never respect Whisperers, but you are a true bastard."

I felt my pulse stop as he hustled off into the crowd with the expertise of an urchin born to the city. He was almost to the door before my numb limbs began to respond again, but when I reached the door to the night time street he was gone, swallowed by the darkness.

I turned back to the taproom, where everyone was pointedly staring at their drinks. In the center of my table, in the middle of some of the meanest cutthroats in the city, the pouch sat unmolested. I gathered up the small package and staggered up the stairs. Theo was outside Aelia's room, alert and awake on his guard. I waved absently to him and entered my room before opening the canvas throat of my package. The scrip contained hundreds of gold coins worth of unset gems and jewels. There also was a scrap of paper:

'They were well pleased. Your fame will grow. Offers exist. Contact soon if ready.'

I read it three times, unknowing of its meaning. 'I never liked you.' the wretch had said. Someone here knew who I was, even if I did not. What offers? Why did I hold a king's ransom in my hand? Alright, it was a knight's ransom, but it was still more money than most people see at one time in their life. No matter the question I asked, the Fog remained silent.

That night I dreamt of walking through a black forest where the leaves were all silent ravens. They all watched me with un-blinking eyes.

TEN

THE TRUE NATURE OF BLACK

THERE were two ways to do this. The right way involved all of us hopping from street to street, moving like mice in a cat's barn– our eyes roving, watching for threats. I should have been picking apart the shadows with my mind, dissecting any place from where a poisoned knife could spring. Even as we would have dodged from alley to alley, half would watch our front while the other half watched our rear. I would watch both ways and up besides. Our tortured pace of doubling back and searching for the perfect moment to move across busy streets would reduce everyone to panting dogs before long.

Would, if we weren't leading three horses, seriously overloaded with gold and wooden trim. The horses alone necessitated plodding along though the streets, coming to a grinding halt whenever animals were driven across the road, or an old lady dropped her basket of fruit, or children decided to come out and play tag between the legs of the horses. In short, we stopped a lot.

Only Theo was keeping pace with me, and he was worn. Then again, from the odor emanating from inside my shirt, I was not in prime condition at the moment. The problem was, we all looked like we were being hunted. This was very bad, but I don't see as you can sell dung as a diamond, even to a blind man. All this before midday. We crossed the street quickly, huddled together like a family of frightened cats. All I could do is set my jaw and glare at any city personage that even considered getting in our way.

The back of my neck tingled and chill sweat raced with the air to frost up my veins. Our group was horribly exposed, and there was nothing for it but to keep our heads down and plod along, hoping nobody noticed the weapons hidden in bundled blankets on the saddles. We entered the rich quarter and found a place to stalk the front of the inn where the negotiations would take place.

The Grand Sage, like all buildings in this town, was built for war. Carolaughan represents the quickest way from the frigid north to the heart of the Kingdom without going around the Sorrow Wood. The taxes and prestige this valuable trade route offers means, no matter how often it is attacked, or how much of the city is burned to the ground, some noble simpleton will always see it resettled, by force of personality or by force of arms. Rich, decadent, and on the edge of the Sorrow Wood where dark fae and worse things held sway, it was virtually guaranteed that this city would be besieged during any and every significant conflict.

Carolaughan has come under fire every time the barbarians had rallied a significant army, but it has never fallen completely. Each time the penetration of the city stalls out a little faster, leaving a few more of the buildings behind. Every time they rebuild the city little larger and a lot sturdier than before, and not just to withstand the siege of the city, but of each and every building.

Eventually, seeing the power offered by the city, it was claimed by the Grand Noble family of O'Riagáin and made the capital. The Grand Sage was richer, and thus more unassailable, than most. A wall, as tall as two men and topped with pig iron spikes, surrounded the square three floor structure. The windows were thin, placed so that if the leaded glass panes were kicked out, they would be serviceable arrow-slits. As my eyes picked out each of the defensive measures, the next became more obvious. From the ornamentation of the wrought iron gates to the wooden bridge that rose over the pool that blocked easy access to said gate, it was all covered by a thin veneer of civility, but was brutally functional nonetheless. Combined with the walls, spikes, and gates, it became painfully obvious that this wasn't an inn; it was a castle. The fact that the great and the good wanted to call it an inn, however, made it an inn. Like a laugh that punctuates a lie, a guard stood outside, resplendent in shining mail beneath his gentlemanly attire.

The guard came to attention, snapping his halberd on the stone at his feet as if we were about to see the King himself. His eyes were sharp and his uniform clean, telling more of etiquette than skill at arms. His rigid back spoke more of servant than soldier. In a crisp, clear voice he sung out. "Approach and be recognized!"

Hey, dung-balls, does it look like we want to be heralded to the whole world? I didn't say.

Aelia moved forward to address the watchman. The miles and the fear and the blisters on her feet melted away until a royal princess stood before the guard. "I am Aelia Conaill, Grand Duchess of Conaill. I have a set of suites reserved for the bidding."

The guard smiled ruefully. "Shove off."

Fine. The princess, Grand Duchess actually, was wearing her old and stained riding clothes. She was also a bit disheveled and suffering from the runs from the meal of roast rat she had eaten last night. She was a week gone from her last bath and at least that long separated from the use of laundry or perfume. Her green eyes, however, had lost none of their nobility, "I beg your pardon?"

His bemusement faded into annoyance. "I said shove off, or I'll have the city watch throw you into the stocks. You have no business here–" He smiled nastily, a highly paid servant looking down upon a gaggle of tramps. "–your Grace."

Now, gentle reader, you realize this is the type of man I wipe my boots on. You also realize I was standing in the middle of the damn street with a damn Grand Duchess who, more than likely, had a damn assassin drawing a bead upon her damn back with a damn crossbow at that very second, right? You also probably remember that I am, by nature, impatient. That is why I took one, swift glance to make sure the guardsman was not wearing a gorge and then backhanded him in the throat.

Gorges are uncomfortable things, bits of bent steel that fit over the throat apple. They make your neck all stiff and sweaty, and they also stop people like me from reducing you to a hacking pile of offal on the street with a fist in your throat as I had to Captain Faux De' La Guarde. I removed the oversized iron key from his belt and unlocked the gates, gesturing everyone inside, slapping horses and cursing at the men. I kicked the herald once to make sure he stayed put.

If you guessed Gelia hated me again, you would be correct. I was beginning to believe you can't please some people. People like Gelia...and the six definitely not ornamental guards who had surrounded us as soon as we had entered the front doors. Their eyes were fixed on me, their breath coming in smooth rushes as their bodies primed to kill. This is a fight I wasn't going to live through–

"Aelia!"

–unless my string of bad luck had finally taken a wee trip to bother someone else. I held up my hands in surrender (and prepared to kick the first bastard that moved on me directly where he forked his horse), and waited for someone else to solve the situation for once.

"Aelia!" The guards melted back into their niches before the boisterous voice. "You look simply dreadful!"

He was made up like a street whore, color brought to pasty, flabby skin only by paints and blushes. His voice could only barely be contained inside his rotund majesty. His voice had exactly the same quality as I had tried to capture on the road with Captain O'Conner. He eyed me like I was some manner of strange beast, then turned back to embrace Aelia like a lost relation. Considering the inbred nature of nobles, that was a real possibility. They nattered back and forth like hens at a seed-pile as we were efficiently, and swiftly, booked into our suites.

I was impressed at the service, not impressed enough to be distracted from the hired swords who had turned out to see Aelia's defenses. Each of the noble families, there were over a dozen here, had their own troops of servants and guards that eclipsed our own. Each also had hired a killer, either freshly purchased or sworn to loyalty, and some had two. It's like wolves, really. We watched each other's movements and weapons: feeling, smelling and posing. Each time, a bit of mutual forewarning went out— a bond of kinship toward another skilled warrior, and an acknowledgment of willingness to die in order to kill. We were professionals and it was our job to die, all at once or bit by bit. The dwarves also had a caravan in residence, though I saw none of them as of yet.

I lent half an ear to Aelia and the fop, who turned out be Horatio O'Riagáin, Grand Duke of the Sorrow Wood and the Golden Hills. If I have ever been impressed with noblemen, I doubt I ever will be again. He was a pattering juvenile, however he did have some information of interest to me completely by accident. The auction was still on for a week from now, even though several nobles had sent word that they would not be coming due to various 'misfortunes'.

Being installed in our rooms was pleasant and surprising. The suites were groups of three or four rooms, linked to other, smaller, and less luxurious rooms for the servants. Baths, privy, bedroom, dining room, reading rooms— all linked together as a hedonistic apartment that could have housed a dozen peasant families. Within the hour our (the boys/men and mine) backs were screaming even more loudly as we funneled the sacks of gold from the horses to the suite. By the time we were done, tailors had been fetched and rushed there to fit us for new clothes.

The boys got new uniforms, the cleric got new robes, and Aelia was measured for a dozen new dresses. The seamstresses, and tailors then turned their attention upon me like a pack of wolves. Only once I was enveloped in a storm of needles, thread, and measuring devices did I see a way to turn them from an annoyance into an asset. I slipped into a mental costume of jovial eccentricity.

I needed several sets of black clothing for formal affairs. Black is the color that makes idiots believe you are a dangerous assassin and leave you alone. It is the color that blends least well at night, or anytime really, and is absolutely the last thing you want to wear for stealth. Funny enough, professionals will be convinced one is not an assassin simply by wearing a lot of it.

An anonymous voice, woven of razor-edged threads, whispered, *There is no weapon so great that confusion cannot act as a shield against it,* before fading into the back of my mind.

And, of course, I have more important things on my mind than making sure my clothing matches for polite company, I thought ruefully.

The servants tittered and pouted. Reds would set off my hair, and blues my eyes, they said. At least some splashes of color? I pretended to consider, and made as if to relent, but the rest of the clothing was all made of hardy cloth or leather, dark greens, browns, blues, grays, and charcoal. Like a Lord in his castle, I gave out my unfashionable orders without mercy. Interchangeable, anonymous cuts of fabric that could blend into a crowd, a chaos, or a shadowy crack. I begged small hidden pockets for secreting tobacco or keeping purses safe from pickpockets. I needed odd cuts with extra spaces for hidden flasks and maybe even a dagger for defense on the wild streets of the mean city. I needed soft, pliable boots to gently cup my tender feet.

Clothes are tools, like any other, and these were suits of armor with numerous hidden pockets and straps for weapons I had plans to procure. While I made my odd requests, I soothed their concerns with jovial speech, and thereby found out those things 'everybody knows' about the Grand Sage.

The most interesting thing was this: the Grand Sage used to be the seat of power for the O'Riagáin family until about twenty years ago, when the need to be fashionably apart overcame the need to look over the shoulders of tax collectors. The new palace, located two days away at Riagáinhead was finished. Sturdier, further away from any potential uprising, and far more comfortable, the royal family lived there now.

It seemed that all of the finest people in the world were here, excepting King Ryan himself. Some whispered the King had enough to worry about keeping a Kingdom intact which had been divided not fifteen years ago. Others thought the army of female servants he had at the capital were progressively taking up more and more of his time as they sprouted bastard children like lice.

On the other hand, all of the Grand Nobles had planned to be present, save those like Duke Flannghaile (He being busy learning to walk, let alone to taking over his duties from his father). His mother, still grieving the death of her husband beneath the hooves of his herd of horses, had taken place as regent. It was rumored that she was torturing a hastily gathered set from the underworld, searching for who had killed her husband. Súilleabháin, Grand Duke of the Southern Marshes, had the misfortune of consuming a roasted swan spiced with too much nightshade. He died blind and mad, but Dochartaigh was struggling in vain to recover from an axe to the back of his skull.

Yes, dear reader, things were getting ugly. Inside these walls was at least one murderer.

I rose from my seat in the entrance to the princess' suite. In the near complete and total black, I crossed the ankle-deep carpet with less sound than a stiff breeze. I twisted the knob to her bedroom, carefully measuring its resistance and entering in as a piece of coal in a pool of pitch. Stealth is partially luck, a bit is skill, but more than anything else, stealth is patience. I took ten minutes to shut the door and cross the chamber, but the noise I made was less than an owl's flight. Even Leoncur did not stir at my passing.

The light was filtering from the single white candle, spreading across the predatory night to splash across the Grand Duchess. Her soft skin was like one of the legendary Elvish queen's dresses, fit so perfectly that one day's worth of growth would make it unwearable. I am clear enough of mind to know I am not in love with her. To say I would refuse her bed if she offered would be a lie, but she would never offer, this I knew. The seemingly paltry sum she had paid me could be multiplied a thousand fold by anyone wishing her dead. I could kill her now for having lied to me. These hollow thoughts alone knocked against the back of my eyes, the ghosts of psychotics that filled my skull with the echoes of their screams. But they were not real, like the demons who tormented me on the road. The thoughts were simply a habit, a suit of clothing pulled on against the cold of vulnerability.

Gelia lay in a smaller, handmaiden's bed, her wrinkled face looking as kind as I had ever seen it. Her sagging, aged breasts rose and fell with her breath, showing the life that stirred within her. Some part of me still pushed me to slay her as well, for she definitely knew more of me than I did. The reason I did not, the reason I was still here, was something flighty and intangible. It was some small seed inside me, woken gods knew when. From the fear and pain it caused me, I also know it used to be dead.

I had taken a vow to protect something pure, this young woman with the will of a matriarch, and I could not let go of the mission. My emotions, my commitment, terrified me in the deepest levels of my soul. Yet, I knew no one would kill this girl while I lived. If I would continue to live was the point in much contention.

My eyes swept the ceiling, the thin windows, and every stone in every wall. Secret doors, hidden panels, odd shadows, sounds, even my nostrils flared to catch any vagabond smells. After thoroughly interrogating the room, I carefully left, locking the door behind me. I crept back into the entrance foyer and sat on an upholstered couch, sinking into the padding. Even if my duty denied it, sleep would have been held at bay by the constant threat of raven filled dreams. My mind began to go over all the information I had stripped from my surroundings. Of course now...

The sound of metal grinding on stone shuffled softly to my ears, banishing even the memory of sleep.

Finally.

The front door to the chambers came slightly ajar and stopped. It moved again, a slight push grinding hinges against the fine sand I had expertly installed there. I rolled off the couch into a crouch, picking the Phantom from where it lay on the carpet. I hefted it, relishing the lethal weight in my hands. I was fully prepared by the time I heard a cork, and a thick liquid (oil?) being poured on the hinges through the crack between door and jam. It helped muffle the grind as a cautious hand continued its business. It was too bad, really; he had picked the lock so quietly I never would have heard him otherwise.

I felt the Beast stir, begin to buck, to roar. Containing the rage inside a quiet shell made a sweat bloom on my brow. I slowed my breath as much as I dared, fearing my thudding heart would cause stars to spring before my eyes as it hungered for air. I squinted my eyes to hide the whites. I took comfort at the dark cloths wrapped around my head like a hood and mask. Then I froze, for patience is the most deadly weapon.

A stain of a slightly deeper hue poked from around the door, barely silhouetted by the candlelight outside. He paused, surveying the room, then he slipped in and shut the door. I lost him in the darkness until he moved again. Like me, he had come into a darkened room, dressed and hooded in dark colors. Like me, he had sat in the night, taking miniscule motions to cross open fields and sticking to cover. His foil, however was luxury itself.

The Grand Sage was an inn so resplendent and costly that all night candles burned in glass flasks down every hallway. It was just a little light, enough that a noble sneaking back from one apartment to another would not have to face the horror of a royal stubbed toe. It was just enough to dull the edge of the intruder's night sight. Worse yet for him, as the invader, he had to move. Movement in deep shadow attracts much more attention from than a stationary blotch. To him I was just a shadow caught between couch and table. To me, he might as well have been walking down a brightly lit street, whistling off key, and wondering out loud what to do with a certain bag full of coin.

If you know anything about me by now, dear reader, you know how fair and honorable a man I am. So it will come as no surprise that I waited until the lumpy shadow got just past me before I struck. The Phantom carved deeply, snapping bone and shearing muscle with equal abandon. The sheer force of the blow caused me to stumble on the table however, and I careened head first into a bookshelf. It ground to a halt having blazed a path from shoulder to navel. The assassin's knife-arm jerked spasmodically in death, the weapon flying from his grasp and sticking into the wooden door to Aelia's room with a deep, woody *thunk*. His only other sounds were a quick, strangled cry of pain and surprise followed by the burbling noise of breath exiting a ravaged lung through a bloody wound, but it was enough. Moments later the armed boys/men crashed into the room.

I had dizzily discarded my hood and stole to the corner so that anyone could see me and recognize me before killing me.

Thankfully no one tried. There are some accidents that just won't be fixed with an apology. Aelia and Gelia also emerged from their room– again against my orders. As both of them looked at the dagger stuck in the door with wide eyes, I wondered if they would ever learn to obey me and stifle their curiosity until I was sure it was safe.

Despite my objections, Aelia insisted on calling in the guards of the Grand Sage. I watched, partially annoyed and somewhat bemused as they came in, tromped over everything with big boots, and poked the body to make sure it was dead. After that, they simply stood around and shrugged at each other, their job apparently done. Finally one asked if we wanted them to take the body away. With some smoldering words, Aelia sent the guards off and made a motion to me that I took to mean 'Do what you want, Crow' as she stalked off to her room with priestess in tow.

Truth be told, I would have taken any sign, no sign, or her just leaving to mean, 'Do what you want, Crow.'

So I stationed Theo and Jon outside the door, gave stern warnings to the other two to get some sleep, and motioned for Theo to help me move the corpse before he went to his station. By the time I started, most of the blood was already on the floor, but I spread out horse blankets on the table to sop up the worst of the leavings.

'He' turned out to be a she, not that it would have made me hesitate to strike had I known. I pulled of the hood, with its thin canvas mesh covering the eyes, to expose a woman's bitter, ox-like face beneath. Amongst her possessions I found knives, vials of poison and oil, garrotes, and three emerald tipped hairpins– all tools used to sculpt murder. If any doubt was left, the mangled remains of some kind of a guild tattoo on her back, even cleft and ripped by the Angel and covered by drying blood so as to be almost totally unrecognizable, left no doubt. The Assassin's guild was now involved.

I had the feeling that I was the only person in the suite that knew exactly how bad the situation was, and this fact became horribly clear as the idiots I stationed at the door let six inn servants in to clean up the blood as the other two morons kept peeking around the corner like children on Pudding Night. Her Royal Highness, the Grand Duchess of Stupid and her nanny insisted on checking back on my progress with irritating regularity. Finally, I slammed my fist onto the table where we had spread the assassin, bringing all motion in the room to a halt. I gave the servants a look that could curdle milk. They stopped cleaning and instead dried the floor with a few hasty swipes and fairly ran out of the room with the dripping, bloody carpet under their arms.

I pointed at Godwin. "Go prepare four horses. Now!" And I stared at him a heartbeat too long, making sure as he reached the door to the suite he was at a run.

Next I... well I didn't exactly point at the Grand Duchess. "Milady, we need reinforcements. Can you please draft two letters?"

She nodded and retired to her chamber to fetch the required pen, ink and paper.

Next was Jonathan, my voice dripping with syrupy sweetness, "Get to the damned door and do not – and I realize that this may be complicated so listen clearly – do not let anyone in!"

The tone, mixed with a murderous twitch of the eye, banished Jon in a blink. Then I pointed at Miller, once again stern. "Prep your equipment and Godwin's. You will carry the letters and his equipment down to the stables. You will ride in a pair toward the Duchy. You will gallop. Kill one horse each, then ride the others as fast as you dare. Do not stop for any– and I do mean any– reason. Eating and drinking is optional. Shit in your breeches. If one of you gets held up by brigand or beast, the other is to leave him behind. Do you understand or do I need to fetch some shorter words?"

Theo took a step into the room, but in response to my contemptuous glare, he only puffed out his chest. "These are my men, Crow..." I loaded an obscenely worded, ego-withering retort that was surprisingly cut off as he continued "...if one of them is going to be sent into danger, I will lead him."

Those words hung in the air like the blade of a guillotine. I nodded once and said nothing, but Theodemar blushed. Miller disappeared into the boys' room, Theo went to join him, but just as I was about to get back to work, Gelia reappeared.

I gestured to the corpse on the table. "Unless you have been holding out on me, I think she's too far gone."

The aged crone's lips twisted churlishly and then reached out quickly to run a hand through my hair. I shied away like a wounded dog, but she held out her fingers to show them splashed with clotting blood. I reached up to the side of my head and found the same. A curse rose into my throat, but then Gelia's hands had me up and guided me to my room with uncompromising force.

I was on the bed like a recalcitrant child. Perhaps it is that I only have memories of bedding down on blanket covered rocks and mud, but these were fantastically comfortable. I had checked and found them to be goose down mattresses held aloft by a rope latticework attached to the wooden frame. It was almost too decadent, and after a night spent dozing on a couch, the feathers called sweetly to me. In just a moment, however Gelia brought in a bowl of warm water gathered from who-knows-where and began tending my head wound, as quiet and confused as I had ever seen her. Her hands were more tender than ever, and her ministrations more thorough. She began to mutter a prayer as she dabbed salves and pressed a thick pad to the wound. As she packed up her kit, my scalp began to burn and itch furiously. It faded moments later and I brought the pad down to my eye level. I dabbed a fresh patch on my wound, and it came back clean. I started to thank the old woman, but something hateful inside strangled the words in my belly. I settled for nodding in appreciation, and she moved to leave.

She made it about halfway out the door before turning to appraise me critically. I returned her gaze, only my flat demeanor met her sad searching eyes. Well practiced walls vaulted into the skies of my soul, cutting myself off from her, but then she spoke. "When I first met you, I felt you were the worst tragedy to befall this good family yet. Then I thought you a valiant savior, then I was convinced you were a stalking doom."

Why do Clerics enjoy being cryptic? Can anyone tell me? The next cleric who gives me half veiled commentary is going to find my boot prints covering the back of their robes! It had been a long night without any real sleep. I had little time or patience for this. "Care to tell me why I am such a threat? I have killed at least two dozen men, I have defied death, done the impossible, and rescued your charge from certain doom at least three times. I have done nothing but great service for Aelia, her men, and you, to put a fine point on it."

Her eyes widened and she shook her head fractionally. Her breath was the only thing powering her words as they escaped past her. "You do not know?"

I felt the Beast stir and my fingers itched for a weapon. My voice was a knife that I flung across the space between us, "Know what?"

She retreated from me, holding out a hand to stay me where I was. Her face mirrored her goddess, a bottomless well of pity. Fangs whirled inside my chest, chewing at my humanity with the need to kill, maim, be feared and thus be safe. "If you truly do not remember, Crow, it is better you should forget. But I do not think your past will lose you as easily as you did it."

Then she was gone. I leapt to the door, but when I heard the lock snick to enclose her in the sanctity of Aelia's room, I knew the conversation was truly over. My skin flushed and chilled at the same time. The thought of going in and beating the knowledge out of her flitted around in my head like a bird caught in a castle. As little as a few days ago, the thought would have been a serious consideration, by which I mean I would be planning it already, but now I simply shot the thought and let it twitch and go still on the floor of my mind.

I was changing, every single day, and I did not understand it. All I knew is that the sheer weight of inertia was pulling me in one direction and I found myself swimming in the other. I was exhausted, becoming unsure, in a word– conflicted. The only thing I was sure of was in conflicts somebody died. My hands went to my belly where a scar rested silently, a testament to the last time I had lost focus at the wrong time. I set my jaw and determined that if I died at least I would have the satisfaction of watching my life replay in front of my eyes. Then at least I would know who the hell I was. It was the least I deserved.

I sat down beside the corpse just as Theo and Godwin met in the main room. I noticed that only Theo was wearing his mail and tabard though both of them carried identical letters in their hands. I started to ask why he would choose to paint a target on himself, and then it became unnecessary as the pieces became a full picture. He saluted me, and I stood to return it with a fair amount of snap. He nodded to me, obviously trying to convince himself that he was, indeed, brave enough to go through with this. I clapped him on the shoulder, and then Godwin as well to not leave him out. They left the apartment like men, without a word until...

"Ride fast. Don't let Godwin spare the horses at the cost of your lives." My first thought was: *Who said that?*

The second was: *You did, idiot.*

Theodemar, a man who was about to make himself a target so

that the man who followed him would have a better chance to succeed, smiled and nodded again.

I wouldn't. My face burned, my stomach twisted, and my heart sank, because I knew this was the most honest thought I have had since the Shadow Wood. He was a far better man than I, and I wasn't sure I liked how that made me feel. Then he was gone.

I stared at the closed door for a long time before I cursed myself for a moon-eyed puppy. I had to roll up my sleeves to avoid soaking my new shirt to the elbows in bodily juices. No matter what you see on stage, death is always a messy affair.

Many hours later, I was sure I was close to gleaning all the information I could from the corpse. That is to say, I found nothing unusual for an assassin except an odd key. I opened the front door to our apartment, almost causing Jon to void himself where he stood, and used the key to both unlock, then lock, the bolt. That was how she had gained such easy access to this place, in the heart of The Sage. Still, it was much more intricate than others I had seen for this inn. I pocketed it for later consideration.

What was of more interest to me at the moment was the killer's multitude of weapons whose nature was stealthy killing. I made note of each, as well as where and how they had been hidden on the body. Miller soon appeared again, but as my face contorted in a snarl he hiked a thumb in a random direction, "Sun will be up soon. I have to relieve Jon."

I nodded and swallowed a nasty comment about how neither the rising or setting sun had anything to do with the direction his thumb had indicated. Unfortunately, he took my lack of insult as an invitation to sit down at the table.

"If she's an assassin, why isn't she wearing black?"

Words swam out of the cloud and out of my mouth, ghostly things that echoed with other voices, "Black is too absolute. It stands out at night, pushing you out of the background. You need things that are dark, but dark in the same way the world around you happens to be."

He fingered the rags that had been tied around her limbs and tools, "Why the scarves?"

The Fog was pregnant with pain, pounding in the back of my head and given license by lack of sleep. "If a shadow looks like a man, you will know it is a man. If the shadow is broken by a lighter swatch, it no longer has the outline of a man and your eye will pass over it. Plus, they silence equipment, act as bandages, masks, garrotes, and some of the longer, reinforced ones are climbing lines."

He pointed at a few relatively large clay vials on the table, "What are these?"

I rubbed my eyes, determined to not be in pain, "Sleeping poison mixed with chicken blood."

He made a face, "Who would be stupid enough to drink chicken blood?"

I gave him a look, carefully crafting it to express the precise amount of insult, "It's for dogs."

He found a long, thin, blackened silver flask, sealed with multiple layers of hard, red wax. "Poison?"

I nodded, still gingerly going through the bloody clothes, "Pastes. Probably sea snake venom, Redcap livers, or maybe pressings of the Death Cap mushroom. You pop the cap and stick your dagger in. It comes out coated."

He wrinkled his nose at the waste of so much money. "Seems fancy for poison. Why not make it out of clay?"

"What happens when you fall on the pouch?"

Miller shrugged.

"Sharp, poisoned shards."

That shut him up for a few more minutes, long enough for me to discover two more long, thin heart pins hidden in the assassin's boot lining. "What are those for?"

I mimed stabbing with one. "Between the ribs and into the heart."

"But it's so thin…"

I sighed and he dropped the subject. Instead he picked up a piece of waxed and folded paper. As I liberated a thin, razor sharp disc of metal from under the heel of one of assassin's boots, he unfolded it. He stared at the black goo for a second before silently folding it back up. I glanced up at him, but he was determined not to ask. He was so determined it hung in the air like an obscenely disgusting fart, demanding attention.

"Tobacco tar. Used in strong tasting foods." I said.

He smiled in victory, "How much?"

"That's enough to kill everyone in this apartment."

"How fast?"

"You wouldn't get to the main hall from this room. Even if you ran."

"Wait, it kills you? Tobacco is healthy!"

And the night's exertions were finally burning my patience down to a nub. "And a chiurgeon's lancets can pierce a heart. Anything that can heal, can kill."

He picked up a nasty little blade attached to a discreet iron collar and turned it around in his hand. "What's this thing?"

"Ring knife," I said from around clenched teeth, head pounding.

He stood as he slipped the collar over his finger with the blade pointed outward and made to punch the air with it. I rose from my chair and held out my hand like a father taking a toy away from a child, "Here."

He handed it over and watched me slip it on correctly, with the blade faced inward. I mimed the weapon's proper use in the air with bloody hands, but Miller just shrugged and shook his head. "It's too small to do any real damage."

That's when I finally lost patience. The haze of pain cleared, and every moment gained a perfect, crystal clarity. One long, angry step brought me around the table. He started to retreat, but a well timed foot caught his leg and put him off balance. That's when my hands snapped out like cobras. Left clapped to the side of his head, but Right, wearing the ring, was resting on the artery in his neck.

It would be so easy.

His eyes flew wide and he tried his best to freeze in mid air, but after a moment he began to fall again. His arms flailed and I alternatively pulled and pushed him, spinning him around until I was behind him. Left covered his mouth and Right slapped into his throat, blade barely pricking the skin over his windpipe. If he swallowed it would cut him.

So easy.

I spun the ring on my finger, then pushed him away, keeping him off his feet so Left could wrap around under his left arm and wrench him to the side. Right traced along his belly, then slapped him on the inner thigh and under his arm. I released him to the floor. He was shaking slightly as he checked himself for damage. Instead he found handprints painted in the assassin's blood on vital areas, each marking a possible death earned from a blade smaller than his thumb.

And the cold realization of the moment punched me in the

face. I was standing over him, sweating with denied release. I felt every inch the monster, but when he spoke his voice was shocked, shaken, but without rancor. "Can you teach me to do that?"

"You haven't finished your sword work yet." *Is there a word for wanting to clap someone on the back, kick them in the crotch, and stab them in the face at the same time?* "Go wash yourself off and take your turn at guard."

He bounced to his feet and did as he was told. Jon came in from outside, walking as if recently dead. I'm pretty certain he dropped to his bed without removing the smallest piece of uniform. I washed as well and plopped onto the seat by the door where I had waited earlier that night. Dawn was coming but sleep would not take me. Or maybe it is more truthful to say I dodged its grasp. There was so much to consider, so much that could go wrong. I was constantly reining in dark impulses that were becoming more and more powerful. I had to out think and out-plan gods knew how many assassins, mercenaries, and at least one Grand Noble. On top of it all, two boys – *MEN!* – were riding into very real danger on the road, and there was nothing I could do about it.

Somewhere, a long time ago, I had lost the ability to hope, and I am not sure I ever could pray. A vision flooded my mind's eye– Theodemar, broken and bloody on the road. Sudden tears stung my eyes and I squeezed them shut against the alien feel of their wetness. And that was it, a simple stumble that sprawled me in the dark forest of my mind, allowing sleep to catch me like a demon and ravage me all day and into the next night.

Eleven

The Shadows of The Great and The Good

AELIA had pled being sickened with fear at the thought of near death and had waved off dinners with the other Grand Nobles on that pretense. She was not afraid, though. She was furious. She stormed about her confines, raging at the unknown employer of the midnight visitor. She was prepared to wage war and in my mind, prepared to enter the negotiations.

That was good because tonight was the first of three grand banquets being held to honor the gods of the guests. Since it included contact with the dwarves, it was the start of the end to this deadly dance. Below, an army of servitors finished rushing about, oblivious to me as they put the final touches below.

The Great Central Hall of the Grand Sage was no less richly appointed than our rooms. Artwork and furniture was either carved in a classical style, or in actuality, antique works (I was betting on the latter). It was an open hall for the entire three stories to where leaded glass windows crowned the roof in a dome worth more than a dozen soldiers would see in a lifetime of service. During the day, this was a happy, lively place that captured the essence of daytime and sprinkled it down upon the meals of the great and the good. At night, with the three chandeliers and fourteen sconces lit, the windows became mirrors behind which I could hide.

As well could an assassin.

Below, the nobles began filing in with horrible slowness, taking places at the table without a thought to how quickly my posterior was losing all feeling against the freezing stone. At this moment, all I had to do was wait. I could say I waited like a hero, calmly and coolly, but that would be a lie. Have I mentioned that stealth is a good portion of patience? Have I mentioned I am not a patient man? Have I mentioned it was cold? Have I mentioned that there was an assassin coming? Good, now you're all caught up with my state of mind.

I shuffled back and forth in my crouch as little as possible, tensing and loosening my muscles to keep them from stiffening up. No such luck. The night crept in closer as the formalities (temporarily) ended down below and the meal had begun its tortured pace. Nobles like to punish themselves with long, drawn out banquets where each bit is served in courses. Each course is just enough to get you really hungry for the next, and has its own rules and etiquette.

The worst thing was the endless time alone in the dark gave me little to dwell upon other than Theo and Godwin galloping into danger at my word. If we were in luck, some enterprising guard in Aelia's employ had decided to chase her down taking the direct path and the boys had already met up with him. To say I believed that would be a lie. Rather than dwell on that, I tried to focus on the job at hand.

I was only there to test a theory. It was a good theory. If I was right, I was saving Aelia's life. Again. If I was a little wrong, I was saving some other noble's life, which I must hasten to add, is not strictly a reason to not do it. At least not by itself. I sighed into the heavy muffler that diffused the steam of my lungs and slowly turned my head from side to side.

The ornamental façade on the corners of the castle, done up to exaggerate the block-pattern of the stone, had provided a sure ladder onto the roof. The merlion blocks around the edge of the roof provided all the shelter I needed, which is not to say as much as I desired. On every side, soldiers walked in bored circles, in cautious pairs, and kept watch outwards in all directions. If any of them even paused to glance inward, I was just a not-human shaped splat in the lee of a big rectangular stone. If you have ever wondered why castles are normally unadorned brutish things with few places to hide, now you know.

I took a long coil of rope from under my light cloak and opened the loop enough I could slip it over the ornamental stone. Then I simply sat the coil down in the snowy shadow at the bottom and hoped I would never have to use it. It did give me a slightly less frozen place to put my butt. Mentally I inventoried my weapons, which made an impressive list but did not include the Phantom. I sorely missed it, but while I could contort myself to press into the shadows, a length of steel that reached from my elbow to the ground was not going to fit just anywhere. I had borrowed the assassin's short sword instead, and I felt somewhat naked for it.

At that moment, Aelia was in the feasting hall, warm and bursting with fine food and better drink as beautiful music tickled her ears and the ears of all the damned, stupid, inbred nobles. Don't mind me, I'm just a little bitter about having to try to stay warm, not an easy proposition on a copper-tiled roof in the middle of winter. I had to stay still, and it had been so long since I had climbed to the top of the keep. All I had to remind me of the hotness of exertion were the dull pains and the freezing sweat caught in my clothes. And it wasn't as if I could wear my fine travelling cloak up here, or even a heavy fur surcoat. I was clothed in various alternating dark and light shades, rags tied to break up the outline of my body so something human easily became separate splashes of snow and darkness in the winter night. Great for hiding, but if you think you can climb even a stupidly adorned castle in the middle of an icy winter wearing clothing that qualifies as warm, then you have another thing coming, likely a fall to your death, but I'm sure you deserve worse. At least the thick climbing gloves kept my hands from icing over.

I knew it would be today that the next assassin would strike. Don't believe me? Well allow me to marshal my arguments:

1) It was the first event where everyone was guaranteed of being present. Protocol required it. Once a strike was made at one of these things, it's not like there would be a lot of chances at the others as additional security was brought to bear. That meant now.

2) It was the perfect place to make a shot. You are hidden from below by the mirror effect of the glass and shielded from the towers and outer wall by the decorative gargoyles atop equally useless merlions that ringed the main keep's roof.

3) The key to the Aelia's apartment proved that the Assassin's Guild had inside help. Now I was just testing out the idea –

A puff of escaped breath erupted from beside me like the roar of a mute dragon. I froze and squinted as a shape clad in dirty white and sooty dark rags slowly and silently clambered onto the roof, provided a ladder by the same artistic moldings I had used. The very same, in fact.

Whoever he was, he knew his business. He moved like an optical illusion, easily dismissed as he crept across the snow patched copper roof to the dome of glass.

He only exposed himself once when he had to shift the crossbow off of his back and lay it on the roof. I tensed, half hoping, half terrified that some nameless guard would see him and raise a cry, bringing retaliation down on us both as they responded as only guards can...

Where are the guards?

It was true. The guards were gathered at the corner towers of the outer wall, accepting mugs of steaming goodness from servants.

Working like lightning, the assassin pulled down his mask, exposing an unshaven face as he spit out a wad of goo into his hands. He split it into two chunks and pressed the ends of a rag into each glob. One he pressed onto a glass panel, the other he pressed onto a copper plate of the roof. Any kind of wax or resin kept warm in his mouth would harden almost instantly, and tether the pane to the roof, keeping it from falling in and alerting his prey.

Some of the soldiers were gulping greedily, honestly trying to get back on duty before they were missed. They would not be in time.

Back on the roof, my opposite was working as invisibly and quietly as a wind full of arrows. Instantly his dagger was in his hand, and he was expertly prying out the lead caulking that held the pane to the metal frame.

I stole a quick glance at the guards, most of whom had not near finished their pints.

I was amazed at the assassin's speed and clarity. He worked quickly, efficiently, without pause or doubt. He popped the pane outward and it fell neatly into his hand to be set on the roof. No gap between this and laying down to use his feet to cock the crossbow. A bolt seemed to magically appear in the notch as he saddled closer to the dome and prepared for firing.

He was an artisan and this was his art. It was beautiful, magical, a ballet of poison and blade and pain. I admired him and sat in awe. Well, that's not exactly true. Still, he shouldered the weapon and prepared to fire, the climax of his silent symphony. Of course, that's when Right closed in on his throat from behind and Left, the cheeky bastard, used my dagger to keep the crossbow from pointing through the opening he had created. His whole body clenched and exclamations ran through his head loud enough I could hear them leaking out of his ears.

"Who hired you and who is your target?" I whispered in his ear.

Dear reader, you have followed my adventures. You have seen my dauntless bravery, endless wit, and unending luck. If you have marked them well, then you know exactly what happens next: the man grabbed Right with one hand, grabbed Left with the other, and let the crossbow fall to the roof, where it went off and sent the bolt into the night. He shot to his feet, dragging me with him, and then planted one boot directly on the arch of my foot. I yelped and let him go. Let go of him, and my dagger, damn it.

Below and on all sides, they carried on unawares, but my opponent drew forth a short fighting blade and lunged, his face contorted in abyssal fury. I drew my own short sword with one smooth motion and batted his thrust aside. He reversed this motion cleanly and came at me again, sending our weapons to kiss again and again like the stuttering ring of a mad bell.

I fully understood his rage. As much time as I had spent getting up here and into position, he would have had it worse. I have no idea how he made it over the outside wall with so many guards, nor how many hours he had waited out in the darkness for the perfect opportunity to strike, nor how often he had practiced for the perfect kill I had now ruined beyond salvage. He focused on me to the exclusion of all else, strikes no longer coming in single swipes, but in legions of hateful flying teeth. He was good, in fact, I daresay that he was far more skilled with his truncated blade than myself. It limited my options greatly.

The thick gloves made delicate blade work difficult. My dagger was on the snow and getting further away every moment. I missed the Phantom Angel more, because it would be useful just now, and less, because the very second I reached for it across my back he would have split me like a rabbit. The moment I stopped blocking his blows and tried to land one of my own, I'd lose a limb. If I tried to move in to grapple he'd have me parting company with my head. Our blades continued to scream at one another like alley cats as he backed me up step after step, coming ever closer to my original hiding place on the corner. I gave ground before his endless fury, even as his rage sapped his endurance faster than the most intense battle. I felt my foot slip off the edge of the roof. He struck again and again, given vicious energy by the nearness to the end.

He abandoned all pretense of skill and gripped his weapon with both hands as I went to one knee. He smashed against the fragile steel wall I hoisted in my defense, over and over, each blow ringing deeply in my soul. Even through the gloves, my hands were weakened and stinging. Then, without warning his downward blow reversed and the upstroke cast the sword from my hand. It sparkled and sang goodbye to me as it fluttered into the open air of the dark night.

But his victory was not without cost. Steam erupted from him in bright clouds, highlighted by the distant moon. His breath, like mine, came in ragged gasps and his eyes boiled with rivers of molten hate as they cooked me.

"What now, fool?" he spat through clenched teeth.

"Now that the guards have their bows?" He spun, in a circle, every direction bristling with steel headed death as I lunged leftward for the rope I had secreted at this corner, "Escape."

When the bards tell this story, I will swing gracefully from the rooftop as guards pierce the assassin with a rain of arrows. Don't get me wrong, twenty shafts left bows with the sound of a cloud of oncoming hornets, and at least fourteen penetrated the frail flesh of the assassin with ease. Using the age old soldier's adage of 'if it needs killed, it can't be killed too much' the shafts were followed by another volley. Many more skipped off the roof, but the shooters continued to nock and fire until the hired killer topped off of his feet. All that will be told in gory detail, and be absolutely correct. No, the error would be once I left the roof assuming that I'm at all safe or graceful.

I plunged a man length before the rope became taut in my grip. Even worse, rolling off the roof had given me some lateral momentum that carried me away from the wall, only now to be slammed back against it. The gloriously torturous yank slowed my fall, but threatened to pop my shoulder from its socket. I continued to descend, dragged upright by a stubborn fist forged in a thousand sword fights. I squeezed for my life, feeling quickly building heat of the rough rope speeding through the cage of fingers and heavy leather. The ground came up too quickly, but I hit it with bent legs as two arrows shattered against the stone above me.

Right plucked the short sword from the ground and slid it into the sheathe without help from my eyes. Beaten and tortured, Left grabbed rags from around my face, unknotted trick ties around every limb, and left fluttering cloths falling like forgotten sins behind me. I sprinted like a madman into the first open door and into the bowels of the inn. As far as anyone would be concerned, I was an assassin, and would take whatever measures required to make me dead.

This is when everything else stopped going my way.

The spiral staircase ahead boiled over with guards from above. Covered in snow, fresh nicks in my sword, rope burns on my glove, there would be no time for explanation before execution. Instead I bolted down a side hall. Behind me three guards sang in unison, booming voices making up in volume what they missed in melody, "WEST CORRIDOR, NORTH END, SOUTHWARD."

And then there were a lot more soldiers.

Cute trick. And my feet beat the floor like they resented it, but thought I made strides on the heavily laden soldiers, behind me they sung, "WEST CORRIDOR, SOUTH END, SOUTHWARD."

Guards sprang into the hallway from all sides, forcing me into the next doorway without even a bit of consideration. Steam and smoke slapped the lingering fingers of cold from my body as cooks gasped and cried out as I slammed the heavy door on the hand of an erstwhile apprehender.

A voice shouted out of the Fog, almost lost in the bustle of a far away marketplace. *The trick to losing people in a busy place is to make it busier. Pick the holes in the crowd and run there. Just make damn sure they close behind you.*

That is why I dove over a table and reached up and yanked down the metal racks holding the cookware down behind me. Food of all types went flying as I toppled baskets, bowls, cauldrons, and pots in my wake. Boiling mush, iced fruit preserves, slippery dollops of fat, and hard dried vegetables slowed my pursuers, but hope, all hope, hinged on the door ahead leading somewhere, anywhere I could disappear.

Of course that's when I burst forth into the Grand Central Hallway, skidding to a halt in front of a crowd of people who's whim could separate my head from my shoulders. The first to notice was the quartet of musicians who broke off their songs and uncovered the muffled calls of pursuit. Given the honored head of the table, the dwarves looked on curiously. Next to them, storm clouds gathered over the gaily painted face of Horatio O'Riagáin. Further down the table, flanked by Jon and Miller and escorted by Gelia, Aelia watched me with wide eyes. She paled visibly. Guards all around the room tensed and practiced killing me in their minds. I did the only thing I could think of, and made the most intricate, respectful low bow I was capable of.

Horatio stood and demanded, "What is the meaning of this?"

I fluttered through a hundred mental costumes but they all frayed into dust in my hands. I smiled, but my mouth opened and closed without even a hint of an explanation. And that was when my pursuers burst into the Hall and tackled me to the floor. I hit my chin on the stone and stars blossomed before my eyes. Under the press of a dozen bodies they stripped me of half a dozen weapons (leaving a goodly number behind) and hauled me to my feet.

But at the exasperated, lilting repetition of, "What is the meaning of this?" had them forcing me to one knee as they all prostrated themselves as a group. Several were shooed out by the ranking man, leaving four to keep their hands on me.

"Sire, we apprehended this assassin."

Miller and Jon, stationed at her side, stood shocked and mute as Aelia bounced to her feet, cheeks flushing as she shouted, "That is not an assassin! That is my manservant!"

Someone took the obvious shot. "Your manservant is an assassin?"

"The assassin is dead on the roof, along with all his weapons of murder. I interrupted him as he sought to slay one of your good and Lordly number," I said. Or, I would have, if right after the word 'interrupted' I hadn't caught a mailed fist to the back of the head, making the world spin drunkenly. My heart began to thunder in my chest, clouding my ears with its infernal beat. The Animal wanted out, tugging and pulling at me to let it free to kill. *Not yet, damn it!*

I shook my ears clear of the ringing as Horatio was saying, "...to understand that there is an assassin on the roof of this very inn, Lieutenant Palmer?"

Again I piped up, "There is, with all his equipment and articles of death, Your Grand Lordship."

Or, that is what I would have said if there hadn't been a quick, "Shut up, you!" and a fist to the side of my face right after the word 'is' passed my lips.

I stared into the glassy, bloodshot eyes of the abusive guard, noticing several days worth of beard, the rotting teeth from too much drink, and cruel set to his lips. A flood of jumbled memories erupted from the Fog and I was filled with such raw hate that only divine providence kept him from bursting into flames under heat of my stare. He saw the fire inside me, and was not afraid.

What I missed was Horatio asking but I was filled in later that he asked, "How is it this man," indicating me, "managed to discover a plot against one of us when all of you did not?"

But the guard that hit me decided to hawk a quick gobbet onto my cheek. The Beast burst forth and, for the life of me, I could not catch him.

The loose, thin, outer shirt had a dozen uses. One of the most popular was if you are held, it is much easier to give guards the shake if the shirt rips when you pull back violently. The shirt sleeve parts, leaving one arm free, and the right man can do a lot of damage with one hand.

My thumb found the face of the man who hit me, nail biting into an eyeball and causing him to let go of my other arm. The remaining guards fought to get closer and put hands on me, tripping over one another as I rolled away and slipped the thick, steel rods out of the fronts of my boots. One guard had his hands on my collar until one rod whipped into his temple and dropped him like a sack of shit. The one behind me closed his hands around my neck, but before he could press the advantage, I thrust the needle sharp point of a rod into his kneecap, shattering it. The next got his sword out, but then a thrown rod pierced his forearm, paralyzing the muscles and causing him to drop his weapon. Lieutenant Palmer got his sword out to en garde, but instead of attacking he backed off before my fury.

Of course, to the audience of aristocrats, he appeared to fear my shin length rod. Somewhere in the room, one of the nobles was clapping. A few others giggled. A couple tossed coins to show appreciation at the wonderful show.

I blinked, vision clearing of the red, murderous haze. Though the royals might have been impressed and amused, their personal guards had drawn in close. Everyone had been caught off balance by the viciousness of my attack, but now they were ready, simply weighing the odds of killing me in one shot. Everywhere I looked I saw spring guns, throwing daggers, darts, and all other manner of missile. They were all ready to dance in front of their respective charges, dying in their stead while hurling my own death back. Only then could I call back the Animal and put him in his cage.

Gelia shot from Aelia's side and ran to me, covering my shoulders with her light cloak in a display of modesty so extreme as to be comical. She tutted and produced a plain, functional kerchief and pressed it to my cut chin. I started to recoil, but she handled me roughly, eyes beseeching me to simply play along. Even before I realized I was trusting her an awful lot, I let her minister to my hurts as if I was a child back from the fields. The sight of the old woman without fear, ministering like a grandmother, sent a titter amongst the great and the good and relaxed the room slightly. I tossed the rod to the pile of crying men at my feet. I spoke around her, gasping, "I found the assassin because I was looking for him, Your Grand Lordship."

Horatio O'Riagáin, Grand Duke of The Sorrow Wood and Golden Hills stared at me with a mix of awe and terror. "You are indeed a man of great skill."

"You are too kind, Your Grand Lordship." Gelia backed away to her place by Aelia and I bowed again. "May I examine the body?"

For the record, that's how you keep from being arrested as an assassin. I'm not sure how you prep the princess, the cleric, and the fop before hand to make sure it all goes off at the right time, but the theory is sound. You see, I asked to see the body and was immediately denied. Horatio wanted his own men to go over the corpse. It was fine with me, I just needed an uncomfortable excuse to be dismissed. Requesting the body was easy, the adamant denial immediate enough so that suspicions were raised. Nobles began asking uncomfortable questions about where the guards had been and why the mulled wine had been handed out to men on duty instead of waiting in the barracks for when they were off duty as was customary. In fact, nobody could really see anything wrong with a warm, spiced drink on a cold night, but distracting the guards all at once cried out for answers. Nobles do not like being made to search for answers by their peers. They like less being forced to find answers in front of their inferiors (namely me).

I was dismissed, but I graciously helped pick up the men I had beaten senseless not minutes before. I took care to wind up holding up the poor bastard who's knee swelled up angrily as it bled profusely. Voices behind were becoming more clipped and measured as we ushered ourselves out, a sure sign that the friendly façade of the feast was collapsing fast. I did hear one name, intoned as a shield against the incoming glares by Horatio O'Riagáin. It was Captain O'Loinsigh.

We were moving as a knot toward the healer's quarters, past the dispersing guards in the hallways. I got a few hard stares, but nobody was willing to move against the servant of one of the Grand Duke's guests just yet. We made it to a staircase and descended below ground level. The smell of herbs became overwhelming, and a lot of banging on a great oak door brought a small wizened man out of hiding. The injured were brought inside and the leader of this little gang and I made to leave. I let the twerp get to the base of the stairs before I tripped him face down and planted my boot into his groin with all the force I could muster.

It took several minutes before he could speak, and when he could, nothing he said would be considered printable in a civilized society. My shirt was torn, sleeves missing, and Gelia had pinned on a white modesty cloak to what remained, an overall effect that was quite ridiculous. Yet I needed to be taken seriously by the young lieutenant. A sharp knife pressed gently into the lower lid of his left eye focused him on the benefits of civil discourse.

Then I asked, "Captain O'Loinsigh..where is his room?"

"I will kill you, assassin!" was not the answer I wanted.

"What? You figure that the four guys you had with you the first time was too much of a handicap?" I removed the knife and sat back on the stair, my posterior inches from his face. I made as if cleaning my nails with the blade. "A compromise Lieutenant– you tell me where O'Loinsigh is and I promise that the next time you unsheathe a sword near me, I will gladly turn you into meat where you stand."

The young man staggered to his feet, his hands twitching for the grip of his sword, but I was so very close, and the dagger in my hand was so very sharp.

"He should be in his quarters."

"And those are?"

"His is the first door west past the barracks." Palmer spoke somewhat churlishly I thought. After all, I could have just cut out his eye and listened to him scream the answer.

"Take me," I said in a voice that stated very clearly that even though it looked like I was putting the knife away, it would forever be in my hand.

Thankfully, he behaved himself as we traveled upwards through the halls to the outer courtyard. This was fine by me because I was working the painful knots out of my shoulder left by the rooftop rope escape. I still had little doubt I could maintain control of the idiot until we turned the blind corner to the rear side of the Grand Sage. Furthest away from the gate, the barracks sat next to the stables, the drafty, yet perversely unventilated wooden structures virtual twins. The reason they were back here was simple: vital to life and security they may be, it would be awful for the nobility to have to see where the horses shat or the dirty soldiers slept. It also, and I am not certain that this was by accident, allowed guards to mount up out of sight of the street and any guests to quickly respond to any threat. And by threat, I mean something big enough that simply shutting the door to what amounted to a castle wouldn't do it on its own.

Apparently this was one such time. Guards, shucked of heavy mail and shield and armed only with swords, worked alongside stable boys to sling saddles onto the backs of trembling horses, only to mount them the very instant the cinches were tight. They left in waves of five or six, necessitating the Lieutenant and I hug the castle wall as they rode forth like a rushing wall of thunder.

Palmer forgot himself for a moment and asked, "Where are they going?"

"To search the roads for the good Captain." I said, moving again.

"Why would the Captain be on the road?"

I sighed, because I needed Palmer along to give me the illusion of being escorted, but I'd much prefer him tongueless. "Let's say if you arrange for all the guards to be busy at the time an assassin tries to sneak into the castle, it is probably wise to be elsewhere no matter what else you had planned for the evening."

The Lieutenant reacted like a upper crust matron walking in on country boys swimming nude in a city fountain, "The Captain would never do such a thing! He is the most loyal man in the barracks."

"I would bet he's the one that ordered the servants to bring the drinks to the roof."

My opposite frowned at me, "What proof do you have, cur?"

In response I just motioned to the chaos all around. Another officer called out to the next group of soldiers mounting up. "Sorrow Road, boys! Keep your lamps bright and your edges sharp!"

And then they stormed off, giving me enough cover in the confusion to loop around the crowd even in the comical cloak. The doors to the long building for the enlisted men was open and soldiers were constantly coming in and out. Beyond there were five doors to much smaller buildings, apartments for the officers. The first one, belonging to the Captain, had been messily kicked open. With no guard, and all the commotion behind us, it was simplicity itself to just walk in.

"The Captain is an honest man. I'd stake my life on it."

"And if someone gave him a waterweight of gold?"

"Never!"

Behind him another officer was rallying his hunting crew. "His Grand Lordship only needs the head back, gents. Gold coins to those that carry it!"

Meanwhile I fixed the Lieutenant with a hard stare, "How about three waterweights?"

At least that shut him up. The sparse room had the luxury of privacy, and little else. Snow was tracked over the floor where the door kicker had come in, looked under the bed and in the wardrobe, and then left. I opened drawers as the Lieutenant made mute protest, and fingered through his wardrobe and chest. So much had been left behind, as if the Captain would be back any second. I poked around, and found what was missing almost as telling as what was left behind: every bit of heraldry or military equipment for sure.

Finally, lost in thought, I sat on the edge of the bed and considered the facts as I knew them. The heels of my light, climbing boots clunked against something under the blanket and I lifted it, exposing large, reinforced boots not unlike those I had worn all through the Sorrow Wood. These, however, were made of leather dyed in Horatio's colors, like those worn by all armed men in his employ. Boots like those would take a man across the kingdom and not give up when the average street boots would have your feet covered in blisters and splitting at the seams after six days cross-

145

country. Heavy boots were worth more than two months wages to any guard, even an officer, and it usually took days to cobble a fresh set. Just then the Lieutenant lost his patience, "The Captain is not here."

"No, and he will not be found on the road." I murmured.

"What did you say?"

And then I remembered I was not talking to Miller, Godwin, Theo, or Jon. Gates as impenetrable as any in the kingdom slammed shut inside me and I exited the Captain's apartment. "You are free to go, Lieutenant. Do stay out of trouble."

Color flushed his cheeks as he realized he was chasing me like a lost puppy, begging for scraps of knowledge. "In the name of the Grand Duke, I order you to tell me what you know, peasant!"

"Try not to get on my bad side until I've had time to develop a proper hatred for you, Lieutenant." I tossed the acid words over my shoulder, not bothering to turn but keeping a keen ear open for the rasp of a blade being drawn.

Instead, another soldier, slightly more senior than Palmer from the looks of him, came and grabbed my puppy by the elbow. "Lieutenant! I need you to lead a party here..."

"But sir, the man from the roof..."

But of course, I was already gone in the crowd– one of my more useful skills.

I made it back to the suite with Her Grace. With dark thoughts orbiting my head loudly enough for all to see, Aelia's party all avoided any contact. It wasn't hard. I returned the cleric's cloak, slept until dawn, and then was up and about. I stayed out all day, trusting the boys to keep the princess safe as I plied my lies to every ear that would hear.

After all, it is not uncommon for an elder brother to inherit the father's estate. And if that estate included a travelling business, the beloved older brother would need hardy travelling boots. As a devout younger brother, it would be an act of love to find out which cobbler was making said pair of boots and pay for them in secret. The shiny silver coins in the hand of the merchant would bring such trust that finding out where the boots were to be delivered was a detail too trivial to be remembered by anyone.

The boots were to be delivered tomorrow.

That's why I was on a roof that night, freezing my ass off again. This place was not unlike the den of iniquity where I had stashed

Aelia during our first day in Carolaughan. Of course it did not appear at all homey from up here. It is still cold and it is still dark. What has changed is my shirt, my camouflaged rags, my location, and my whole perspective.

Soldiers do not change. Take a dozen and set them loose on a town with a pocket full of coin and they will be drinking anything that burns, bedding anything dazzled by coin, fighting anything that gets in their way, and betting on any game they can lose. Reduce the number to one, and the roar of debauchery becomes a cat's cry—more annoying than dangerous. This one, Captain O'Loinsigh, sat in his room all day. He paid hard coins for the serving boy to bring him at first the finest spirits, moving on to the strongest, in the run down little hole. No company, paid for or otherwise and no tips for the serving boy either, which is why a few copper bits easily bought his habits and room location.

I crept across the slate roof, careful of a thousand things that could send me tumbling over the edge to my death. I watched for a thousand more that could slip, tinkle, crack or shatter and give me away to anyone inside. Again I looped a rope over a chimney, but this time I brought the end with me across the top of the building to the overhang where his window lay.

I tell you this, if a man is sitting around for a whole day, drinking progressively stronger libations, you can assume three things: he is being consumed by sadness or fear, he is probably emptying his thunder mug out of the window every hour or so, and lastly, he's extremely unlikely to remember to latch said window. A quick peek over the side confirmed at least the last of these, which is good because I was tired beyond reckoning of being wrong.

Without guidance from my head, my hands twirled the rope flawlessly around one leg, cinched tightly by hand and knee as I gently rolled off the roof and expertly hung upside down just outside the window. My free hand poured oil out of a long, thin vial on the hinges, and then skillfully worked the pig skin shutters open a bit at a time to minimize any chance of a creak, groan, or squeal. It opened onto a room with no less than four candles burning into pools. In the light, a still form sprawled in a lonely chair at a table strewn with bottles. My knee loosened as my hands pulled me inside with all the sound of a gliding owl. The soft boots Aelia had purchased for me, comfortable and useless for long treks through the woods, made little sound on the floor. I stalked forward and

147

removed the heavy climbing gloves. Then I pounced.

Sometimes you want quiet. Sometimes you want subtle. Sometimes you want to grab a sleeping man and tilt him back on the rear two legs of his chair to keep him off balance. You want your left hand to grab his right arm to keep him from grasping a weapon and slashing blindly at you, you want to grab him by the throat with your right hand to first squelch any cry, and to let him know that you are absolutely, irrevocably in charge. And if you had a bad experience the last time you tried this, you wear a blade ring on that strong hand.

"Tell me who paid you off," you would say. Most likely he'd tell you, unless he was me. Then, in that case, you would pull him off balance, grasp his hand with a fist seemingly made of steel, and grasp his neck to cut off any scream and let the blade ring nick his neck ever so slightly

Then you would say, "Tell me who bribed you."

That's when you realize you have been told that your target had been drinking all day; you had counted on it. And now, as he wakes up, thrashing and drunker than you have ever been in your life, all he can say is, "Wha? Girroff! Isumin. Iscampn da DUKE!"

And while his lids droop and head lolls bonelessly to the side, you silently scream out curses at every god you have even heard of. I should l know. I did.

So I took the chance and let go of his arm to slap him across the face. The clap resounded in the tiny room, and it brought him around a bit, but it was clear that if the Duke's army didn't catch him, he would likely drown himself in drink. Still, I controlled his sword arm and throat as I enunciated very clearly, "You have the guilty thirst of a traitor, O'Loinsigh."

He reacted like a branded horse, or at least a drunken branded horse as he yelled, "Imma nottaraior. Iamma not. NOT!" But at least his anger was clearing his head slightly.

"The Duke's men are out there looking for you, O'Loinsigh. Tell me who paid you and I may find safe passage west to the border."

The Captain leered at me knowingly, anger fading back into the comfortable haze of alcohol, "Shove yooour safe passage. I'mma goin' to Riagáinhead."

It was as if he slapped me back, "The Grand Duke's palace? Horatio O'Riagáin's guards will kill you the instant you set foot on his land."

But he simply rocked further back in the chair, suicidally letting my bladed hand keep him from toppling over as he sung, "Ooooooooopen arms. Ooooooooooooopen arms."

"You are mad. They will hang you from the walls as a traitor."

My first clue was the sharpening of his eyes, the clearness of his voice as rage poured through him, "I am no traitor."

While I was holding O'Loinsigh's right hand to keep him from attacking, it very suddenly became clear that he was left handed. The dagger came out of nowhere, sweeping across my vulnerable belly. Instinctively I recoiled even though I tried to grip his neck tighter as he slipped out of my left hand. He hit the floor hard but bounced to his feet unsteadily, giving me plenty of time to try something else. I leapt away, sweeping a thick curtain of blankets from his bed over his head and using the momentary confusion to break his nose with a vicious kick. He collapsed immediately, dropping his dagger.

I swept the knife under the bed and watched him closely, but he lay still, allowing me to sit for a moment. Say what you want, but scaling a building, hanging from a roof, gaining entry to a building and then wrestling with a drunk is enough of a night for anyone. Now all I had to do was drag him somewhere his screams would not be heard, let him sober up, and break fingers until he told me who had bribed him to distract his own men.

I shook my head, walked over to the table, and searched for a bottle that had more liquor than backwash in it. That's when I realized that the leather covered jug in the middle of the table was not a jug, but a pouch stuffed so full it sat upright. With trembling hands, I opened the drawstrings and released the contents to glint in the light. It was a fine scrip, made with several internal pouches for bits of copper or silver, but instead of whatever kind of bric-a-brac the center chamber of the leather vessel was meant to hold, there were instead golden coins.

"You are a man after my own heart, Captain." Each coin was thin but heavy, and bent easily to the tooth, testifying to the content of pure gold. "You were expensively bought."

But there was something off... I brought forth a fresh coin and examined the edges, experimented with the minting marks and held the gold up to the light so it could catch every sparkle cast by the candles. It brought a chill to my skin as I saw every perfection on every gold coin.

The whole bundle disappeared into my oversized belt pouch next to a dozen bits of equipment and I turned to the still recumbent and blanketed form of O'Loinsigh.

"I know who paid you, Captain." I jostled him with one boot but he lay without twitching. "The game is mine, Captain, get up and I can get you to a place of safety."

I kicked him lightly, and then not so lightly, to the same effect. I drew my short sword with my off hand, but he did not move. I felt my scalp prickle and I planted my heel on the thumbnail of his exposed hand. In seconds, I was pressing with my whole weight and getting no response. That's when I used the tip of the sword to flip the blankets aside to expose his pale face and the explosion of blood leaking from his throat. I opened the turncoat Right hand, the hand that had tried to stop him from falling back even as I pulled away from his dagger, the hand I could not use to draw the sword because it was the hand with the finger with the damned ring blade on it. It was just a small nick, but the artery was large and the blood thinned from excessive drink. Now, the only link to the person trying to have Aelia killed was also dead. And I was willing to bet that my escapades on the roof had not been forgotten, but instead were creeping through diplomatic apparatus like caustic chemicals in an alchemist's lab.

I had to find a connection that couldn't be dismissed due to rank or station. Failing that, I needed Aelia to send me after the man with the money. Or even whoever controlled the assassins. A sharp knife in the dark would solve...

Pain exploded across my back, a lifetime of lashes compressed into a few minutes. I could only make a strangled cry and fall to the floor. My limbs trembled. My vision blurred. It felt like venomous insects crawled underneath my skin, pulling out chunks of skin from the inside, hollowing me out into a bag of useless flesh.

Fists of agony pounded me again and again, dropping me to the floor where darkness leapt on me like a predator.

The world was in color, bolder and richer than I had ever seen. Every splinter and stain of the run down room gained a beautiful random life of its own. Everything seemed to fit into a master puzzle I could only guess at, where this rats nest of an inn was so squalid, not because of abuse or neglect, but because it was in its very nature. It could not be anything else, but perhaps it could be more... I lifted my head from the floor to stare at a cloaked angel standing above me.

I had always known he was there.

Something began to scrape my heart with veins of frost as the figure raised his arms. Two hands, carved of aged alabaster, emerged from within the robe woven of webs and night. He held a crooked staff topped by a regal raven in his right hand, carved of ebon wood so pitted and worm-eaten it seemed to wither and crumble in his grasp. His left held the most powerful weapon I had ever beheld. Easily ransomed for a king's crown, the gold and ruby blazed in the shape of a lidless eye. Set in a golden lattice of razor sharp metal, every time I judged I had the hilt marked, the precise method to wield it escaped my grasp. He seemed to be offering the statuettes to me, waiting with the patience of one who has no life left to trickle through the hourglass. Power. Secrets. Wealth. I reached for the sword...

And the door to the room smashed open. Corpses, dressed in rags, piled in with hands clasping poisoned blades. Chained to the floor by thick links bolted to my back, I had nowhere to run as they piled upon me, teeth flashing black and rotten.

I awoke too frightened to scream. Then the room swam into focus, a plain place of dirt and desolation. I shook off the vision, or at least pushed it back into the Fog. The pain didn't stop. Not really. It just started to fade until it was tolerable. I sat up, tears and snot streaming off my face into my lap. It faded further and further, but it never went completely away, never. For all I knew it would always be there, a phantom agony waiting to pounce and torment me forever. It had kept me prisoner until morning, and if the man at my feet was not a wanted criminal I would be in a lot of trouble trying to explain his unlawful exsanguination.

But right now I needed a way to get back to Aelia and convince the other nobles that I had sat all night on the roof and caught an assassin, because I am a hero, not a scoundrel. After all, in a dragon's cave you will find dragons, but also you will find knights. The Captain would help greatly to that end.

Then I remembered that O'Loinsigh was dead. But I also remembered a head was easier to carry than a body.

TWELVE

THE MISSING PIECES

THE jugglers, musicians, and acrobats looked quite entertaining. The bear baiter was a bit much. Every bodyguard in the room watched the bear intently, perfectly willing (the only question was able) to turn the damn thing into a rug the instant it twitched toward the nobles sitting behind the feast tables.

I strode into the great hall without fanfare or much in the way of cleaning. I had the look of a man who had ridden far and wide in a short amount of time. In fact, I had gone to a dry patch of dust in a back alley and splashed my clothes to make sure that's just what I looked like. Once the damned bear and his owner cleared the way, I pushed past the next series of acts, the functionary trying to keep everyone in line, and the two guards at the entrance to the makeshift stage, and stood at the center.

The murmurs of the great and the good pattered on the ground like the last lingering moments of a contrarian rain. As their disapproving stares grew in intensity, I stiffly went to one knee before them. Horatio left me there for a good, long time before he recognized me, "Ah, the rooftop bodyguard. Why have you interrupted our entertainment?"

People starving, barbarians sacking and burning farms, nobles dropping like flies, and he's worried about delaying his entertainment. By way of answer, I walked to the front of his place, causing all four of his bodyguards to coil for attack. I pretended not to notice and I sat the tied bundle of blankets on the table. "Your Grand Lordship, a gift from your cousin Aelia Conaill, Grand Duchess of Conaill."

I left without being dismissed. I smiled only a little when I passed by the doors to the corridor beyond, for the great hall behind me erupted into exclamations of all kinds as Horatio unwrapped O'Loinsigh's head. By the time I made it back to the apartment, a warm glow was growing inside my chest. The idea of shocking a room full of blue bloods, and especially laying the head of his traitor at the feet of his employer, brought a smile that filled me from beard to boot leather. I passed Jon on guard duty on my way into Aelia's suite. He started to say something, but a raised hand stopped him. Fine, the fact that the raised hand was covered in Captain's blood may have stopped him more than the hand, but he shut up and that's what mattered.

I was delighted to find a basin of lukewarm water on my dresser, yet aghast I had left the door unfastened so that any random functionary could gain entrance. It was unlike me, so unlike me in fact that I checked every fingerlength of the room. Then I sniffed the water, but detected no traps or poisons. Still, the nagging voices that echoed out of the Fog spurred me to toss out the contents and go fetch fresh myself from the kitchens. Each time I passed Jon he acted like a puppy with the bladder of a mouse. I made it a special note to stop him from talking to me each time.

It wasn't mean, not really. I had enough on my mind and now I just had to figure out the next step.

Once again ensconced in the safety of my room, I carefully removed the heavy weight of gold from inside my shirt, as well as a dozen means of stealthy death. I stripped down and washed down, careful of the old wound that must lay, buzzing, across my upper back. The skin felt slightly textured, but otherwise unbroken. I pushed thoughts of the malady aside, however, because the auction would begin in four days. Four days was a long time with a price on one's head. Before one more poxy bastard was allowed to try to kill me, I was going to eat like a noble and then sleep like a child. I pulled on warm clothing across my damp skin and fastened only three blades to various locations, practically going naked as I strode out into the common area and right into Theo who was sitting at the table, eating thick stew with gusto.

I exclaimed wordlessly as he came to his feet and he embraced me like a brother. I felt a cold shock as he touched me, but then relaxed and embraced him back, feeling nascent tears press at the back of my eyes. I held him at arm's length and stared at him up and down, finding no hurt nor malady, but then a doubt. "Godwin?"

"Still abed. He's been denying himself sleep, making himself sick with guilt that we killed the first set of horses." He smiled as he ladled out stew into a bowl for me.

I accepted it gratefully and set to it. "One set? I would think both. You are back far earlier than any could have hoped."

"Captain Roehm had decided it had been too long without word, and started toward Carolaughan with a hundred men. We met him on the road and joined him for the return trip."

Another army outside the gates, just what we needed, I thought on one hand, but at the same time a great, crushing weight was lifted from my shoulders. Well, a few weights. Theo and Godwin were safe, and suddenly I wasn't solely, or at least mostly solely, responsible for the good lady's safety anymore. I was suddenly very cheery. "Well one thing's for certain, you're assured of a promotion after this! Bravery in the field and... and.. and why are you making that face?"

Blessed with the talent for concealment reserved for particularly naive nuns and surpassed in dissembly by toddlers, his face had twisted around his mouth as if he were chewing on bitter herbs, or perhaps bitter words. He sat there for a moment, trying to contain himself until I arched my eyebrow, the tiniest of actions that pushed him over the cliff. "I'm being punished."

I nearly gagged on a mouthful of stew. "Punished? For Gods' sakes why?"

"Three month's pay gone..." Godwin's sulky voice slopped over my shoulder, "...for leaving the Grand Lady Aelia in your care. Your care."

I don't know if he meant to repeat that as a way to underscore my part in Theodemar's newfound poverty, or if he repeated it because he repeats everything, but Godwin stared at me in a distinctly unfriendly manner when he came and joined us. I shook my head, willing my ears to leave me and go get a pair that would do the job properly. I dredged up all my wit and witticism to blurt, "What?"

Godwin got his own bowl of stew and picked at it as if it were made of horse meat. "He was the ranking man and it was his responsibility to stay, to stay here with her. Here with her."

Another problem. Fine. I mentally ticked off how severe a beating I would hand out for this transgression against Theo. "On who's authority?"

"Captain Roehm," Theo said. "He led the party himself."

I smoldered in my seat, and suddenly Theodemar wasn't quite as hungry anymore. "Have I taught you boys nothing? Question everything. Question everyone. There is nobody looking out for you but you, and everyone, including and especially the nobles, will use you as a cobblestone rather than twist an ankle. You must look more deeply!"

Both boys stared at me like I had gone insane. Quite possibly I had, speaking so much bold truth to them so blatantly. I slapped Theo on the back and motioned for him to take another serving. "Eat. You too, Godwin. This is my mess and I will address it one way or another."

Theo smiled weakly and went back to eating, but Godwin's smirk had more than a dash of nasty to it. "You will address it, will you? I'm sure. Sure."

I had ordered him to ride one of his prize horses to death, and so I suppose it was inevitable that Godwin was to be slightly peeved. I would have to talk to him about it later. That, or slap him until he saw things my way. Still, punishment meant authority, and that meant a new commanding officer in residence. "The Captain, what kind of man is he?"

"Old and pressed," said Godwin.

"Old and unforgiving," said Theo.

"Fond of his rules," said Godwin. "Rules."

"Strangely enough, he wasn't a soldier until after the Grand Duke died," said Theo.

"Was his personal bodyguard since birth." Godwin spooned a hunk of beef into his mouth and spoke around it. "After the Duke was assassinated, Aelia made him commander of the house guard. Commander."

And then she left him behind. That's telling. Telling what, precisely, I cannot say. "I will make him see reason."

Theo reached across the table and caught my spoon hand midway to my mouth. "Do not tangle with him, Crow. He has killed more men than the pox."

Normally when people say things like, 'He's killed more men than the pox,' it is a rhetorical flourish, a play on words, a little game with language to drive home a point. When Theo said it, however, he did it with utter, literal, certainty.

Jon opened the door to the apartment and the Grand Lady herself entered unannounced. She came into the room, steaming over something, and when the boys shot to their feet, I waited half a beat before following suit. Aelia shot past in a blur of blue velvet and pink silk, trailed by the worried white form of Gelia, who cast me a pitying glance before disappearing into the Lady's room. Striding proudly in their perfumed wake was House Captain Roehm, who both needed no introduction and deserved none. After all, I was probably going to murder him before I learned how to spell his name.

He was as if cast in iron: gray, weathered, and dulled from age. His lines were still clear, his uniform sharp, his long moustache well manicured, but he had the brittle stiffness of a man who has determined he can scream at the universe and make it do what he wants. His back was straight, his gait long and proud. Though painfully thin, I had no doubt of the strength of his limbs. The pommel of his sword was excessively decorated with inlayed silver roses and virdigrised copper leaves and stems; but the whole thing was hard to distinguish since it had been used so often they had nearly worn down to nothing. He had the discipline to become dangerous with a blade, and further strength of will to continue practicing into his advanced years.

Pox indeed.

As he closed in on me, I wondered if I could really kill him in a fair fight. Thankfully the chance of me engaging him in a fair fight was fleetingly slim. He towered at least a fingerlength above my head as he brought his formidable stare down upon me... where it shattered on my indifference. He growled quietly, making Theo and Godwin jump to a whole new level of attention with his words. "The next time you fail to come to your feet when the Grand Lady enters the room, I will cut them off."

A familiar viper raised its head inside my gut, slithering around with the need to bite him in undignified places. I looked downward and then back up to his cold, grey eyes. "Strange, I thought I was standing. Betrayed by my feet again. Taking them would be a blessing."

Both boys gasped. His eyes became specks of flint beneath brows that would be long and wiry bushes if he hadn't been intimidating them into behaving since shortly after birth. "Jest all you want, fool. I will be keeping my eyes on you."

But he had exposed the chink in his armor— his unflagging, and largely unwarranted, pride and dignity, "I am flattered beyond measure, Lieutenant, but I think I can do better than you."

He wheeled upon me like a wind-borne death. "I am Captain of the house Guards to the Grand and Noble House of Conaill and you will..."

I Know Not

I love it when they tell me what I will do. "Actually, I heard that you were the bodyguard to the late Grand Duke. So, how is he?"

Godwin and Theo stood agape, literally at attention with their mouths scraping the floor. As for his captainess, blood infused every exposed inch of skin. Veins began to pulse across his neck and forehead. His fingers twitched with the need to feel cold steel. I planned six ways to kill him before the blade left the scabbard. Then I planned on taking that sword. It had class.

"If you were under my command I would have you flogged," he whispered

"Being under your command would be flogging enough," I responded.

He wanted to lash out, but instead he stalked toward my room and tried the door handle, shocked to find his entry denied. He kept his voice low as he demanded, "Why is this locked?"

I decided I had had enough of the game, and I sat down and continued to eat, "So I don't have to kill any nosy bastard I find inside."

Control comes hard for some, easy for others. For all the levers I had just shoved under his skin and pried with all my might, Roehm managed to get himself together while I watched. It took real practice to do that. "I do not care for your tone."

As much as I could use an ally, I just couldn't get around a man walking in on a situation I had held together for weeks by force of arms and will, and started acting like he was in charge. "Imagine the bereft desert that your hurt renders my soul."

He smiled unkindly. "You are not too old to beat, peasant."

I smiled back, a promise of later reconciliation. "And you are just the right age to toss into a pig pen."

Roehm lunged forward and planted his fists on the table with a resounding thud, his voice echoing off the walls. "What did you say to me?"

I picked up the still steaming bowl of stew, planning to throw it in his face before engaging him with steel, because fair fights only exist for bards. "I said there are things even pigs do not eat and you, sir, rank just below offal on their list."

Of course that was a lie. Pigs will eat everything, including a corpse, and leave little but hair and teeth behind. I think he knew it, too. There it was, the narrowed eyes, the slight tremble of bloodlust and bile floating just under the surface. This was the edge of his control. "You think you can bleed me, whelp?"

But I just couldn't let well enough alone. "Assuming that, when I cut you, I get more than dust?"

Fortunes in any gambling hall can change with a single roll of the dice. That's when the door to Aelia's room opened up and she entered the room, forcing me to once again come to my feet. She stood in the doorway for a few seconds, trying in vain to find a diplomatic way to say, "Have you two come to any understanding of who is in charge?"

I hooked my thumb at Roehm as he said, "Yes," and interrupted with, "He thinks he is."

Aelia affixed me with an icy stare. "And who do *you* think is in charge, Crow?"

I reached through the many disguises in the back of my head and chose the perfectly ingratiating, winning smile and slapped it on my face. "Why you, of course, Grand Lady."

"Quite," she said, managing to fit a lifetime of disapproval and disbelief in that one word. "You have caused me quite a bit of trouble."

My tone was light, my words were not, "I am sorry, Grand Lady. Of course I should have let the assassin take his shot at you from the rooftop. He may even have missed."

Roehm hissed, "Speak to her with respect, cur!"

Fighting men (and whatever his former position, Roehm was a warrior through and through) are really sensitive about honor. If you convince someone they have to go off onto a field of battle and die in horrible, painful, long, and drawn-out ways, they better have a reason. I figure that someone just like me came up with honor so they would have a reason to do it. Sadly, it does become awkward at times like this. He had placed Aelia above himself in his great view of what is. By failing to kowtow to every whim, living in the same suite, and generally treating her as an equal, I was placing myself on her level, and thus above him.

"No, Crow. You did not capture the traitorous captain alive, said Aelia"

I shrugged. "Those were not O'Riagáin's orders, Milady."

Roehm made a sound like an aborted bark, probably at my use of Horatio's name without the fifteen titles attached to be properly obsequious.

"Be that as it may, now he will never give up his cohorts. And, by placing the head of Horatio's Guard Captain in front of him in public..." Aelia threw her hands up and paced the room, agitated as a juggled beehive, "You might as well have accused him of ordering him to sabotage the patrols."

"If the head fits, Milady."

Her shoulders fell. "Horatio is my cousin, Fox."

"Name one noble here that is not at least a cousin to every other."

"No, he is a close cousin. We spent summers together. He is my friend."

Words, not mine, came bubbling out of the Fog and out of my mouth. "You can only be betrayed by those you trust, Milady."

"Stop it, Crow! It is not Horatio. He would not have had my father murdered." She had grown pale and shaky, her voice drained of strength by the very thought that someone so close to her could have plotted to destroy the person she most loved in the world. "Unlock your room and gather your effects. You will be moving into the boys' room." Roehm made to protest but she cut him off. "They may be young, Captain, but they have proved up to the challenge of safeguarding my life. Sending them to the guard camp now would feel ungrateful."

While they began to start what was obviously a rehashed argument, I went to my door and dug through my pouch for the key. I felt kicking me into the crowded room with four snoring youths slightly ungrateful, especially since Roehm would be much more comfortable in a garden variety coffin. Still, Roehm argued that he had men of far greater experience available to come and provide close support. She replied that she felt better with people she knew. At least, he argued move me (who nobody really knew) out to where trusted men could watch me. I stifled a retort that would cause sailors to flinch and unlocked the finely crafted Dwarvish lock.

The key I had just used caught my attention.

I locked the door, then unlocked it, then locked it again. I took another key out of my pouch and tried it. Well tended and well oiled, the lock opened and latched without a hitch.

Roehm frowned at me, "Quit wasting time and move your effects, peasant."

I turned to him, eyes not seeing him at all, "Front door."

I brushed past him as he developed a really good belly of fire and yanked open the door, causing Jon and three men in Aelia's colors I did not know to jump. "Key," I ordered.

Dutifully Jon handed it over, and received a tongue lashing from Roehm for his trouble. It didn't last long, just enough for me to test three keys on the front door. Two opened it without fail. I raced back to my door, where again two of three worked the latch. I remember the hot water, and the door I thought I had secured.

"Roehm?" Perhaps it was my boldness in questioning him mid rant that had him stumble to a stop. "Did you request water be brought for this room?"

He nodded, and I turned to Aelia, hand out. "Your key."

This caught Roehm's attention, and he came at me like a bad tempered terrier. I insulted him still further by ignoring him, going to Aelia's room and trying all four keys. Only two worked. One worked them all, without fail.

It was the key I had taken from the assassin.

Roehm remembered he needed to punish me for something and came at me, but I stopped him with a pointed finger, "Roehm, you hate me."

The old warrior stopped, glanced at Aelia for permission, then smiled. "More than any other man, living or dead, has hated anyone. More than drunks decry the dawn, more than soldiers despise the chiurgeon, more than prostitutes hate the pox..."

"Yes, yes, I have heard you are far more deadly than any prostitute, but it is your hate that makes you the perfect man to come with me."

"And why should I do that?"

"Because I have known the Grand Lady for several weeks. She knows when I get like this I am always right, and if I ask her she will order you to. This way you get to save some face and look like the better man." *Or would have, had you not made me point it out.*

But, moustache trembling, he came along without being ordered. We spent a half an hour checking the handful of keys in dozens of locks all across the castle/inn. Only one worked, but that one never failed. I handed it to Roehm.

He examined it closely, then slipped it into his pocket, "What now?"

I wanted to bristle as he took what was clearly mine, but instead I pointed down the hallway. "We have to beg an audience."

"What?"

I Know Not

Two minutes later we were in front of Horatio O'Riagáin's door. That isn't true: we were in front of six guards, in front of four servants, in front of one haughty nose wipe, in front of his door. I had no hat to hold in my hand, and the mental costume I was wearing really required one, but still I was already here longer than I needed. It was important to disguise the reason for the visit, though. Thankfully, I was about to be dismissed by the chamberlain, or seneschal, or whatever they called haughty functionaries in this castle, "I was sent by the Grand Lady Conaill, Grand Duchess of Conaill to apologize for the audacity with which I brought the traitor's head to the festivities."

The functionary sniffed twice, as if I stunk. "I am sure a letter will do..."

Then the door was flung open, and a disheveled, red faced Horatio stared out into the hall, focusing on nothing but my characteristically contrite form as everyone went down on one knee.

"What is the meaning of this?"

I swear, that's just what he said. As everyone else looked at their mental maps to make sure they were currently located nowhere near the place at fault for the Duke's displeasure, I started in a shaky voice, "Your Grand Lordship, I am to confer the most sincere apologies of your favored cousin, Aelia Conaill, Grand Duchess of Conaill, and I am to beg for forgiveness. I, lowly creature that I am, sought to remedy the harm caused your house by taking the traitor to your table, unknowingly implying–"

"SILENCE!" He shrieked, but after a pregnant pause, seemed to regain some of his composure, "Please tell my sweet cousin that her," special emphasis, "apology is not needed. I just hope you are going to be flogged for your impertinence."

I bobbed my head toward Roehm, "The Captain is tasking me now Your Grand Lordship."

Horatio looked pleased, but he was a moon to Roehm's shining sun. "Very well, carry on."

And he retreated inside, shutting the door firmly.

Roehm and I rose and we left in haste, but as my mind finally got the last few pieces into position, Roehm was busy being amazed at the wrong thing. "To take a flogging to protect the reputation of the Grand Duchess, I never thought you had it in you."

"Forget that, you dolt. Did you see the lock?"

"The lock?"

Why, why, why must everyone around me be so dim? Before I kill the next assassin I am going to have to have a lengthy conversation with him or her so I might at least have a chance of finding an equal! "The lock. The lock. The lock on O'Riagáin's door!"

"I fail to see..."

I took out a knife, causing Roehm to blink and wonder where it had been stashed. I scraped at the lock on one random door. Years and years of age gave way before the blade, leaving shiny, silvery steel beneath. "Do you understand?"

Roehm did not understand, and was coming upon a very foul mood, but that was because he was becoming more and more convinced that there would be no flogging after all. But it was much later that things got worse.

That was when I approached Aelia and said, "I know who's paid to have you killed."

THIRTEEN

MISDIRECTION OF THE LAW

SWEAT flowed from my brow in steady streams. Well, that's not true; it flowed from everywhere. It was just the brow that kept my eyes full of stinging droplets, so it was most noticeable. It was predawn, too early for most people to be up and about, which suited me just fine. I was making music. The straw packed hard mats were quiet underfoot, but not so quiet they completely muffled the percussion of my feet as I danced. Voices reached tongues from the Fog, tickling my internal ears with half remembered lessons.

The Phantom Angel was a lonely falsetto, singing in my hands as if possessed by the souls of the elves that forged it. The burn in my muscles was a silent chorus that tried to drown out the fire of my humiliation. The symphony built and waned, climaxed to crashing crescendos and faded to deadly diminuendos. It was flawless... flawless but in vain. Still I pushed, harder and faster. Then there it was, an opening in the defenses of my imaginary foe. A hunger blossomed inside and I leapt to the imagined kill. A final thrust vibrated in the air, the thunderous echoes of future violence fading from inside my mind.

I closed my eyes, hoping for clarity, for stillness, for an end to the yawning chasm inside. I got none of these things. It shouldn't surprise me. I had wanted to be alone and I hadn't gotten that either.

Gelia sighed, shattering the thread of concentration I had knotted to snare any fleeting serenity. I opened my eyes and there she was– distant, matriarchal, disapproving. I sighed in response, careful to fill it with just the right amount of frustration. It is important to speak the same language, after all.

I gathered my sword and belts, each laden down with a forest of sharpened steel, and slung them over my left shoulder. That was when she decided to hand me a thick, black, leather vest while giving my sweat-soaked white shirt an even more critical eye than she reserved for the rest of me. For the life of me, I didn't know where her obsessive need to make me cover up every inch of skin sprang from, but it wasn't worth an argument. Well, it might have been, but I was too tired to enjoy it. I put on the vest and re-shouldered my load. "I prefer to practice alone."

"Every time I'm not there you start bleeding, Crow." To that, I couldn't argue.

We left the practice room in the depths of the basement, very near the healer's room in fact, and began the long climb back to the apartment. Gelia followed modestly in silence as I took the long way around to the room, and then a longer way, and then yet a longer way. I had gotten trapped in these hallways by the guards and, as long as I had the cleric as cover, I would memorize as many of them as possible. Given the chance, that's the lie I would tell others as well.

"Not in any hurry to get back, then?" She said, flaying my excuse bare to the truth.

I decided not to answer. I became determined not to answer. Then I absolutely refused to answer. Shortly thereafter, the word "No" escaped all on its own.

And that was all the opening any guard, inquisitor, or cleric needs. "Crow, she trusts him. They've been friends practically since she could walk. I personally used to watch them have grand adventures with imaginary unicorns, throw balls for the queen of faeries, and whisper secrets together on cold winter nights. I hope that explains her, somewhat."

Explains a bit about him, as well, I didn't say. To my chagrin, what did come out was petulant and childish. "I am right, Gelia."

"I know you think so, but..."

I darted into an alcove and pulled her after, drawing the curtains close to muffle our voices. I raised a fist in front of her face, which she stared at warily until one finger sprang out. "First, the Grand Sage is owned by his family. The assassins had every advantage because they were given information by him or his staff."

Her face showed that she, like Aelia, was unconvinced. A second finger sprang out to join the first. "Second, the Captain was carrying money, obviously some kind of bribe, or maybe a bonus. It was all locally minted coin."

"But that just means the architect of this evil got his gold from a local moneychanger."

I drew forth one bit of the offending gold from my belt pouch and tossed it to her. "Do me the justice. She did not and look at the thing, woman! It is pure gold, a nail weight, easily. What moneychanger in the city will have access to so much pure gold? And not just pure, but virgin, for it has never been circulated. It is untarnished by skin, unscratched by time in a pouch next to harder coin. It is too much to believe anyone but the Grand Duke had access to so much fresh coin, coin carrying his bust, at hand."

Her eyes pierced me with thinly veiled hostility, her voice pitched too low to carry beyond our covert spot. "Then why use it at all?"

And it was at this moment that I realized she, like Aelia, did not want me to be right, didn't see the things I took as obvious, did not understand how the path I showed them would lead out of the confusing forest. "Because, Holy Mother, he never expected us to get this far. You are looking for a magically grown plot set well in advance of our coming. Everything since we have arrived has been the scurrying of rats looking to murder our Lady."

She blinked, "Our Lady?"

My ears still rang with my words, but I shook them off, fighting off the irrational anger that rose unbidden. "Please, focus! He had the coin at hand, that's what he used. Captain O'Loinsigh said his plan was to go to Riagáinhead. He expected to be welcomed when he got there. O'Riagáin–"

"His Grand Lordship, please."

"Damn it, Gelia! He paid his own captain to distract the guards and gave the assassin the exact time, place, and seating so he could take that shot. I was there and," I flicked out a third finger, "that assassin knew just where to be. He didn't have to search for the right window, he knew it from memory. The Captain just gave the order and skipped out, attempting to wait in the city as Horatio sent his men outside the walls to put a good show of searching." A fourth finger rises. "O'Riagáin gets to look like he's hunting down a traitor, and if things get too bad he can just produce a corpse, re-pocket the gold, and proclaim he has solved the question of his own betrayal. It was perfect!"

"Why not just have the assassin attack in her room?"

I felt like screaming. "They tried it, and I was ready! That's where we got the master key."

"Master key?"

"The key of the first assassin. She used it to get into the suite and could have used it to gain entry into Aelia's room as well."

"I don't understand." I dragged her from the alcove and we passed by dozens of doors along the length of corridors. I pointed at the aged locks, taking special care to note to her the identical Dwarvish runes that marked them. We found another niche and she hissed, "They are the finest locks money can buy."

"Yes, and the key the assassin had opened every one of them I tried. They must be made so that every high ranking servant in the castle may come and go, clean and service to the contentment of the nobles and merchant princes that stay here."

"Crow, that is insane. There is no way the Grand Duke would hand over the keys of his castle to an assassin."

Restraining my emotions flattened my voice and deadened my eyes, and for a minute I think she was honestly frightened of me as I said, "And that is why Roehm was supposed to notice that the fat bastard had replaced the locks to his room with a human made lock, making sure the Dwarvish master key was useless to gain access to him."

"But the cost of replacing..."

The intensity of emotion swelled inside me like a dragon, spreading its wings and casting her belief in shadow. "Gelia, if he wins the contract for Red Sky, no cost would be too great."

She left our hiding spot and I chased after. Tears peeked out from under her eyelids and she discreetly daubed them with her cuff as she murmured, "I don't know. I just don't know."

I dodged past Gelia and stood in her path. "I know. You have to get Lady Aelia to listen to me. I know how to end this."

Gelia's eyes said that she believed me, but didn't want to. Mostly she didn't want to because it meant the only way to end this would be to kill Horatio. Dry up the money, and the flow of assassins would be cut off. It would save her life, but at the cost of what everyone still wanted to believe was a dear family friend. All my convincing words were so much wind against the heavy stones of memories like those. It would be a lie to say that this was anything other than a lost cause.

But as I watched, a miracle occurred. Gelia, the woman who hated me most and trusted me least, looked at me with eyes full of emotions I found strange and alien. She reached out and touched the side of my face in a manner that could only be called tender. She nodded and wiped at her tears again. "I will talk to her."

I can't remember if anyone ever told me that when someone reverses their position, you get them to make good on this decision as soon as possible, but it seemed like a good idea. I steered her down the stairs and over to the wing where our suite was located. We made it to the master entryway of the Grand Sage before we even saw anyone else. Dawn was just around the corner and the army of servants was beginning to stir.

I admit it, I was hurrying and not watching all the dark corners. I acknowledge that my plate had been pretty full for the last day, and I may have let things slip. I concede that I didn't see coming what happened next.

"ASSASSIN!"

But I should have. Gelia did exactly the wrong thing. She froze and looked for the source of the voice, which meant I couldn't leave without leaving her. That meant I had to turn and face the disheveled Lieutenant Palmer.

Fine, I beat him and three of his men badly in front of the Great and the Good. I had taken one of his men's eyes, and broken another's knee, and made him look like a coward, and gotten off with a spanking. Next I humiliated him, dominated him, and got him to show me his beloved Captain's quarters, only to impugn said corpse's honor with entirely accurate accusations, and return the next day with said Captain's head. Still, doing this now, in public, seemed a touch showy.

"Assassin, I have you now." Well, to tell the truth, what he actually said was, "Ashashin, I ha' you now," but you get the point. He was waving a sealed letter festooned with ribbons and seals and big, fancy writing. My stomach turned as he half staggered and half sauntered down the staircase, brandishing it at me.

The Fog was screaming danger and my palms itched for a hilt, any hilt. I compromised by lazily stepping between the cleric and the soldier, slinging the belts of death from my shoulder and holding them low where one hand could snatch out some steel fast enough to cut a blinking eye in half. I nodded at the flourished parchment, "What is that Palmer, a warrant?"

There is a certain quality in the voice that tells a perceptive man that the words would normally be crisp and proper, if wine had not totally demolished that talent. The Lieutenant was, indeed, far gone as his sword slurred from its sheath. "Of a sort. It is permission to challenge you to a duel."

And again, he said, "Of a short. It ish permishion…" But you get the idea, and it is far less cute and folksy when the man doing it has an arm length of cold steel deployed. I reached back with my free hand and pushed at Gelia, but she only retreated to the base of the stairs as I kept the drunken bastard busy. "Have a sense of fair play, man. You are drunk. If I lose, I die. If I win, I've killed a drunkard and that's hardly a feat one boasts about. Go to bed. If you want to commit suicide, at least have the decency to do it sober."

The pressure of the words built up inside him until, red cheeked and veins popping, they burst forth. "DO NOT MOCK ME!"

For the record, that was clear enough. "Dueling has been outlawed since the war."

I watched as he directed music only he could hear with his sword and paper batons. "Dispensation. From his Grand Lordship"

I glanced over my shoulder, a risk I took because I could not afford to be disobeyed this time, "Go get her."

Gelia had no doubt to whom I spoke, or to whom I referred. But before I could see her go, my ears picked up boots being set on marble with distinct purpose. I spun back to my opponent, who had struck a stance that is highly effective if you happen to have a shield and are fighting with a dozen other men, and will get you killed if you are fighting alone. He screamed, "I will have you, scullion!" and half lunged as his sword made a high arc toward my head.

The Beast wanted out, needed out. It rattled the bars of its cage, but I kept it captured in my chest. Killing this guy should be easy, but the death of the Lieutenant would greatly complicate things. Not killing him would take a bit of my skill and completely ignoring every one of my instincts.

I slid the Phantom Angel from its sheath and batted his blow aside, then followed up with a boot to the fork in his legs. The most difficult part of it was getting out of his way as he dutifully collapsed on his face, sliding forward to a stop against one pristine white wall. I don't care how drunk the man slinging the steel is, steel is still steel. To that end, I needed this to be over so I bounced toward him, lashing out with one, booted foot to the side of the head. He lurched upward unexpectedly, and his sword stuttered uncertainly in the air. The wild but weak strike sliced a piece of leather from the side of my boot and forced me to retreat.

Have you ever wondered why a cat toys with its food before it kills? It's because even mice have teeth, and nobody likes to be bitten. He gave a few tentative swipes as he stood, and I batted them aside with ease. An unexpected lunge came less than a finger-length from my nose, and without even thinking about it I struck back in earnest. I swatted his blade upward, out of my way enough to slip the blackened tip of the Angel under his guard and stick his leg. Most importantly, I avoided his wild counter swing as he slapped one hand over the wound, rivulets of blood oozing between his fingers.

"I don't suppose that license to duel is only to first blood?" Sometimes I don't know what my mouth is thinking. The slight jab lit off his temper again, and he redoubled his efforts. He cried out something incoherent that echoed against walls and ceiling. I looked around desperately, I swear for the first time in my life, for anyone wearing a uniform to come intervene. No luck. Instead, showing how sheltered a life they led, servants were appearing at doorways and staircases.

I skillfully retreated and parried, watching as Palmer's swings devolved into a tired, predictable pattern. I waited until he was staggering, wheezing, and then the Angel flew forth again, drawing a long red line along his right bicep. He screamed, one hand holding onto the wound while the other was ever so slowly losing its grip on his weapon.

I took a deep breath, desperately trying to ignore the chorus of opportunities singing for me to kill him. Instead I concentrated on keeping my voice calm, reasonable, "It's over, Palmer. Put down your sword and we can get you to the healer."

But everything I said caused his smoking pride to burst from coals to fire. He raised the sword to a sloppy guard, "You louse ridden dog, I shall end you on this blade!"

The Beast roared. The Angel came out of nowhere, ringing against his sword and sending it fluttering loudly down the entryway. Everyone watched it fly in shock. Only once silence returned did I say, "I apologize, were you not ready to kill me?"

Palmer's mouth made a perfect 'o', his eyes wide and skin pale, though that could be from the blood that now painted every step he took and fell from his elbow in a trickle. I shouldered the belts of weapons again and backed away one step, then two. The

Lieutenant's face fell, then he bowed his head, shaking with some alcohol fueled grief for reasons beyond my knowing or caring. Then he almost fell, staggered forward, staggered again on the bad leg, instincts that had been telling me to kill him for minutes now screamed like a chorus of burning cats. That's when he lunged, dagger in hand.

I dropped it all; Angel, belts, attitude, mercy. They hit the floor faster than drops of rain in the wind as I took his wrists in my hands and brought the blade out of line with my tender flesh. We wrestled for half a second until the dagger was trapped between our faces, ineffective for the moment. Of course he was bleeding badly, so all I needed was hold him until his limbs weakened and I could yank the damn thing away from him and–

Palmer came close, the smell of the unaged corn whiskey on his breath watering my eyes as he hissed, "I know what you are, killer. I have seen your mark."

"My mark? What are you sloshing on about, fool?" The words were dismissive, loud, brave. Inside, rats made of ice awakened and cavorted as they chewed at pieces of my stomach.

"Wrestling, Assassin. Wrestling you to the ground, I saw it." His strength was fading, his grip unsure. I could hear the tromping of a dozen booted feet as men descended upon the sounds of battle. Gelia had long since raced up the stairs. Though every sign was that I was winning, every word that left Palmer's lips said I was going to lose. "It watches you, slave. It sees you. "

And everyone saw as he gave a titanic lunge. I cried out in dismay as his blade slewed left, right, then back across my face, gouging my chin along the left side. I kneed him in the guts, expelling air from his lungs and causing him to crumple on his feet. Finally the dagger came free into my hands. It flashed for a second in the early morning light before twirling in a wide circle up and under Palmer's ribs and into his vitals with all the mercy of a hungry viper. The force of the blow straightened him and pulled him into a deadly embrace with me. I felt the meat part grudgingly, fibers cut deep and set free from bone.

Palmer did not scream, he did not cry. He simply stared at me, a horrible truth burning on his whispering lips, "You are damned. Doomed."

The blade came out and flew in the light, sprinkling red rain against the walls as I danced around Palmer, lifting his arm to expose another artery and plunging the iron tongue in. He gargled on blood and bent over backwards. But then my knee was there, supporting him like a short table and offering his chest to my rage as the blade shot down over and over. I drew it back, hot and wet, from its business as his mouth worked silently.

Then he said, "I saw it on your back."

The blade flashed forward one last time, entering one side of his throat and exiting the other, cutting off any more thoughts that sought to escape. There was no need to bend my sword tempered arms to pull the dagger out the front, spraying blood in a deadly fan even as I stood and spilled him onto the floor.

I did it anyway.

Battle-worn mental walls held me apart from the moment, kept me above it as he bled across the snowy white marble. Everyone had seen him attack me one last time, and die for his trouble. I was completely in the clear.

No matter that I had been the one to yank the dagger in his weakened grip, that I had cut myself, that I had calculated his murder in full sight of twenty people in such a way as to appear blameless. It was all crystal clear, now, clearer than any thought had been in my head since I had awoken weeks ago: this is the kind of man I am.

Horatio's guards, suspiciously fully armored for war, burst into the vaulted entryway from three sides. No one wanted to talk as they came cautiously forward with weapons bared.

"Keep still," one of them growled.

I stepped smartly on the crosspiece of the Angel, flipping it onto the top of my boot. A flick of my foot sent it spinning into the air where my hand snatched the hilt like an acrobat at the circus.

"No," I replied.

It is a well known fact that guards do not like to be told "no". In fact, it is one of those things they like to beat out of peasants using truncheons. It is NOT something that they use as an excuse to point naked weapons at the bodyguard of a visiting noble and advancing menacingly. "I am the bodyguard of Aelia Conaill, Grand Duchess of–"

One took a tentative poke at me with a spear. The Phantom Angel lashed out, beheading the spear, cutting in half the haft of the man next to him, and ringing off the helmet of the next in line. I leapt back, over the body of the late Lieutenant and giving myself a few seconds to talk, to escape, to–

In my mind's eye I was seeing myself open up every one of these tin coated cans and spilling the blood trapped inside. I wanted to cheer at the images.

I shook my head violently, feeling caught between conflicting urges, being acted on by forces written in stone barely hidden in the Fog. *No! I have to focus, have to stay calm.* I pointed the bloody tip of the Phantom Angel at the beribboned letter on the floor, only now being overtaken by the spreading pool of Palmer's blood. "He had a dispensation to duel and attacked me."

The guard didn't even bend over to pick it up, didn't even look at it, "The Duke does not authorize dueling."

Palmer was not the trap. He had been the bait. Now there were many, so many. *So this is it?* I raised the Phantom Angel, but they kept coming. One last try, "You have to wait. The Duchess will be here in a moment..."

One swatted at me with a sword, testing me. I expertly caught it on the hilt of the Angel and twisted viciously, bending the blade off true and snapping it at the base with a disturbingly musical tone. That guard retreated, but was replaced with two more, and they kept coming. They were not intimidated, and they did not hesitate.

I felt the drumbeats begin inside, the music of death that kept time with my racing heart. The Beast inside howled once and then went silent, cowed by The Dark Thing that blew in from the Fog and curtained off my mind. Cold, exacting, it plotted a course between the heavy, slow soldiers that left four of them dead in the first three seconds. My chances were fifty/fifty to be alive to face the rest. It didn't matter. Nothing mattered. Nothing, but the dance.

My hand tightened upon my sword, then loosened as I took a deep breath. I raised the Phantom Angel in a parody of a salute. Following some unspoken command, four of them stepped forward as one. Still I retreated, back, back, showing them weakness so that they would overestimate their own strength. I led them into the corner, let them crowd one another, let their arms tangle and their feet touch. Then I struck.

The servants finally ran as blood fountained in red rivers and scarlet spatters. Steel pealed as the Phantom Angel slammed into vambracers, chest plates, helmets and paltroons, splitting them open and exposing the red goo inside. Three wounded men retreated before my onslaught, one dragging the man who could not make it on his own. More of Horatio's men yet were coming into the room, but cautiously now, afraid now.

Soon bows would be fetched and I would die, but until then, I would kill and be filled by their deaths. Their words meant nothing. Time meant nothing. Every one of them could see the darkness flying behind my eyes and feared my sword. That was all that mattered.

Fear. Mayhem. Power.

A crystal scream, pure and resonant, called out. It slammed into me, billowing the Void and casting the Dark Thing back into the fog, obscuring the Animal within. It caught in my mind and funneled into my chest where it built up power, echo after echo; shattering the fortresses of ice and hate within me. My soul emerged red and raw, bleeding and sending shocks through me. A stabbing pain thundered from between my shoulder blades, worse than any before. I fell to my knees, retching as the guards leapt back, expecting some kind of trick.

Then one gathered his spirit and raised his axe.

Aelia's voice resonated like a church bell, "Do not touch him!"

But the guard did not even pause to listen. He was intent on his prey. He raised the scarred and slightly rusty weapon above him as my head erupted in blinding misery. It started to fall as a cool rain washed the agony from behind my eyes. A silver sliver shot forward and rang against the axe, halting it midair a few fingerlengths from my upturned face.

I saw the acid etched roses on the blade first, and groaned as I saw the wrinkled but powerful hand that held the sword. *Not him. Please not him.*

But it was. He had his sword in one hand, holding off my death with a perfect block, while the other hand held a long, thin dagger that was perched with the tip just inside the visor of the axe wielding guard. Roehm took a deep breath and let his voice echo off the walls, colored by his distain, "The Grand Lady said not to touch this worthless cur."

And even having just insulted me, there was not one heart in the room that did not wholly believe that he would kill anyone who even attempted to defy her.

My back spasmed again, and the world lost focus. I shook my head and the whole room had changed. The guards had backed off, Horatio was on the stairs, a deep frown creasing his round face.

Gelia was over me, her expression unreadable.

"Lay still," she said.

Again it felt like flat piece of steel, white hot and horrible, being inserted between my vertebrae and twisted. I don't know if I screamed, but the whole room was empty when I opened my eyes. No! It was not empty, it was filled with easily a dozen men: O'Loinsigh, Palmer, O'Conner, the assassins, and many more. Bandits from the trail were there, and the soldiers at the fort. No, not a dozen, many dozens, hundreds.

Gelia used a cool rag to wipe the images from my eyes, bringing me back to the here and now. Everyone stared at me as if I were mad, and a few even made signs to ward off evil spirits. My ears stopped ringing long enough to hear Aelia say, "Get him to his room."

But as Jon (where did he come from?) lifted me and my back clenched again. I squeezed my eyes so tight that maggots twisted behind my eyelids, spiraling across the world in a wiggling white blindfold. I opened my eyes, or I tried.

The world was in color, bolder and richer than I had ever seen. Corpses stood, eyes angry and wounds still fresh, packed impossibly deep in this hallway, stretching for a mile in all directions. Two statues held me in mid lift: Jon sharply carved out of innocent marble and Roehm cast in dull metal... I lifted my head from my chest to stare at a cloaked angel standing before me, towering above.

I had always known he was there.

Something began to scrape my heart with veins of frost as the figure raised his arms. Two hands, carved of aged alabaster, emerged from within the robe woven of webs and night. In one palm sat a silver ring, worth a few coins, but old and so blackened with age I could barely make out the crude raven carved in the surface. It hardly mattered in his left there was a golden crown adorned with rubies and ivory, built into patterns that twirled in endless knots of gold and gems. Every facet, every curve, led one to stare at the grand star on the brow of the crown, gold and ruby blazed in the shape of a lidless eye. He seemed to be offering both to me, waiting with the patience of one who has no life left to trickle through the hourglass.

But I felt the crowd pressing in on all sides, their hate an army of hot pokers that bounced behind hollow eyes. I could only smell dust and the dead, could hear their screams whispered at me in deaf ears. The Eye called to me, but I could see the nails sticking inward from the brow, crusted with old blood. I recoiled from the crown, and the bodies began to press in on all sides, their hands turned to talons and breath so cold it burned.

I came to on the floor of the suite, hands clasping my head so hard the nails were close to drawing blood. I let go, but I could feel my hands still, nightmarishly like the grasping claws of the dead. I thought I was alone, but I should have known I wasn't that lucky.

"You could have at least told me you had the falling sickness. If you have infected Milady with your malady I will end you, cur." Roehm towered over me, Phantom Angel in one hand, his other sword on his hip.

I rubbed my star-blinded eyes with the palms of my hands, trying to crush out the gritty pain that still echoed inside them. My fingers found the deep cut I had inflicted on myself with Palmer's dagger, sealed shut by one of the priestess' balms. "Where's Gelia?"

He obviously debated, but he answered. "The nurse has stayed with the Grand Lady. They have entered into negotiations with Grand Duke O'Riagáin to discuss your punishment for the murder–"

The words were propelled out as if from a heated kettle, "He attacked me!"

"You seek to play games, Crow. You know nothing of discipline or the law." Roehm shook his head. "You may have helped the Grand Lady on the road, and for that I will not kill you, but the Grand Duke will likely as not see your neck stretched yet."

The reaction inside me was equal parts sharp ice from the sky and rampaging forest fire. "He will try."

Again, Roehm shook his head, as if at a village idiot for not knowing he was covered in dung. He snapped his fingers, summoning four of Aelia's soldiers from behind me. None of them were the Boys. I looked, and all of them looked at me as if I were a particularly unsavory piece of meat. Going along quietly looked like the simple answer until Roehm said, "Take him to The Grand Lady's room."

Real panic began to set in, then. My mind raced, "She said to take me to my chambers!"

Roehm was adamant, his eyes casting upon me the way some

people look at sewage. He didn't even address me. "No, Gods know how many weapons he has secreted in there. Take him to the Lady's room. We will move him to the camp later."

"You're going to leave me in Aelia's room without a guard?"

Roehm smiled, obviously feeling the better man, "We moved her effects into my quarters while you were unconscious."

I felt a deep hatred stir inside me for Roehm, for while he was stupid, he was proving an inspired enemy. "She ordered that?"

His smile widened slightly, telling me all I needed. He opened the door with Aelia's key and stood to the side. The soldiers bodily took me inside and dumped me onto the floor. It was, indeed bare to the rafters of most everything but a bed, a wardrobe standing empty, a smaller servant's bed in the corner, a wide glassed window to let in light, and sumptuous mirrored vanity, "At least give me my things. That's my sword, Roehm."

He held up the Phantom Angel as if he had never seen it before. "Is it?"

Old wounds bled from inside the Fog, leaking building rage across my boots. "Give me my sword, or I will kill you."

"No," he whispered back.

From the Fog, a fake self poked out his head and I snatched him like a murderer. I lunged forward, pulling on the disguise. Roehm raised the blade, only missing my jugular by a hairs breadth as I grasped the front of his vest, tears welling up, "We've had our differences, man, but you can't cage me here like an animal!"

He lowered the weapon, the sneer on his face had an odor. "If I had my way, you would be caged like an animal, not in Milady's quarters."

I banged my head hopelessly against his chest, "But you can't–
"

"I can and I have." He twisted my hands from his clothes, then thrust them back toward me without catching the hint of silver in my palm. "Now have some dignity, fool!"

He turned and tromped out of Aelia's room with his men. He was happy to lock the door and march off, his world once again taking its rightful shape, unmindful of the marginal lightness of his belt.

Moving the chair to block the door was child's play, sliding under the bed even more so. The mattress of the bed, like mine, was held from the floor by a long, twisted length of rope woven back and forth through holes in the frame. It came free easily. The rest of the bed frame created an excellent anchor point for the hemp, though I had to snatch the chair from the door to smash the window before tossing out the rope. In seconds, Roehm was unlocking and opening the door, he and his men piling into my makeshift cell.

Sometimes stealth is about painting a picture. If a guard enters a room, sees the window shattered, the furniture dismantled, a rope leading out of the window, they are going to think only one thing. While they will look out the window and not see you, they can't assume that you haven't already found the ground.

But the skeletal bastard may not be a complete fool. The first thing he will do is scan the open rafters above, but you are not there. His eyes may probe left and right around the room, pouncing on the only bit of furniture big enough to hold a man and fling open the door. But you wouldn't be short sighted enough to be in the wardrobe. Then he and his men will obviously prepare to leave when he turns back, sword in hand, and madly slashes and stabs at the mattress laying dejectedly on the floor, his men joining in. The explosion of feathers will be spectacular, and more than a little humorous, as goose down is attracted to men with the highest level of undeserved dignity in any room. But goose down is all they will have slain.

The jailor you have just foxed may or may not growl, "Find him!" That is not guaranteed.

If you are very lucky, however, they will pile out of the room to go looking for you. Even better, the walking corpse may take a second to relock the door, figuring that, if you circle back around, you would still be stuck in the makeshift prison.

That is when you silently climb back in the window, fingers and toes raw, legs and arms shaking from the effort, and secure in the knowledge when someone sees a rope leading down, they very rarely look up to the sill above.

There are basically three components to a prison: walls, doors, and guards. I waited ten long, slow breaths as they loudly made plans to go find me, and left the apartment with the tromp of big, heavy boots. Then I reached into my shirt and brought forth the master key, taken from the assassin, confiscated by Roehm, and then cleverly liberated from Roehm's pouch as I begged him for mercy. With it, the door opened easily.

Now if I had a bit of advice for the novice escapee, it is this: be wary. If you exit into the common areas of a suite and your gear, as well as your sword, are sitting on the table, you should ignore it. No, really, there is no reason for it to be there, so do not focus upon it. It is not just a weapon, it is a symbol of power, and in taking it from you, your opponent is assured that you will chase him down to get it back. All he has to do is hold onto it, and he is assured to have another shot at you.

That is why I ignored it. *No, I should leave it alone. Really, damn it!*

But, of course, Left and Right had other ideas.

Of their own volition, my feet crossed to the center of the room and my hands picked up the Phantom Angel like an old friend, a first love. The balance perfect, the edge immaculate, the dark surface of the steel smoky and warm. When the sibilant sound of steel on leather came from behind me, I wasn't surprised. I wasn't even disturbed. And, to his credit, he had gotten rid of all the goose down. I knew I was going to enjoy killing this man.

I was even a little delighted, because of course, whatever I might think of his rigidly simple ethos or single minded morality, my jailor was not a stupid man. He was a dangerous killer, and he was even now constructing a situation where he could murder me with no culpability. Just like I had with Palmer.

I spun, Angel leading the way, and the heavy hand and a half sword clanged off of Roehm's rosy short sword. I leapt away from the table, having to spin the Phantom in a tight circle to meet no less than three lightning ripostes from the Conaill family bodyguard. His face was blank, purposeful, his sword moving in tightly regimented drills. His perfect form could have been lifted whole from woodcuts on the proper methods of swordplay. He came relentlessly, probing with a steel finger for any weakness in my defenses, only to be swatted aside by the larger, heavier Phantom.

He did not say things like, "I have studied the blade for thirty years", "You have no chance", or "I am a master of five fighting styles with this blade alone". He certainly did not ask for surrender, or promise to end things quickly. He did not have to. He was a man who had spent his life on the drill field and dueling floor, honing his edge to razor sharpness. The problem with too thin an edge was that it would shatter the first time it met real resistance. His timing, while precise, was regular. His thrusts, while deadly, were disciplined to the point of predictability. If he wasn't so damned fast, I could have killed him already.

His arm blurred as he stamped his foot down, bringing the rose sword within a fingerlength of my face. I cursed myself for missing the block, and then being too slow to capitalize with a counterstrike. His sword lashed out again and sliced open my shirt, leaving the thinnest of cuts across my chest. I was tired and wielding by far the heavier blade. Worse, I had already winded myself with exhausting practice and then fought a duel and then many men already today. That was to say nothing of hanging out over the window of my cell by fingers and booted toes alone. This had to end quickly for my sake, or it would end finally.

I tried one last gambit, but to be honest, a large part of me was hoping it would fail. "Aelia will be upset with you, Roehm."

He shrugged. "You will never compromise the dignity, safety, or ambitions of the Conaill family ever again, vagabond."

His comment hit a nerve. I batted his sword aside, but before he could bring it back to bear, I used my off hand to sweep up a decorative vase from off of a side table and hurl it at him. He started, staring at the missile and attempting to block it as if it were an incoming blade. The porcelain shattered on his sword, turning into hundreds of shards that rained against his face and chest.

And then it struck me... the man was a duelist, and though in command, he was not really even a soldier. He was used to regimented, civilized battles with tightly controlled forms, and rules, and an audience. He wiped dust and sharp bits from his face and came again like a whirlwind of death, but I was not there. I moved around the common table and used my greater reach to thrust playfully at him, daring him to come round to meet me. Come around he did, but he was not ready for me to grab the extinguished lamp off of the wall sconce and slosh the contents in a sloppy splash that collided with him from left leg to right shoulder and face.

He stumbled back around the table, desperately clawing rancid oil from his eyes as I pursued him. He got the goo from his eyes as I struck, Phantom singing in a tight arc. He blocked, but the bigger, heavier blade slung his aside like a reed in the breeze. But I did not stop there, instead forcing the Phantom into a wicked dance of tight circles that built the killing energy inside the blade and intersected with Roehm several times a second.

I figured he should appreciate the technique. He seemed like one of those people who go on and on about the art of the blade. I have never seen a man spitted on the end of my sword mention one thing about how pretty it was when it happens.

It came back around and he blocked again, his sword ringing painfully. Then again, and it was almost tossed to the side. Again he blocked, now fully on the defensive, and he brought both hands to the grip and squeezed tightly to focus more strength. He also transferred far too much of the slippery, smelly animal oil from the hand that had wiped it from his face to the hilt and clean hand. I struck once, swords ringing like bells, then again, sword twisting, vibrations building and rattling his teeth, and then one last time as the rose sword leapt from his oozing grip and skittered across the floor under a random piece of furniture.

Roehm stood proudly, moustache still dripping with rendered animal fat and twitching with the power of his rage. I knew he felt I had cheated. I knew I had, in fact, done just that. Of course I had won the fight so it didn't bother me near as much. But as he stood, tall and unapologetic, there was a moment of utter clarity.

He had barked his knuckles sometime during the fight, and the blood was moving sluggishly. Sharp little pieces of vase peppered his clothes up and down. The oil was beginning to stink as his body heat warmed it. His hair was lank and drained of color, his face craggy with wrinkles that told of an austere life spent in worry and duty. I had not lied; he and I served the same woman, though from vastly different means and ends. He was a sad, old man who was only standing upright because of the starched discipline of his legs. With another life, I might have become him. May become him still.

Then the silent appraisal shifted too much weight onto his shoulders and he blurted, "What are you waiting for? Kill me, kna-"

That is when I kicked him in his fork, and followed up with a vicious elbow to his nose. He collapsed wordlessly and stayed there, which was good, because I was already regretting not tossing him out a window.

It took only moments to tie him up, a moment more to throw my gear messily into a bag and hoist it onto my shoulder. I made sure to go into the boy's room and get my heavy travelling boots. I was sure to need them. I cast a longing look at the clothes and other gear left behind, but I had to travel light and fast. The door outside was unguarded, unsurprising since he would hardly want witnesses to complicate his plan to kill me. Was he planning to cast me as a murderer, saying I struck first? I knew not, but cared not, since I had to quickly find a place to hide.

Thankfully still wearing my soft boots, I padded through the Grand Sage like a ghost. The morning routine had begun, but suppressed in light of the violence already this morning. Guards in chain armor clinked and clanked as I melded into nooks and crannies as they passed by. No thoughts plagued me, only an animal sense of urgency that pressed on both sides of my head like a set of massive jaws.

I descended to ground floor unseen. Then I saw a side passage and the genius of Captain O'Loinsigh struck me, hiding so close as the net was thrown far and wide. The next set of stairs came quickly and I took them. I continued past the healer and past the empty guard station at the entrance to the dungeons. I pulled a candle from my pack and lit it on a torch up on the wall, feeling assured that nobody would be on station in this area. The empty cells were relics of the Sage's old purpose, no need for prisoners at an inn after all. They stood strong and ready but unused for ages. What I was looking for, however, was deeper, darker, and further into the bowels of the rock foundations.

I found the wide, spiral stair and stood shocked at the numerous footprints that disturbed the light layers of dust leading downward. I strained my ears but heard no voice, scuff of boot, or sign of ambush. It was absurd, after all, since I hadn't even known I was heading here until moments ago myself. A gong sounded faintly from above, showing someone had discovered something, and it was likely Roehm which meant they were again after me. I descended the staircase, careful to make as little noise as I could, and painfully aware that the candle in my hand would announce me more effectively than any footstep ever could. Soon my breath clouded the air, and a faint whiff of rot wafted to my nostrils.

The stair finally splashed into a cold chamber deep in the ground, silent and dark. When this was the Duke's seat, this was where the royal family would have lay in state waiting for heirs to gather for contention of the throne. It was deep in the earth, farther than light or warmth would reach. Stone sarcophagi lay on shelves carved from the ancient rock, marching onward into the darkness, but this is not what I wanted. Near the entrance there was a rather small, unassuming room with dust covered implements for preparing the dead for a dignified state burial. Silver bowls carried stale herbs that had long since given up their fragrances. Large mirrors reflected my candle and my face stared out of it accusingly, eyes more hollow than I can ever remember them. There were stone tables carved out of the wall for the corpses to lay on as they were prepared. Most disturbingly, four were occupied with the bodies of the assassins, Palmer, and O'Loinsigh.

Normally these would have been hung from the walls of the castle, or the city, as a warning to assassins and traitors. Then again, at least Palmer deserved some kind of burial and should have been sent to a local church for preparation. Next to him sat the blood stained letter he had flourished at me. I set down my equipment, perched the candle in one of the mirrored holders, and slit open the parchment with a thick nail.

In pursuant to the Law of the Grand Duke Horatio O'Riagáin, Lord of the Sorrow Wood, Sovereign of the Folded Hills, Warden of the... I skipped ahead... and *the peace needing to be kept within the walls of Carolaughan, and this peace being declared by the Sheriffs, the Grand Duke, and King Ryan...* I skipped more... *Lieutenant Patrick Palmer shall be granted the rights, immunities, and dignity of a state champion...* garbage, garbage, garbage... *and be authorized to carry arms to keep the King's good peace in the name of the...*

Nothing. The letter went on and on and on, and constantly mentioned special permissions, rights and immunities, and the names of many powerful people, but it never actually said anything. It was a piece of puffery, the kind of thing you can wave in front of a drunk boy and send him off to murder an inconvenient person. If he succeeds, you can blame or back him as you like. If he fails, you can execute his opponent for dueling. At the bottom was the signature and seal of Grand Duke's Horatio O'Riagáin.

I tossed the bit of evidence aside disdainfully, knowing it to be as useful as a glass of water to a drowning man. The Great and the Good would ignore it in course, like everything else. I slipped off the sliced shirt, dabbing at the dried blood from the scratch on my chest. A quick flash of movement behind me had me spun around with a dagger in my hand, but there was nothing but me in the distorted mirror behind the candle.

I turned back to my business, but saw a dark shadow again. I spun back around, wondering if one of my victims here was shamming, or his uneasy spirit coming back for revenge, but nothing appeared. I set the dagger down slowly, turning away from the light only by degrees as I scanned left-right-up-down, looking... searching.

As I turned, my back was reflected to own my eyes, and for just a second I saw a twisted pattern, something not quite drawn on the skin as drawn in the flesh, something that looked at me even as I looked at it. Then a pair of dark, haunted eyes appeared in the mirror.

Shaven headed, sunken cheeked, the ghost that had followed me in reflections across the kingdom appeared and silently screamed. I grabbed my sword, but he was gone.

My back suddenly started to burn, to twist as if the skin was reshaping into new and hideously wonderful shapes. I fought past the pain and reached back with a hand that found no dagger or pin, no arrow or stinger, only slightly rough flesh that even now was bypassing misery and heading toward agony.

I remember what Palmer had said, *"I know what you are, killer. I have seen your mark."* I stumbled to Palmer's corpse. I twisted his stiffening form onto his front and pulled aside his shirt, but there was nothing there. *"Wrestling, assassin. Wrestling you to the ground, I saw it."*

Pain building against the walls of my tolerance, I lunged at the female assassin who I had cut down in the apartment. Death had ripped away all sexual connotations of her naked body. I turned her over, dismissing flaccid muscles and icy blue skin. Across her back a huge gouge, provided by myself, interrupted her flesh and bone to the middle of her chest. Coming from back to front, it cleft the area between her shoulder blades messily. The area was ravaged, but there were clearly lines of ink that formed some kind of intricate pattern. My eyes followed the lines, familiarity blowing the Fog in my head until it became frustratingly thin. I was breathing heavily, nostrils flaring as my heart thudded as the only noise for a dozen paces in any direction. I dropped her carelessly to the stone. *"It watches you, slave. It sees you."*

Then I dove to the last assassin. Bearing a hundred ugly kisses of bloodthirsty arrows, he still oozed fluid as I twisted him up and used the angry swipe of a knife to split his rag-adorned clothing. What I saw there saw me back, an ornate tattoo that twisted over and over to the mind, folding in upon itself like an unknowable maze, on top of which was drawn a lifelike eye that stared into the depths of my very soul. I cried out and dropped the body, but I felt it stare into me, still.

I glanced at movement in the concave mirror behind a dead candle and saw that same sunken eyed demon that had chased me since I had woken on the Northern Ridge. He was smiling. *You are damned. Doomed.*

I lifted another mirror from an unlit bracket and angled it over my shoulder remembering the tortured words gurgling past Palmer's bloody lips, *"I saw it on your back."*

The mirror showed me the intricate knotwork, sacrilegious ink stabbed into the flesh to mark it for all time. The all seeing eye that watched me back as it steamed angrily in the cold air. I looked back to the strange, crazy man in the mirror across the room and I recognized him. It was my face. The demon, it was me. Then the pain came in thundering waves that dragged me under, the calling of crows was everywhere.

I remembered everything.

FOURTEEN

THE HIDDEN HISTORY BEHIND ME

THE world was in color, bolder and richer than I had ever seen. Corpses stood, eyes angry and wounds still fresh, packed impossibly deep in the crypt, stretching for a mile in all directions. I stood, pulling myself from the cold stone floor before turning to a cloaked angel standing before me, towering over me.

I had always known he was there.

Something began to scrape my heart with veins of frost as the figure raised his arms. Two hands, carved of aged alabaster, emerged from within the robe woven of webs and night. In one palm sat an old, withered heart, as if taken from a man's chest and plunged into a jar of salt. The blackened, saddened thing was strewn with black feathers, and it beat pitifully against the fingers that restrained it. In the other hand was a monstrous, malevolent thing, an organ that never found home in any sane man's chest. Tentacles sprouted from the surface and reached for me, eyes opening up across the powerful muscle, weeping streams of blood that broke into thorns and shards of glass against the floor. He seemed to be offering both to me, waiting with the patience of one who has no life left to trickle through the hourglass.

Then, for the first time, I turned, and ran.

I burst through the crowd of my victims that pressed in, screaming curses written in guilt and death. The voices rushed at me, filling my head. My mind spun like a crippled bird, whirling and dying and screaming. The Animal inside me roared like the primal thing it was, shaking the rafters of my soul and flooding me with its strength. Then it was no longer in me, but beside me, a huge, hairy thing of claws and fangs, reaching out for me in its endless rage. I dove beneath the grasping talons and made for the stairs, which became a forest in the wild places of the Kingdom. No, it was not the *kingdom of today. It was, the split Kingdom, before King Ryan, during the Reunification War.*

I had a family, a loving upbringing I can barely remember. I was ten when I joined up with the baggage train to Ryan's army. I wanted to fight for my country, to follow a real hero into battle, but the quartermaster placed me where men have placed boys for centuries... in the rear to distribute and manage the supplies needed to run an army.

I was cold, and hungry, and very, very tired. I was young and terrified. The wave of corruption and power before the battle lines of the Kingdom's finest troops reached in and twisted me. An old toothless man, leader of the baggage train, spit black juice from the shredded root he was chewing and watched grimly.

"Will we survive?" I asked, my voice so small and vulnerable.

"If they live," he replied in a cancerish voice as he gestured to the wall of men between ourselves and the massed barbarian horde, "we live. Those demon beasts won't recognize the articles of war. If they reach us, they will slay us."

"Will Ryan save us?"

He laughed, wheezing like a bent and broken tree, "If he lives he will try. Our well being is in the hands of Fate now, boy, and Fate cares not if you be a hero, or a fool. She is cruel, or kind, all the same."

I saw the brave soldiers die by the thousands, but more heralded to Ryan's banner to take up the fight than died on the spears and swords of the western barbarians. I saw the scavengers who came and picked over the bodies of the dead. They grew rich off of the blood of other men, not risking any of their own. I saw the soldiers, too tired to stop them from killing the few poor bastards that were still alive when the damned vultures got to them.

I knew then it was better to be a scavenger than a soldier. Watching the butchered men scream for healing that would not come, seeing entire cities burned, seeing the very earth burned and spooled beneath the feet of barbarians– something died within me. I remember watching the redcaps climb from their dark places and feast on the fallen heroes at night.

I was only ten years old.

A roar behind me caused me to turn and bolt. I dodged past the scene and ran through the woods to the foot of the mountains, leagues flying beneath my feet. There I saw Ryan, bloody and desperate, leading those last few men on the charge that made him King, reuniting the Kingdom, and driving the few surviving enemy back over the mountains. I was there when he thanked us, and paid us in debased campaign coins, and rode off for his throne and his palace, leaving us in the dirt. I watched myself looking left and right, to the face of each man, hoping for orders that would make everything make sense, that would tell me where to go next, orders that would never come.

I followed the lost boy across the Kingdom as his debased coin was stolen, spent, or swindled away. The nightmares pressed in on me as I traveled, cold and alone, towards a half-remembered hovel. Ryan got a parade to each capital while I trod on frozen feet to a burnt, abandoned place I once called home. Winter pressed in as I lay, screaming, in the clutches of my parents bones. The Barbarians had been there, or Ryan's abandoned soldiers looting toward home. I had been spared their fate by my foolishness.

I trudged along the icy, mud-covered roads of the newly re-minted Kingdom trying to find food and shelter. There was none. No one had any use for another mouth to feed, at least not until the following fall when the harvests could be brought in.

I stumbled through Dreaming Forest which became an alley in some unnamed city. Four boys were savaging a fifth. The victim was so small, so defenseless, and though all the fight had been knocked out of him the older boys continued to kick him (me!) mercilessly. I did not scream, did not make a single sound. I only stared blankly out into space, tears crawling down my face and imagined their deaths over and over and over.

The Beast broke into the alley and I leapt, my hands grasping a low windowsill. In seconds I was moving upwards, but the Beast did not follow. It had been distracted by the bullies, whom it tore into ribbons of flesh that splashed from the walls. It saved the younger me, still laying on the ground, for last.

I heard my own screams as I shattered a window and crawled inside, finding myself at night, in a building I knew intimately. The long shadows and sharp edges were more horrible than any creature of tooth and claw. I saw myself in bed and I couldn't breathe.

Those were long nights in the orphanage where I resided under the cruel hands of the masters of that place. We were hired out for jobs to earn our keep, dangerous toil in inhuman conditions.

I Know Not

We did it to earn our gruel and a place on infested straw mattresses. I remember the punishments of Master Niall, sometimes given in the middle of the night for offenses not remembered. We didn't understand it for what it was. We just saw it as another kind of beating.

The next year I was one of the boys kicking smaller children. It wasn't much later that Niall came for me in the middle of the night. The smell of his breath was like dog shit. I snatched a sharp knife from his bed stand and severed his dangling fruit. His screams echoed off of the walls like a nightmare that propelled me off into the winter cold.

Faced with starvation and frostbite, I killed a sleeping man for his food and his gold. The feeling of power tickled my senses and pushed back the utter impotence that had taken me. By the time I was twelve, I was a petty murderer on the streets of a city, any city, every city, in the Kingdom. I would kill and steal until the bounties became too high, then slip out for another place where I would start all over.

I was fifteen when one of the derelicts of the city came to find me and offer me gold in exchange for a life. I did not want to believe him, but a handful of silver convinced me he may have a coin or two of gold to spend. It was not a simple murder, and it was not done subtly, but the man died and somehow I escaped. Payment was made, as promised, but it was delivered by a man with the gaunt face of the dead. He moaned that I had been noticed, and that I had potential. If I was willing to pay... I looked at the short stack of buttery golden coins in my hand and closed my fist over top of them. I wanted more.

The Beast shattered into the room and reached for me, claws dripping with a hundred vile humors. I gathered the dark curtain into a net and tossed it at the thing, and it became a thick straw mat upon which an older me was fighting.

During this time I drank other people's lives like cheap wine, hunting for and against the law to catch lesser criminals to gather the gold for my training. I was soaking up the arts of murder far to the south. A fantastically ugly woman, made up of sharp points and cutting edges, looked at me from over a rooftop as my legs cart wheeled into space. Now I remember why I wear my sword on my back. I remember her name was Elidra as she sneers, "The moment you cut a corner, it will leave an edge sharp enough to slit your throat."

I shuddered. The unfamiliar voice was colder than all the winters throughout time. I absently wandered to a fire in a forest where a man built like a razor blade spoke intensely, "Not all stealth is quiet. The ears hear danger in the unfamiliar, boy. If an ear is used to a creaking mill, no creaking will disturb the sleeper."

I turned away and there were dozens of others, each one bore me no love, but taught me in exchange for the gold I earned by murder. A huge weight slammed me and I hit the ground. Suddenly I was laying down and a man was jabbing an inked needle into my back hundreds, and thousands of times. He was drawing the lines that bound me into the Ragmen, the symbol of the Great Murderer and Master of Secrets, Isahd.

There were whispers that the tattoo would grow, that it would twist, and that it would burrow into the very soul.

I heard, "Are you going to get up, or am I going to kill you here?"

I rolled to my feet but the teacher I expected was not there. Instead, a great, bearish, western barbarian, Bjorloff, was beating me badly with some wooden weapons. He picked me up and shook me like a mastiff with a drunk rat. "'Ero's die boy! You 'ave to do better!"

He threw me to the mat, but an even older me stood up into my own head. It was not Bjorloff teaching me, it was the Beast coming in full force. But I did not fear. Since the days of my training, I'd had hundreds of lessons, thousands of victims. The rage inside was my tool, not my master.

The Beast lunged– hateful, hurtful, and hungry. I simply moved to the side, lashing out with a whip made of black steel and drawing a bloody line down its flanks. The whole body shattered into dust, but as I turned the Animal was exploding out of the cloud of chalky cloud. I went low, flinging the blade overhead as the storm of teeth and claws blew past. His roar changed to a scream as he fell and destroyed another wall within myself.

There are some men who see a rock and know there is a sculpture inside. Those that see a blank page and can feel the soft curves of the story and wishes to bed down upon it. Those that listen to the wind and the rain and can capture the notes in fleeting puffs of air. The Dark Thing is like that. I am like that. Assassins are like that. Our medium is death.

The Beast blew by again and I cut it three times, spilling blood, bile, and viscera across the entire road.

Road?

It was not the Beast. I was carrying a crossbow. I had shot a Knight. No, it was an Inquisitor like the knight of Amsar I'd encountered on the road to Carolaughan. I had pierced this holy judge's foot to the ground, then calmly reloaded as he sought to free himself. I laughed as he succeeded, mangling his foot in the process.

He drew his Angel-hilted sword and struggled toward me as I punctured his lung, crushing his chest-plate in. I took the bright sword from his numb fingers and hacked his head from his body with the impossibly sharp edge. It flashed and crackled, hot lightning clinging like fire as the blade blackened and my victim's head tumbled down the hill and splashed into a pond surrounded by fir trees. I looked at its darkened surface and raised my prize into the sky, cackling with triumph. I brought the blade to my eye as the interior shadows deepened. My hair was shorn short, my eyes red and sunken from weeks on short rations while on the hunt...

I blinked as a trail of blood seeped from my scalp. I wiped it away and looked back at my reflection. As the smell of dried bones slammed back into me, the candle danced in a wind that wasn't there. The shorn-haired crazy man was staring at me from the safety of the mirrored candle stand. His head was cut and blood flowed into his face. I glanced at my feet and saw long, fashionable tresses spread across the floor. The Phantom Angel was in my hand. Hairs were stuck to the bloody edge of the supernaturally sharp blade.

I looked back into the mirror, realizing that I was the man who had been chasing me. The man from the roof was Kenneth and the axe-faced woman was Claire, Knife of Bannon. I knew them, of course. They were assassins, Ragmen of the Guild. The marks on their backs said as much, marks like mine. I turned and angled my head and shoulders so I could clearly see the mass of sharp metal and soft tentacles tattooed into my back between my shoulder blades. In the center of the mass was the all-seeing eye, symbol of Isahd, patron devil of murder.

I had always known it was there.

But as I looked away from it, The Lidless Eye blinked, and unknowable agony shot through me like a boulder dropped from a mountaintop. It went on and on, and the unbending rage threw hooks of hate into my skin and pulled like a leash to remind me of my place.

I heard wings, and I blacked out.

The candle said I awoke an hour later, but it felt like centuries. Having a naked chest flush against the carved rock of the tombs left me with a bone-deep chill, but still, the cold trickle of water across my back was a soul cleansing relief. I heard a rag being rung out and felt it spread across the obscene tattoo, immediately quenching the fire and barbed claws.

The memory of the bounty doubtless on my head flooded me with wordless panic. I tried to jerk around to challenge whoever was with me, but I only managed to thrash sluggishly. Gentle hands pressed me back down and Gelia whispered, "Crow, you can't get up yet. Crow. Crow!"

Then all fight went out of me. The pain, the hurt, the sheer weight of all my memories crashed into me like every waterweight of stone between me and the sun. It shifted and churned like the sea underneath a winter windstorm, building currents that poured into my head and exploded out of me as pure misery. I fought for control, but sobs slipped through my fingers and shattered against the walls. Gelia moved my head to her lap and stroked what bristle was left of my hair.

She tried levity. "I told you, every time I leave you, you start bleeding."

I felt the weakness coming, and I hated myself for it. I cried against her, and I don't know for how long, pressing into her kind warmth as if I could not believe that such a thing existed. Inside my head the Fog continued to retreat, fingerlength by fingerlength. It had only just begun, but I had a feeling I knew where it would end.

"So now you know." She did not ask. Of course she had seen the tattoo weeks ago while tending me, and had known what I was, even though I did not.

"My name is Simon.". It was still foreign in my mouth and my head was full of dung-stained cotton. Gelia reached over me and pulled the cloth from off my back. The stinging needles began again, only to be quenched by another application of whatever tincture she had placed in the water. "Will the hurting ever really go away?"

I Know Not

Her face, so often pointed at me as a mask of barely bridled angst and loathing, was set like a mother with a sick child. "I do not know. I think there is something inside of you screaming to get out. That mark on your back is a baleful thing. Something powerful is trying to reclaim you, but you will not let it."

I had known all the poisons by sight and smell, known the weapons and methods of an assassin. If I had been less busy trying to stay alive, I could have seen it a long time ago. I rose from her lap, and the cloth slid to the side, exposing me again to a hail of burning wasps as I threw acidic words in a torrent, "I won't let it? Who are you trying to fool? I've been stuck without me for so long I don't even know who I am!"

My fury would have had as much effect on a mountain. "Maybe that is what the Gods intended all along."

The pain was like being staked out under a stampede. I had to choke the words out, "I am not who you think I am!"

Again, she was placid. "I know. You never have been, and that is what gives me hope." With those cryptic words she gathered me to her aged breasts like a child and rocked me back and forth. A seed within struggled and twisted, tearing at the cascading fabric of nothing within me.

"Fight for it, Crow," she whispered, giving the seed teeth and claws, a wolverine fetus that was swimming in the sea of my own apathy.

"My name is Simon." My own voice was distant, detached. It was as colorless as all my memories from the age of thirteen, and before a few scant weeks ago.

"You are Crow. You have always been Crow. You always will be Crow." The seed roared like a dragon, shaking the pillars of my mind and cracking the dam I had erected against insanity. "When I called to the Goddess in fear, she spoke to her Father and he sent you to us as a deliverance."

Waves of emotion built and began to swirl, taking the last vestiges of the Fog from me and beginning to arc along my spine. The pressure in my head was amazing, cracking the mask of quiet I wore against the world. "I am a killer, Gelia."

"You are a hero, Fox Crow..." She began to stroke my hair as if I were a long lost child. "...and you always will be."

Again the rag quenched the blinding pain like a storm obscures the stars. And even at that instant all other things were becoming clear. I was not a good man. I was not a hero. I was not a protector of old women and boys. I was a murderer.

Five hundred gold had almost bought the life of Sir Walden, Marshal of the Sorrow Wood. Had the barbarians not attacked while I was convincing Walden I was a third son of a noble turned mercenary for hire, he would be dead all the same. I would have killed him. Had I been paid a few coins more, I would have killed his daughter and wife as well. Even his infant son could have been purchased as easily. Ten coins more, after all, what's one more?

I was trying to fight my way out of the castle, not defend it. I am not a good man. I am an assassin, and if everything weren't dead inside me, I supposed I would be sad. I shifted and the rag fell away, exposing the tattoo and starting another whipping. But even as Gelia soaked the rag and replaced it, the hurt felt half hearted, as if the lesson had been learned and now there was only the inertia of ire causing it to burn

"What medicine is that?" I wheezed, frightened by the weakness in my own voice.

"It is only water," she replied.

"Just water?"

"Well, it is the blessed water from my silver flask. It was all I had at hand."

I sat in mute shock as she adjusted the rag again.

Head bent, I felt the stirrings of bone deep shame bubble through my flesh. Twin drops slapped silently into the stone. I touched the corpses of my tears gingerly as the final dregs of pain drained from my back. I saw the salty water, certain they were not borne from any wound. These were tears of loss, and knew they meant something profound, if only I could decrypt it.

Then the final wisps of Fog cleared, revealing the dark and dangerous cloaked stranger. It was me, had always been me, the cold murderer inside of my mind that held the wild Beast in check. It calculated everything... it felt nothing. It was as much protection from the world as the thickest castle walls. It spread its arms, showing me its hollow core and it did not embrace me so much as lunge.

Simon opened... *I* opened... my eyes, finally devoid of the taint of Crow. The rag fell away and my back tingled with the cold and nothing more.

Gelia still stared at me, pale blue eyes pitifully beseeching me for some hint of hope. My memories soaking into my mind dissolving trust and hope into a meaningless soup. She leaned forward, waiting for me to say something, anything, to give her mind rest. My eyes flicked to a dozen deadly and innocuous items strewn about the tomb chamber. Each was more tempting than the last, but she was much more of an opportunity than a threat. I would need her to move forward.

The changing room of my mind blurred behind my eyes and I reached in and effortlessly plucked the right personality from the speeding throng. It easily slipped on over my emaciated sense of self. I smiled, carefully portraying quiet embarrassment and a certain amount of frayed nerves, "I will try to be that man, Gelia. I will try."

And the breath she hadn't known she was holding whooshed out of her, signaling her boundless relief. I forced my posture to relax a little and a self deprecating smile to flirt with my face. She smiled back and hugged me tightly as I wondered if anyone had heard me screaming. It was a thought that brought me back to the desperation of my situation, because I could not hide in the tomb forever. I shrugged, "So how high is the bounty on my head?"

Gelia blinked twice before giggling like a young girl, erasing decades from her face. "Crow I was there. I saw the Lieutenant attack you. I may just be a sagging old woman to some people, but I am a Priestess and my word carries a lot of weight. I testified before the Grand Duke." Then her tone slipped into being more than slightly reproachful, "You were a free man before you beat up Roehm and escaped to here."

Inside of me there was a slight bounce of joy at a deception well executed, and more for my status as a free man, but it definitely had an iron chain clamped around its ankle. I shook my head as if in disbelief, but I was trying to get rid of some nagging feelings that hovered like smoke behind my eyes. "And Aelia?"

Her countenance soured, "Furious, as you might expect, but at more people than just you, which you might not."

I looked back and forth, forlornly, desperately trying to project half-hidden consternation at the news. Truthfully I was wondering... "Gelia, how did you find me down here?"

She was worried again, reaching out a wrinkled hand to cup my face, "You've been screaming for hours like the living dead. In fact they believed the dead down here had woken."

"And yet you came down."

She gave me a knowing look. "I have heard you scream like that before."

That brought a hot flow of something foreign and frightening oozing into my chest. I clutched my heart and shook my head violently.

"Does it hurt?"

I nodded, lying easily as I pushed her away. "It will pass."

She looked from one disturbed corpse to another and laughed dryly as she gathered up her bundle of herbs, balms, needle, thread, and cloths. "When I first saw you here, I had feared for a moment that your victims had come back to life to take their revenge upon you."

I picked up the Phantom Angel from the floor, marveling at the brightness of the silver robe and golden wings next to the blackened blade. Now that I knew what to look for, I could see the trails in the surface, marking the bloody death of a holy man. My voice echoed off of the walls, "Who says they didn't try?"

Anger welled up inside me as I could not deny the hint of loss, of weakness disrobing in the echoes. I remembered being that little boy beaten in the streets by bigger boys, being hungry enough to eat garbage in the winter snows, of watching half dead men being eaten by redcaps under a harvest moon. I remember holding onto the bones of parents long cold and dead.

I won't go back to that.

So when Gelia touched my arm tenderly, I let her embrace me even though the closeness made my skin crawl. I hugged her back, calculating the pressure of the contact to maximize how desperate, how pitiful, I meant to feel to her.

At the same time, I stomped on something warm and humble inside my chest, and I resisted the very real urge to drive a dagger into her heart. She pulled away and primly began to gather her supplies. It was best she did not see as my hands shook violently as my insides churned like the boiling sea. I caught the reflection of my tattoo in a candle mirror and I swear the inked eye turned to glare at me.

I am Simon. I am Simon. I must be Simon, or I will not survive.

I started to gather my own gear together from where it had been scattered during my madness. I brought up a tunic to slide it over my head, and my hands brushed the bandage across my chest. It marked the newest member of a forest of old scars, but the newest stood out, white and content, against the others. Each one was a memory of this old woman and her wisdom putting right what I had broken.

The dark part of me spoke, *Don't be sentimental. She would not have healed you if she knew who you were.*

Gelia turned to me and saw my face before I could control it. I don't know what she saw, but it worried her. She reached out and gripped my arm, trying to impart some strength to me.

Something else inside me replied, *That's not true. She knew from the beginning. You served your master... she served her master, nothing more.* And to that I had no answer. All color drained from her inside my mind, leaving her a hollow form, easily disposed of. I slipped into a numb fugue as I pulled the tunic over my head and followed it with a leather doublet. The calculating part of me fell silent to a host of ghostly chattering memories as I laced the arms tightly and pulled on my breeches and heavy boots.

"Expecting trouble?" she asked, a touch too innocently

I looked down, and while my mind had been picking through days gone by like a child with razor edged toys, Left and Right had been busy boys. My quick eyes picked out a dozen hidden blades, spikes, needles, vials, and the one deadly ring. Crow socked Simon, sending him reeling and saying, "I don't think you've ever seen me expect otherwise."

But rather than settle her, Gelia puffed up further, "Crow, you had better put those thoughts to their grave."

My fingers were paralyzed, desperately trying to pull my hands apart as they went in different directions to reach a weapon. Guilt flooded me, freezing cold in my gut, boiling hot in my face, and completely foreign to my soul. I cleared my throat. "What–"

"I don't know what you have remembered, but I doubt you suddenly found out you are a scion of King Ryan." Gelia kneeled before me and took both little murderers in her two tender healers. "I know she fancies you. I know you are smart enough to know how much. Please, please, tell me you are smart enough to know that this cannot happen."

And suddenly what she was saying crashed into me like a dying man dropped from a parapet. I blinked hard, squeezing my eyes with the palms of my hands. Fires raged inside me, and Simon could not catch all the sparks before they raged into bonfires. The thunder within rolled like an angry god, shattering my walls like kindling. For a moment, I was thirteen again watching the horrors of war unfold all around me.

Gelia embraced me and whispered, "I will wait for you on the landing."

Then she left. It was best she had, for behind her was the shaven headed maniac who had stared at me out of every reflective surface since I had awoken. If she had stayed, there would be no doubt– I was going to kill them all.

FIFTEEN

A WORLD OF PALE SHAPES

THE Grand Duchess looked up from her dispatches, her beautiful eyes weary. So young, and chained with such weights, and yet she rose to the occasion like a...

She will betray you, I remembered. *She will betray you again.*

Aelia glowed in bright colors. Her cheeks were in full flush even as the paleness of her neck pulsed in the lamplight. Her auburn hair fluttered like memories of autumn as she pored over missives, lists, and maps. I felt my pulse quicken as I calculated how many gold coins she was worth dead.

Aelia had been planning on safeguarding herself; now she was planning a war. She had discarded the complex whalebone corsets and skirts for something that more closely resembled the riding clothes she had worn on the last weeks travel. It was a good thing, since trailing skirts and long sleeves would definitely spill papers and demolish colored blocks stacked on a map of the Kingdom to the floor. At a glance troops were being marshaled northward. It was not hard to guess why. Nor why such a move was complicated.

Even at half the age of most of the men in the room, she still commanded them around like the noble born she was. They were all shadows, echoes of threats unworthy of my attention. Each would take a single cut or trust to turn aside as empty bags of blood and gold. In the corner, Roehm scowled at me through a puffy visage, and I blanked my face as I marked him for certain but slow death should the opportunity arise.

Aelia saw me and I was comforted by the arrows inside her gaze. She began to pale in my mind, and I took courage from the distance. This would be combat, and I knew combat. Her entire day had been taken up poring over maps, trying to deploy forces to contain the border. Well, those parts of her day not taken up with dealing with the destruction I had left in my wake.

"What?" Her words were like the crack of a whip. Too bad for her I have endured real whips, and only feared them when actually present.

I stepped up to the table, but Simon inside my head waved off all mental costumes. I answered calmly, "I am here at your service, My Grand Lady."

She dug into her belt pouch and took out a cheap bag of sewn canvas and tossed it onto the table. A single small disc escaped and rolled toward freedom, but I caught it before it ever had a chance to fall. "There, Crow. That's all I owe you. Take it and go. You are dismissed from my service."

The buttery, beautiful golden coin popped to the top of my fist with only a few movements of my fingers. The light sparkled across the surface like a winking woman, but then Aelia shifted and I focused upon her again. Suddenly she seemed much smaller, so much more fragile. "How will you fend off assassination without me, Milady?"

She became painfully aware that everyone in the room was gawking at the two of us. "Out!"

Nobody moved.

"Milady?" one of the functionaries, either a general or a handmaiden from the complexity and puffery of his uniform, asked tentatively.

"OUT!" she roared, and the room emptied with passable speed.

She turned and gave a meaningful look at Roehm. Even with his face swollen from my beating he managed to exude injured loyalty. He stood stiffly and began shuffling out with a pronounced limp.

He paused when he was abreast of me and mumbled, "If you touch her I will kill you."

I affected a light tone and smiled dangerously, "I'm sorry, didn't catch that. Food allergy? Or did you bite off too much to chew?"

He was glaring at me for long after he left.

As the door shut, Gelia let herself in and stood in the far corner, seeking to become invisible in the manner of servants of a noble house down through time.

Aelia straightened out her dress, feeling uneasy of a sudden. "You shaved your head."

I felt at the ragged stubble, confused. This was how I should always wear my hair, short and harder to grab by an enemy. The only time I grew it long was to ingratiate myself with nobles. "It seemed practical."

"You remember now," she said, and it was not a question.

Now I can say for certain that I have a rule– when sharing a secret with another person never, never, never, ever say anything even remotely like, 'She told you.' It is much better to just nod and say nothing. So I did.

"Will I like you now, Crow?" Aelia stood straight, swirling her hair up in a simple knot held together with a single pin. She was acting brusque, but her eyes could not lie. They dripped with equal parts loss and fear. "Will I respect you? Will I trust you?"

Her questions splashed to the floor around her, leaving interesting patterns just by marking the void of where she stood. It wasn't what she was asking, but what she didn't. Then she was in my arms, warm and soft, strong and beautiful. Her scent enveloped me. My hands tingled, wanting, needing to pull her into me in an embrace that would never end. I wanted to protect her, to have her accept all of me. This is what I had come to want, as much as I wanted to keep breathing. But my mind belonged to Simon and he just stood there and gave her no comfort. She stepped away, leaving two tearstains on my shirt.

I felt a pull from behind me as powerful as any primal urge. I turned and caught Gelia's pleading eyes, and something moved in my heart that Simon could not totally squash. I turned back and bowed my head slightly to the Lady. I spoke the truth, "No, Milady."

She nodded and Simon throttled the ghosts of loss that rose inside my head. "I understand."

Crow wanted to take his leave, but Simon needed more because he was planning to return. "What happens now?"

She gestured to the room around her. "King Ryan has sent back word. Sir Walden has fallen, and I am to work with Horatio to contain any activity in the Sorrow Wood and North Ridge Mountains..."

"...using your combined troops." I interrupted, "That's very clever of Horatio."

Aelia banged her fist against the table, "Crow..."

"I am guessing that with troops committed to the Northern Ridge and along the Sorrow Wood, you'd be hard pressed to fight a full scale war in memory of your father."

"Crow." My name was a tired plea.

"He asked for this, Aelia. He knows that you know."

"Crow." And this time is was a firm request.

"You must strike at him now!"

"CROW!" And now an order.

I felt the truth of my words cut the ties between the princess and myself like an icy knife. "My name is Simon."

She sighed, "Then gather your things and leave, Simon."

At that moment, the only thing that kept her alive was the promise that someone would pay me to kill her later. I swept the pouch of coins from the table and popped them into my shirt. As I walked past her my own thoughts mocked me. *See? After you saved her life, safeguarded all that gold, your reward is a few fingernail scrapings from the treasure and the friendliest of dismissals.*

The burn on my soul sent smoke up my throat which formed into too honest, too hurtful words, "He will have you killed, girl."

She drew her tired form upright, summoning courage and power from Gods knew where. She clenched her fists to keep them from trembling as she set upon me with her beautiful green eyes, "I am Aelia Conaill, Grand Duchess of Conaill, and if I'm to die then I will do it with dignity."

And in her eyes there lay worse; a kind of hurt so deep not even the light of the sun could plumb the depths. My chest felt tight like a formation of overdrawn bows. Simon cut the strings and reveled in the welts they caused as they flew free.

I walked past her into the room the boys shared, where the rest of my things had been stored. Inside were the remaining caravan guards that had survived Aelia's march around the Sorrow Wood: Miller, Theo, Godwin, and Jon.

Theo bounced to his feet as if I were his commander, and not a stranger off the street. He managed to hold off the salute as he asked, "So, you're going?"

They shuffled like children, staring at the floor with long faces. I knew they had heard, and I guessed that at least one had peeked. Both of those I could appreciate, but the threat of imminent weeping disgusted me. They were nothing but pale shapes, hollow bags of muscle and blood. They were little bags of gold waiting to be collected, or tools ready to be used, broken, and discarded. But even small gold is gold and tools are sometimes useful, so I swallowed my harsh face and tried on a bright easy going voice from the wardrobe in my head.

"We thought you had gone," said Godwin, "Gone."

"You sure this is it? Maybe if you apologized to Roehm?" suggested Jon.

"What happened to your hair?" Miller asked.

"I'm going, and I'll probably be on the road for some time. No living like a noble, caring for long, flowing locks. But before I go, you have all been dedicated students, stalwart comrades, and good friends." It took real effort to reach into my shirt and produce the coin that Aelia had given me. I held it out to Theo. "Here, this will make up for the wages you're being docked by that bastard Roehm."

The boys crowded around as he opened the pouch to see the gold coins inside. The amount of gems I had hidden in my pack was enough to make it a paltry sum, but it still stung. What hurt even worse was setting the much larger and heavier pouch containing the dead captain's bribe. "And this is to be split amongst all of you. Call it a going away present."

Two gasped, Godwin almost fainted, and Theo involuntarily sat down, but the boys kept enough of their wits about them to not hoot and holler like idiots. This needed to be our secret. It was, in fact, a gamble, or maybe a down payment to pave the way toward future earnings. I picked up my pack, heavier now with clothes and boots, but lighter for gold, and embraced the boys like close kin. They said nothing, because they thought themselves men and if they spoke they would cry. I said nothing, because the best lies are never spoken.

I left them and crossed the main room, Theo in tow. The Generals had returned, but Aelia was gone. I cursed silently, because I had needed....wanted her to see me go. I paused by the front door where Gelia wept silently. She pulled me into an embrace that I returned no matter how much it made my skin crawl.

"You must help her, Crow. Put this right."

I set my jaw, breathed deeply, and spoke the complete truth, "I will return and end this, Gelia."

"There is the final feast before the auction tomorrow night. Everyone will need a chit from the Grand Duke to get in."

I nodded to her, "Then I shall have to do something to get a chit, won't I?"

I reached to her side, and absently lifted her silver flask of holy water.

I shook it, it was mostly full, and gave her a questioning look. She nodded emphatically as I packed it away. She smiled at me, not understanding, and I walked out into the hall. She watched me go with a beatific smile, Theo with a puzzled look. Then the door shut and I was free.

Fools.

The world is full of them. They have gone to the playhouses, listened to bards in the taprooms, and clapped at the damned puppet shows. All these things tell them that everything will be all right. They say that a hero always appears. They say that a young boy won't be abandoned by the noble warrior king as he tromps off to his coronation. The poxy bards don't tell you his parents are dead. They don't tell you he almost starves over and over and over.

They lie.

Because what happens is the boy grows up in a world that doesn't care, and somehow even just surviving is called a crime. And once you are a thief, what matters a few more thefts? After those thefts, what matters a murder? After the first, murders are much easier to forget. Besides, a wolf is not evil for devouring the child. It is simply hungry. I have been hungry, and I devour who I want and the nobles are only angry because the sheep belong to them.

I heard quick steps on the stairs behind me and the pommel of a knife fell into my hand from up my sleeve. It turned out only to be Theo. I waved him back and made to tell him to go back to his duties, but his voice plowed over mine, "What happens now, will they give up?"

I eyed the sack slung over his deliberately set shoulders. I still needed him to get close to Conaill so I overlooked his harsh tone and told him the truth while I looked for a way to twist it to my advantage, "No, the assassin's guild will never give up unless the target or the employer dies."

"So Lady Conaill will be forever watching for a knife in the dark, then?"

There is the opening. "I won't let that happen, Theo. I may need your help, but we can keep the Lady safe."

His next words had a definite edge, "And that's what the gold is for?"

I acted wounded. I acted offended. I was neither. I was shifting the knife in my hand. "No, and how could you say such a thing?"

"How are you going to stop the next assassin?" And that

question had a honed point.

There was a pressure in my head beginning to build, pushing at my eyes. "I don't know, Theo!"

"Because you are always a step ahead of them, an expert on all of their methods and all of their equipment."

"Would you rather I had let her die, Lieutenant?"

And though his voice was lowered, the force of his heart pushed the words into my face like fists wrapped in iron, "How many of their knives do you have on you even now? How many vials of poison?"

I felt storm clouds gather over me, and dangerous thunder rumbling in my voice, "Watch your tone, boy."

"I am only following orders, sir," he replied, soft voice dripping with sarcasm. "You told me everyone uses everyone else for their own ends, so who are you using, sir?"

"I drop a weight of gold in your lap and all I get is veiled accusations in return."

"You told me to question everyone, so I ask... the inquisitor mentioned that sword belonging to one of his fellows. Where did you come by it?"

Involuntarily I backed down one stair. "I don't remember."

And like a hound after a fox, he followed. "You're different. You look at people different. You act different. You are not the man we met on the road. I think you have remembered."

I looked down at his right hand and saw he had a knife concealed there. Feeling my own knife in my own hand, I felt a strange surge of pride in the boy, that he had learned what I had to teach. Now he was finally a man. He was a person, he was real, and I could feel insubstantial hands pushing on me to look out for his wants, for his needs. I shook them off and prepared to murder him as my mouth stalled for time. Since my near death and resurrection, I have found I have a talent for saying the worst wrong thing at the precisely wrong time.

"What do you want of me, Theodemar?"

Slowly, he removed the canvas sack from over his shoulder and held it out to me. The movement created a miniature musical slide of coin on coin. His face, however was not giving, but stony and distant, "Nothing Crow. I want nothing from you."

I took the satchel full of the pouches I had just given the boys, and my practiced hand counted their number by feel alone.

Theodemar began retreating up the stairs, still facing me. "My men and I are not for sale."

Your friend is afraid of you, Simon whispered into my mind. *I would say your first new friend, but there are no others.*

And then Theo was gone.

See how easily you are discarded? See how much you really mean to them?

I glanced down at the hidden knife in my hand and suddenly I knew why Crow eschewed the safety of self delusion. I am a liar, the biggest liar. I have fooled nobles and sheriffs, peasants and priests. Given enough rancid self pity, I could nearly believe myself.

I slipped the knife back into its hiding place and continued downward. I left through the front door, passing the guards without another word.

I betrayed him. I betrayed them all. Those thoughts rolled like the thunder of an angry god, shattering my mental walls like kindling. My insides ached and I stumbled on the street until I could find the safety of an alley where judging eyes could not find me. There I leaned in the shadows and hurt for a very long time.

I went back to the slums and found my way to a bar. It didn't matter which bar; they all had Whisperers in them.

It took her less than an hour to find me. There were eyes everywhere. She was a mousy, twitchy woman. Not unattractive, but the angry red pox on her face would ward off all but the most foolish of lovers. She blinked incessantly as she scuttled up to the table, never looking directly at me. She fiddled with her soiled clothing and mumbled fractured nursery rhymes to herself. The barman yelled for her to leave as she sang to me, "Eyes are here, ears are there, Ragman must go and give up his share."

Her message delivered, she listlessly turned to go. I stared in horror as her colorless form filled with detail. I could feel the disease ravaging her mind and body. I could hear the screaming parts of herself looking for long lost dreams from childhood. Of its own accord, my hand shot out and grasped her wrist. She gasped and tried to pull away, but suddenly I was standing there, so close she could feel my breath. I could feel every bad decision and every lapsed opportunity weeping out of her dirty pores.

She struggled weakly, but I held her tightly. Her beautiful gray eyes flew open, radiating fear like two stars. I may never have seen her, or maybe I have seen her a thousand times, but this was the first time I had accepted her as a human being. I leaned close and whispered, "Go to the healers and get them to help you. Then get out of Carolaughan."

Her breath was coming in short gasps as she felt a dozen heavy coins quietly slip into a slash in her tunic. There was a spark of something, maybe recognition, maybe understanding, inside of her. Then I let her go with a small fortune hidden in her shirt as I turned to collect my pack.

Her message had been delivered, however, and I knew my life could very well be coming to a close. The dozen gold coins I had just given away left a hideous hole inside of me, and I felt like a fool, but I had been unable to stop myself. Crow and Simon were both inside me, and unless I could get rid of the unintended result of my broken skull, I would surely be dead by midnight. There was no room for Crow in this world.

Five minutes later, I bought a room from the bar man. A half an hour later, steaming water was brought up to fill the big wooden bath. A minute after that, I was nude, looking into the face in the water, eyes tracing every stitched together slash and the angry green memories of bruises and breaks.

You are a hero, Fox Crow.

Gelia's words ambushed me and shattered all other coherent thoughts. I fell into the tub sending water sloshing in all directions. I opened my mouth to scream and water rushed in, looking to fill my lungs. The vision of the Phantom Angel swam into focus. He was holding out two things to me. I screamed out a silent stream of water as I erupted from the tub. My hands were shaking and the world seemed to erupt into white sparks. I coughed until my throat was raw and then shook hair out of my eyes before I remembered I had shaved it off.

I glanced around the room, but there was no cloaked apparition, no ghosts of murders past. There was only myself and the clear knowledge that this was not over yet.

Sixteen

The Estuary of Murder

THE lamp in the run down room picked out the blue cat's eyes on the Phantom Angel as I hefted, spun, and sent it home in its black sheath. I looked upon the bed where I had spread the captured implements of death. Quietly, I armed myself. Knives and pins and poisons and daggers, caltrops and garrotes and the deadly ring.

I started to run my fingers through my long, black hair and found nothing but bristle. I stared at my hand for a moment, then forced myself to focus on the matter at hand.

Next came the rags, subtle variations of muted colors layered over and across the body, turning a man shape in the night into nothing more than a trick of the light. Rags across the face to not just hide, but obliterate the identity, to remove doubt, to become something supernatural in the night.

I went to the window and smelled the frigid night air, eyes scanning streets and rooftops, bearing death warrants for any errant cloud of breath or misplaced shadow. But no matter how cautious my gaze, it was eventually drawn up past the houses, past the hills, to the great lonely spire of Orphan Peak. Ten minutes later I was on the roof, leaping from one ramshackle collection of tile to another.

But even at my best, I felt the lead weight of unseen watchers pulling upon me like chains of debts unpaid. The slight movement from an alley, a beggar shifting his head just so, a half-seen face behind a curtain that drew away– these were the hallmarks of the watchers, and now I was their prey. My movements were their feast, each nameless agent a spy for Isahd, the devourer of secrets.

Ragmen live around us as shadows in the walls. I should know, I've been one of them for nearly a decade. Sometimes we are business men, sometimes watchmen, prostitutes, mercenaries, bounty hunters, soldiers, actors, or noble sons who are destined not to inherit. Some, like me, are simply men too small to care how they make their living, and too good at murder to do anything else. We have our meeting places, through they are smaller than you might surmise.

They call us assassins, but that is only part of who we are. Some sneak into the locked rooms of the world, escaping without trace. Others smash through doors like an avalanche made of hammers. Others put on thousands of different faces, working closely to a bag of coin and slitting its throat at the moment they need us most. I've done all three. I'd mastered them.

I leapt silently from upper stories to lower, and then from low roofs to the street. I approached the public fountain cautiously, feeling dozens of eyes upon me even as I failed to pick out their hiding places. They had to be more Whisperers. Still, they hid from me as I went to the fountain and circled around to the alley behind. It took only a second to locate the concealed catch, less to pull the secret door open and disappear inside. I closed it behind me, plunging myself into blackness as my boots found slippery purchase on the age-eroded stairs on either side of the main flow.

I walked blind for many minutes, the unrelieved darkness pressing in like a shroud as I continued to climb the slight slope. The incline became more pronounced and the flow more determined. I had to hold onto the walls and progress upwards slowed to a crawl as the water-cooled passage throbbed with numbing cold. I fought against it with single minded determination.

Soon after its founding, just after the population boom, the nobles discovered there was not enough water in the wells for the people of Carolaughan. They had an aqueduct built to bring in fresh water from Orphan Peak. These pipes, dating back to before the Kingdom split, funneled the water to the city's many fountains where any may stop and fetch water whenever it pleased them. The pillars and archways that held the massive structure aloft may have been a vulnerability of the city, if the barbarians could build a war engine able to scratch them.

Then I saw the light. It grew larger and larger, and then enveloped me as the path leveled out. Once past the city walls, the builders had given up roofing the massive aqueduct, and the night air seized on the dampness in my clothes to jab at me with needles of cold. Behind me the waterways spread like the veins a dark and forbidding god, but the water sent across the city came from one location where it was collected from the mountain and distributed—the Grand Cistern.

Built into the rock face of Orphan Peak, the system worked on the simple principles of gravity and needed little to no upkeep. Any problems that arose were resolved by the Ragmen with the idea that no one ever bothered to check on a system that was functioning. The cistern had been the meeting place for the Ragmen of Carolaughan for as long as I had been alive and probably much, much longer.

Nobles and fools assume an assassin waits behind every tree and curtain. In reality there were only five for all of Carolaughan. Two were now dead, and I used to be the third. *Used to be?* Thoughts like that one would see me killed. I stood foolishly, silhouetted against the sky. I felt empty and directionless, but I was sure that this would be the last time I would see the cistern alive. As I approached the small, man-made cavern, the smells of food reached me and I knew that Finnegan, the Master, was there. He always was.

Finnegan was surrounded by braziers, all but one burning a foul, too-sweet incense that clawed at the eyes and lungs. I always caught hints of rot underneath the sickening smoke, but figured it came from the expensive meat on the last bowl full of coals.

I pulled myself up onto the aged, virdigrised grate that acted as a floor above the water rushing from mountain to city. It groaned under my weight as I closed the distance between us, passing bas-reliefs of naked women pouring water from ever-full jugs.

The Master of the Assassins Guild was cleaning the meat from a turkey leg. His doublet was strained at his waistline and his jowls rested firmly on his chest, swallowing his neck completely. But do not think him simply fat— Finnegan was immense. He was easily a head taller than me and as wide as two cart horses. Calling him fat was as much an embarrassing understatement as calling him a small mountain range a slight exaggeration. He wiped plump, nearly spherical palms against velvet pantaloons that were stretched nearly full. Wide, useless feet wiggled in satisfaction as nameless Whisperers toiled at the braziers to prepare a never ending march of food. He flopped back a mop of greasy, stringy hair and shoved some fried potatoes into his face.

Four of the five Whisperers, their flesh drained of color and their limbs devoid of fat or muscle, moved around him on his wooden throne to adjust a pillow here, a blanket there. The last of the zombie crew was providing the constant stream of food and drink. If he ever left, if he had a home, or another life, I didn't know of it. I have never seen him otherwise than he was right now, being fed and pampered by his slaves in this waterway in the mountains. Of course if he ever left, there would always be the question of how he would ever get back up here.

Between the platters, a large, leather bound and iron-shod book sat like a tombstone in a feasting hall. The spider web of thin iron plates created a twisting impression of worms bearing an all seeing, lidless eye. I had never seen inside that book, had never even cared to. I had always believed it carried the records of every assassination committed by Ragmen in Carolaughan. I knew I was about to find out.

His black, pig-like eyes alighted on me, finally torn from the silver plates laden with steaming feasts. He spoke from around a mouth full of half-masticated meat, but it would not have mattered, his mouth always sounded full. "Simon! I was about to send some more Whisperers to fetch you. I have heard some rather disturbing rumors from the Grand Sage. I thought you might be able to shed some light upon them. Please eat something."

I towered over him, his over-wide and bloated body laid out as a perfect target, but he pulled out a large leather pouch and laid it on the table just past the iron shod tome. The dull, glassy clink spoke volumes of its hidden charge. It was a sack of gems. Small shadows within began to reach for me and clench my gut with hunger for it.

The lump of flesh before me waved off his servitors and leaned forward, his huge belly straining his clothing at odd angles, pulling at his white under tunic as his fat jiggled grotesquely. His sausage-like fingers opened the pouch with astonishing dexterity, spilling precious stones into my sight.

With enough gold, no man holds sway over any other, no drought, no blight, no sickness cannot be bought away with it. Sweat sprang from my brow as a dull throb started between my shoulder blades.

"I have a most dangerous mission that has met with some... difficulty." He swallowed a mouth full of beef, but it didn't help the words escaping his mouth, "There are rumors that the difficulty is you, Simon." But still I stared at the pouch. Gold was the master of men's lives, mine as well.

He paused for a moment. "I do not put too much stock in the tales of Whisperers. Informants can be so undependable, you see."

I managed to shake my head as my breathing quickened with the anticipation of wealth. I barely caught Finnegan stroking the dark book on his table.

He leaned back as if relinquishing the treasure to me and folded his hands on his massive, lumpy chest. "Perhaps, given time, I could forget the rumors that seek to rust your reputation of cold steel, but I have a contract that needs to be finished and it must be done tonight. A noble lady needs to meet you, my friend. There is no time for your usual game of infiltrate and betray."

He produced another pouch of gems and discarded it next to the first. They lay like a pile of rings pried from a thousand corpses. My need for them was a physical pain.

Finnegan continued, "And we have no inside man. We have no time to plan. No time to scout. But you are the best we have, perhaps the best there ever has been, and I have these sacks here that say you will reach her."

He produced another pouch and dropped it next to the other two. My world had spiraled down upon the gems flowing from the purses. The wealth alone was a shining castle, a warm hearth, protection from the long and bitter trek from my broken and burnt home...

A crystal scream, pure and resonant, called out. It slammed into me, bringing back the faces of all those I had ever betrayed, all those I had ever abandoned, all those I had ever murdered. I saw the face of Aelia so clearly it obliterated the world on every side. My back exploded into the familiar field of dagger tips and barbed claws. I collapsed to the grate.

The scream continued, undulated, resolved out of a thousand echoes into a raven's cry. But Finnegan was now yelling shrilly, his voice ragged and fearful. "Where is it? Kill it! Kill it!"

The echoes faded into silence, but I did not waste the respite. I dug frantically into my belt pouch as I struggled to my knees. But Finnegan was there, speaking in a voice both soft and brittle to me, "Come now, Simon. Eat something, you look very pale. Just take the purse, drink some wine, and I will let you know the name of her."

My life was a graveyard filled with the corpses of other people's families. My road had been washed with blood and paved with skulls. All I was, was a pit; a pit with a mouth wide enough to swallow anyone worth coin. I tried to talk, but the pain was enormous, and it swatted the air from my lungs. Finnegan's brow gathered promised retribution, his lips pursed as his voice became firm, "Sit down, Simon. You have work to do."

The invisible knives still ravaging my back, I stood straight, defying the pain, defying Finnegan. I could hear the fat man clench his jaw, further hobbling words that sounded strangled past a tongue swollen from foul poison. "I don't know what you think you are accomplishing, Simon. You cannot ignore your bondage."

I heard the ghosts of words hidden in the echoes of the cistern, *You are a Hero, Fox Crow. You always have been, and you always will be.* The pain became a blinding torrent of broken glass showering me from head to feet. Still my hands fumbled blindly with my belt pouch. My eyes saw nothing but the intertwining lights that blotted out the entire world.

A Phantom Angel holds out to me Thomorgon and Isahd, the poor raven, and the all seeing eye. A horde of nightmare creations smashed the walls to the cistern with terrifying ease. The stars behind them were not far off at all, and when they blinked they did so with bloody lids.

A boy cries in the night for a hero that never comes.

The sword in my hand sputters and flares as it is corrupted in its purpose by my blackened soul.

The eyes of a beautiful, powerful woman who's respect I craved, who's love I did not deserve but she had still felt, still held like a secret for me. A scream, crystal pure and resonant, shatters the half-remembered indifference to the plight of my fellow men. The hidden crow cawed again, and while Finnegan jumped, he still said, "Isahd will kill you, Simon. All for some noble trollop."

My hands found their treasure— a small silver flask. Left wrenched free the stopper and Right dumped the contents over my back. The liquid purged the army of insects feasting on my flesh, quenching the fire and resolving the world into crystal clear focus. I slammed Gelia's empty bottle of blessed water onto the table, shaking with the sudden release from misery.

"Her name is Aelia. She is a Grand Noble to the Kingdom," I said, my voice sounding stronger, purer, than it had any right to.

The crow cackled, and Finnegan jumped, his eyes chasing every shadow. "So you know of her? Who spoke of this? Perhaps we can find out the spy that..."

"I am your spy."

I know what I have been, what I am. I am no Hero, but I am no longer an Assassin either. Something inside me awoke, neither Simon nor Beast, and began to paw the floor of my soul. I opened my eyes, and quite suddenly I was no longer a fragmented man, but whole.

"I am your spy," I said again. "I am your difficulty, and I don't work for you any longer."

I would like to tell you he folded like a shoddily made privy, but it would be a lie. His face, troubled by the threat of ravens, resolved into a dark glower. He pursed his huge, bloated lips for a moment and nodded sagely. "I thought as much."

I half heard the taut line snapping, and I knew I was a dead man. The world was caught in amber, creeping along even as I threw myself to the side. Lazy tendrils of incense simply halted and spun about me like ghosts waiting to collect my soon wayward spirit. A slave was turning her dead eyes to me. A gobbet of grease was edging off a hunk of pork into the brazier. I watched the bolt, fired from a dark passage, rush to me like a longing lover seeking my heart.

The bolt was expertly fired, and carefully aimed. My reaction was secondary and off balance, a wild gambit to prolong my life a few short breaths. Heedless of my effort, disdainful of the thin cloth covering my heart, the bolt was about to core me like a soft fruit.

I shook my eyes clear as the familiar sound of a bolt shattering against a wall was punctuated by a meaty thump. Then I slammed my head on the grate. My eyes blurred with pain, but the swirling black-feathered bodies resolved for an instant into the corpse of a single crow. I felt at my chest, but as impossible as it seemed, the bolt had passed straight through the thing, knocking the life clean out of it but deflecting the missile just enough to spare me.

The sight of it lit a fire inside me as I stood and drew forth the Phantom Angel. A strange feeling flooded every drop of my blood, every part of my flesh. I had a purpose.

Finnegan smiled luridly at the dead raven, his cheeks seeking to smother his eyes as he licked overfilled lips. "And so it has come to this, Simon. Sad. You made me a lot of money."

The fourth ragman of Carolaughan, Brogan Kalinstein, pulled himself into the cistern from a darkened water pipe. A long, muscular man, he discarded the spent crossbow without even a second thought. With theatrical flair, he removed his heavy grey cloak and cast it to the corner like a broken-winged bird.

Stripped away of all the pretty chains of civilization, he wanted the fortune of jewels on the table, and I stood in his way. He would crush me like a bug and never think of me again. Then he would go kill Aelia and anyone else who got in his way. We may have both been Ragmen, but neither of us had any love, nor hate, for the other.

He drew his two swords as I hefted my Phantom Angel. Brogan, bedecked in coarse, utilitarian clothing, looked more a mercenary than a poisoner, but the gray paste that coated his weapons told another tale. I had to assume that even the slightest nick would be deadly.

I had one major problem: from the time we join the guild, we buy our lessons from our seniors, we pay them from our contracts to teach us how to kill. Each successive generation of the guild is thus more deadly, filled with techniques from all its members down throughout time. I know fighting styles from all corners of the known world, places I have never visited myself. Unfortunately, so does Brogan.

He came in cautiously, but purposefully, edging in for a fast kill. "I can make it quick, Simon, for old time's sake." He waited a half beat for me to reply, then attacked, swinging his swords in from both sides.

He was hoping to catch me with my mouth open and my weapons silent. Instead my blade met his, the heavier Phantom ringing clear and crisp and pushed his first sword out of the way fast enough to reverse direction and block the second strike.

The opening he left me was a classical mistake when people fight with two weapons. Never strike with both weapons at once, as the enemy will parry them both, and you will be standing there with your middle hanging open for all the world to see, just like Brogan here. It was a simple mistake, a flaw in training anyone could make.

Not a Ragman, not Brogan.

I feinted forward with my foot, making as if to caress his groin with no small force. Immediately his widely spread weapons screamed inwards to draw the edges against my calf and thigh, if my calf and thigh were there, which they were not. His eyes twitched in irritation as I moved in mercilessly, a wind of storming steel.

Our strikes began to ring inside the cistern like a nightmare chorus of bells. Each echo bled into the next peal of laughter from our razor-edged femme-fatales. We were intent upon each other, shutting out the moon, the city, the streets, the pipes, the cistern. All that existed in our duel were two masters of death, waltzing toward oblivion. I pressed ahead again, but found no flaw with his footwork, no lack of timing in his strikes.

He recovered well, slinging his blades about himself, attacking and defending with each in turn as he rocked on his feet. But this was not a winning fight for me. My arms would soon start to flag as his took turns absorbing my blows and making his own attacks. A single cut from his coated blades meant my agonized death, a single kiss from any of my weapons may kill, but would more than likely only slow him. I had to change the calculation of my odds. Minutes distended into hours as we fought.

The next time he made to disengage, I let him and did the same, ensuring distance from him by swinging the bastard sword in a wide arc as I spun away. He did not follow, and it was easy to see why. His lank, blond hair was plastered to his forehead above his empty eyes and his chest was heaving from the exchange. Thankfully he paused for a moment, catching his wind. I wasn't in any better shape than he. As my arms burned from the exertion, and my head began to swim, I knew I had to do something inspired soon.

The tip of the Phantom Angel went into a gap in the grate and I kneeled behind it. Brogan's eyes widened, then narrowed as he took in my new stance. He decided attacking was better than waiting for whatever I had in store for him. It was too late; the hidden knife was already in my hand. He grit his teeth and took a single step when I flicked my wrist and sent the little sliver of steel tumbling like a deadly acrobat towards his chest.

It hit him in the gut. He staggered and I heard the knife clink harmlessly against the grate before disappearing into the water below. I snatched another knife from my boot, then one from my belt, and a spike from up my sword arm. Each one flew true, and each struck arm, thigh, and chest. Finnegan chuckled from behind his big, full desk as Brogan smiled and lowered the swords and startled hands, revealing glints of metal beneath his clothes.

Whisper mail is expensive, and therefore rare. It is made by taking a sparsely linked mail shirt and threading the spaces between the rings with black leather cords. It does not jingle, it barely shines, and it is usually worn without padding so it fits beneath generously cut clothing. It's good to turn against a dagger, or even to stop a cut from a lighter sword, and while it won't do much against a hammer or the Angel, it is perfect to stop light throwing blades.

Brogan came at me again, and I quickly ran out of options. He stopped being conservative with his strikes and came at me as fast as he could. There was no way I could block them all with the heavier Phantom, so I began a prancing dance of retreat and dodge, further sapping my reserves as my muscles begged for rest and my breath became ragged and uneven.

I leapt away from a vicious lunge and slammed my hip into the large desk in front of the Master of Assassins.

"I was feeling sad to have lost you." Finnegan slurped at a mug of beer, all worries forgotten with the death of the raven. "It turns out you aren't much of a Ragman after all, Simon."

The thought flitted through my head to hold the fat man hostage, but all I'd be doing is threatening to promote Brogan. My opposite struck mercilessly, dispassionately. He may have been a murderer, but it was just a job for him. He was just looking to get paid.

Paid in a small pile of jewels laying fast at hand.

I parried a strike with a large fraction of my fading strength. Then, with a free hand, I swept up the piles of gems and flung them at Brogan, turning them into a glittering wave of stars for a brief instant.

Brogan screamed incoherently as my body finally gave in to exhaustion. He dropped his swords as he clutched at the few baubles that landed on the folds of his clothes even as he watched the rest drop through the bronze grate into the water flow. There they tumbled like faeries in a glass of white wine before being swept downstream toward the city.

He watched them go like an abandoned child, his entire world collapsing under the weight of lost wealth. In fact, this would have been a perfect time to decapitate him, or run him through, or even try to give him a really vicious head rubbing with my knuckles. Any one of those would be perfect... if I weren't collapsed in a heap in front of Finnegan's desk.

Just as you can whip a horse to run only so far, you can force a body to swing four waterweights of steel for only so long. For those precious seconds while he screamed, I lay as defenseless a few paces away. My eyes never left Brogan has he mourned his loss. The burn in my muscles started to fade and the chill of the icy night began to penetrate again. I went to flip my hair from my face, and discovered only a forest of bristle inhabited by sweat. I slung the hand dry and gathered up the Phantom from the grate, but then Brogan was there.

He slammed into me like a rampaging bear, and I barely engaged one blade and forced it into the other out of the way as he shouldered me back across Finnegan's feast. Swords, axes, spears, all of them, require some distance to use efficiently. Face to face, punching and kicking while rolling on the ground, a sword is worse than useless. So it becomes a necessity to watch how close you let your opponent get, because if he has a sword and dagger, and you have two swords, he will gut you. Sadly my dagger was in my boot, my blades lay in the water beneath the grate, and anger was lending him strength as mine faded. Now that we were nearly face to face, even his swords were hard to wield, and the Phantom near impossible.

The thick gray paste coated the edges a fingerlength from my face, and Brogan growled as he slid his blades against mine, trying to find an angle where he could get steel into me. There were weapons of a sort nearby, and Brogan had pushed me twice within reach. Again, I flung my hand back to Finnegan's table, knocking into the iron bound book, snatching up a two-pronged fork. I slid the small, iron implement along the greasy gray goo on Brogan's blade, then plunged it into the back of his hand.

Brogan screamed and backed off, allowing me precious seconds and space to regain my footing. I need not have bothered, for he was already sweating and his skin turning gray. I backed off as the sword in his right hand tumbled noisily to the bronze floor.

Brogan had forgotten the foremost fact about poisons. Like fire, they call no man master and spare no man their deadly embrace. I watched him tumble to the floor near his weapons, his legs giving out even as he tried to wheeze past the fluid filling his lungs. He did not weep, did not beg, but he did vomit messily into the water flow. The practical part of me made a mental note not to drink the fountain water in Carolaughan for a while.

Then he died. Inside of me, for the first time since I was a boy,

I felt something stir. He had tried to kill me, had killed countless others, but I had still killed him. It felt like he deserved some kind of ceremony, some closure. What I got was Finnegan clapping his overfull hands together behind me.

The other thing that spoiled the moment was that, for once, I had managed to live up to my reputation and exit a face to face battle without being stabbed, shot, crushed, or cut. Unfortunately there was no one around to see it. No one who was going to live through this, anyway.

"Simon you have done the impossible!" he proclaimed, waving the servants off down one dark corridor. "You have eliminated a generation of assassins in Carolaughan. You will have the pick of whatever contracts you desire. You will earn a tithe training every junior Ragman and hopeful Whisperer looking to come up the ranks. You will be wealthy beyond measure, powerful and feared. And one day, one day, you will take over this seat and rule as the master yourself."

My stomach turned as he took another bite of pudding. He talked about continuing it all, of returning to his fold as if I had done all this just to consolidate power. I was angry at him for giving me an out, for tempting me with things that whispered out of the back of my head.

I bent down and picked up the deadly eating tine. I had little time left. The familiar dangerous tingle was starting up now that my shirt was drying, "No, Finnegan, I'm here to cancel the contract on Aelia Conaill."

I set the fork on his desk, pointed at his heart, but his face was twisted into a hungry grimace I was having a hard time believing was fear. "Hmmm, it is too bad, Simon. I made a lot of money from you." The last of the Whisperers shuffled in a panic out of the cistern as I lifted the Phantom Angel, "But, I suppose all good things have to end... Schlimonnnn."

Paralysis washed over me as Finnegan's voice, normally distorted, became nearly unrecognizable. His smile spread, wider and wider, nearly touching his jawline as two slimy pink growths launched forth to frame his teeth. He stood, his mammoth proportions more evident than ever as he stretched, sending shards of velveteen and silk flying in all directions. His jowls were gone, replaced by a skeletal head with a mouth sprouting a halo of tentacles tipped with blinking eyeballs. Six more flailing, boneless tentacles unfolded from around his chest, arms, and legs, robbing them of his mountainous girth. His chest was barely big enough to contain his spine and ribs, warped by the presence of these extensions of his assassin's tattoo.

Where his body was inhuman, he was covered in dense clusters of huge pustules, and the tips of the tentacles were bulbous and discolored. These disgusting limbs pawed at the floor, bearing his starved body aloft. He loomed above me, his own flabby feet and pudgy hands hovering above the ground as he was borne aloft by his nightmarish parts. These extremities parted down horizontal lines and the sheath of flesh pulled back to expose massive eyeballs.

"Why would you abandon us, Simon?"

The eyes began crying, raining black ichor into Carolaughan's water. Huge suckers lining each tentacle sprouted a wickedly curved tooth, and every cluster of boils on the opposite side opened into an army of eyes that stripped me down and lay me bare. The thick balls on the ends of the tentacles opened into eyes with sharp teeth as lashes. The irises were hollow, endless pits that wanted to swallow every hidden part of me. "Why would you choose doom?"

And my total and utter destruction it was. Icy hands grasped at my innards, twisting my intestines with hands made of broken glass. My heart refused to beat in the presence of the demonic thing bearing down on me. His voice sounded like rough stones being ground in the stomach of a giant as he laughed. I ducked one tentacle even as another lashed out and tossed me into a wall with cavorting nymphs carved into the stone.. The Phantom Angel went spinning away into the darkness as I landed. The world rocked and spun as my much-abused skull began to seep a trail of crimson into my collar. Like a tortured animal, I scrabbled to my feet on base instinct alone, slinging my dagger from its sheath to defend myself from The Master of Assassins.

"Could you ever conceive of me, Simon?" I hurled my body to the side, sprawling away from the creature as it tried to hammer me with one massive mouth/eye. I plunged the dagger into it, but if he noticed, he gave no sign. Another tentacle descended from above and I rolled clear as it shattered the bronze grillwork. Shrapnel kissed my face like stinging wasps. I regained my feet only to face him again, his tentacles sliding him from place to place with the speed of a galloping horse.

"Did you ever think your pact with Isahd for body and soul would be so literal, so powerful, so permanent?" I barely managed to bat away one of the ichor-dripping eyes from my face before it struck, sending shock waves through my left arm and into my shoulder. I lunged forward in a desperate attack at his torso, but the endless supply of barbed talons and suckers were held too far in front of his body for me to reach.

"But I have to ask WHY." he continued. Another damned tentacle swatted the dagger from my hand while another gripped my middle and began to squeeze.

"All the others had doubts. For two decades I have been the master and I knew every one of their petty, weak doubts running like stray dogs between their ears. But not you." I felt the world spiraling in upon me, the Fog coming to claim me whole this time, spirit me off to the land of Death, where Isahd doubtlessly waited to claim me as his prize. Talons pierced me as he slammed me into his eating desk, sending food scattering in all directions. I began to hear the buffeting of thousands of wings, ravens wings, the souls I had sent to death before their time. "You were always the perfect little killer."

As the blackness tried to fall forever, Right hand, always the over achiever, flailed through the seas of overturned food, knocking Finnegan's thick book of contracts and names onto the floor, and found a little friend I had put there earlier. Right closed over it, and then jabbed the poison covered eating tine into the tentacle.

Finnegan roared and flung me to the side, but as I clawed the wall to get my feet, he had not died. The tentacle had slowed, but as the poison diluted in its black blood, it was quickly regaining use.

"Clever," he said in a voice devoid of humor or admiration, "but you made a bargain Simon! You took the mark. You made the pact."

I don't know where the hit came from, but I sailed through the air and crashed against the wall, crumpling in a heap at the bottom. My joints and back felt as if I had been run over by a herd of horses and it was all I could do to paw at the grate beneath me as my blood mingled with the water, drop by drop. My life was seeping from me in a half a dozen places. The Fog rushed in again, and I pushed it back, but not so far. It haunted me, waiting to finally take me whole.

"For a man who's soul is already sold, I would think you would want to live a little longer in this world." The Animal roared within me, urging me up and moving my body against its desire to lay back and die. I wrenched knifes from their hiding places, hurling them with the Animal's pure abandon. They sunk into the massive, rubbery flesh of the tentacles. Eyes burst, suckers bled, flesh oozed, but it mattered not even a bit to him.

The cold, demonic man that resided within me for so many years read off my odds of survival as just short of pure suicide. He smiled within me as my legs buckled, knowing he had been the only rational part of me all along. He was the part that sold men's lives, judged their worth, and clinically absorbed their last breaths. He was preparing to do the same to me.

"You are an assassin, Simon." Finnegan hissed. His black-eyed gaze leveled on me again, his ravaged face leering from around the hungry tentacles that seeped drool.

"And you belong to both of us!" He rushed for me, a demon on slithering, snakelike legs.

"You belong to me!" My hand closed on the Phantom Angel's hilt. It had been thrown here when I was first struck, and now it was in my hands again. A few weeks ago, I had died with this blade in my hand. I supposed it was only fitting I do so again, this time for good. I managed to struggle to my feet...

...and I felt the Seed inside me begin to sing.

"You belong to Isahd!" He was rushing in at full speed, his extremities arcing back to strike.

I lifted my eyes to his monstrous visage. My hand tightened upon my sword, then loosened as I took a deep breath.

I dove to the side, trailing the sword behind me to cover my flank like a shield. I felt one of his boneless limbs impact the blade and heard a scream that brought dust from between the rocks of the walls. It hit me like a physical force and sent me sprawling. I slapped the ground with my free hand, absorbing some of the shock of the fall, and rolled into a crouch.

Finnegan screamed with pain as one severed tentacle flopped about like a landed fish. The blade of the Phantom Angel wept blue flame, the fire dancing about the steel, burning the dark corrosion from it in long streams. It burned like fire, but flowed like water off the blade, extinguishing as it fell to the grate below. The room was bathed in its blue glow as Finnegan shook the whole cistern again with an outraged roar.

Witch-fire, the inquisitor had called the sword Witch-fire.

His many limbs shot at me, one pinning me to the wall as I tried to escape. The Angel lashed out, and severed it like a torch parting fog, its mate found my thigh. It was one of the mouthed eyes and I felt the teeth bite deep even as the bone snapped. I screamed, but somehow swatted at another deadly limb as Finnegan yanked me from the wall and sent me through three of the braziers.

The intense pain, the horrible sound of sizzling fat, or the smell of burning flesh woke me, and after I was awake it didn't matter which had done the job.

"Drop it!" he shrieked, picking me up and slamming me back first into the pile of coals. "Drop it!"

One tentacle pressed down into the center of my chest, pushing me back into the irregular pile of coals. I glanced to my right and saw that I did, indeed, still have the Angel in my fist. As the fire seared the nerves in my back to death, I found the strength to use it.

Finnegan screamed again, spurting black blood across my chest as he recoiled with a truncated stump. It burned like acid and hissed on the coals with the sound of tens of screaming children. I struggled to my feet as numbing waves flooded into my shoulder and sent the world into an unfocused blur. He picked me up by one ankle and drew a line of barbed tentacle teeth across my fist, finally separating me from my weapon.

He slammed me into the center of the room, across the body of Brogan, and a lifetime away from where the Phantom Angel fell. Finnegan leaned in close to my twitching form, opening his mouth and spreading the halo of small eyed tentacles wide to crush my head. "It is a shame you have become so corrupted from your true path, Simon."

As he came close to me I pondered the dead raven on the grate near my face. Whatever reason Finnegan had feared it, as a sign, portent, enemy, or avatar, it was dead now. As he pulled himself completely upright and spread himself to blot out everything else, I came to a moment of absolute peace. Maybe that was the answer, the reason I had been spared so many ignoble deaths so that I might die here instead. This one bird had died and so spared my life and turned the tide for a moment. Perhaps history, perhaps Aelia, needed just one moment more.

I let the whole world go and lived from heartbeat to heartbeat, as serene and deadly as I had ever been in my life. I managed to say, "My name is Crow."

Somewhere inside, the Seed caught fire, burning into my soul past the pain and blood and tears. My eyes snapped open and burrowed into his twin dark pits as he made his lethal lunge for my face.

Left hand closed over the hilt of one of Brogan's poisoned swords, waiting for me all this time at his dead feet. The blade came up, the point aimed unerringly at Finnegan's heart. Finnegan, for all his power, had forgotten he may have had numerous tentacles, he had only one body, only one heart, and his size meant he had weight. He simply could not veer, could not stop.

I heard a scream that sounded like a mountain itself had split asunder, then everything went black.

The world was in color– bold and rich. The fir greens reached into me and pulled at me, the sparse clouds above were no mere white, but a brilliant mother of pearl. The water of the steaming pool was warm, silken, and wet like a virgin's womb. The trees above captured my attention as they played around each other, the skeletal hands of dancing lovers. I lifted my head from the coal-black loam to stare at a cloaked angel across from me standing chest deep in the pond.

I had always known he was there.

Something began to scrape my heart with veins of frost as the figure raised his arms. Two hands carved of aged alabaster emerged from within the robe woven of webs and night. He held a regal raven in his right hand, carved of ebon wood so pitted and worm-eaten it seemed to wither in his grasp. His left held the finest sculpture I had ever beheld. Easily ransomed for a king's crown, the gold and ruby blazed in the shape of a lidless eye. Sparkling facets caught fire in the too bright sun, lighting an unending fury within it. He seemed to be offering the statuettes to me, waiting with the patience of one who has no life left to trickle through the hourglass. Power. Secrets. Wealth.

Seeing the riches before me, I paused.

The eye was heavy, an anchor that would pull me into the mud at the bottom of the pool. I saw in the multifaceted gems along it's back a thousand different fates for me, but all of them ended the same. I would end my life empty, soulless, and alone. I began to drink in the deep, rich, ebon wood of the raven. It was not worm eaten, but the was made to look so from the whorls of the wood's roiling grain. Each of the paths in the wood was a mystery, a new path, another quest, another deed, another hope. Wisdom.

I solemnly accepted the raven to my breast.

I opened my eyes and there was Finnegan's book, lying dejected under the ruins of the desk.

SEVENTEEN

THE MOST POWERFUL WEAPON

THE last grand feast had begun. A bonfire erupted from the fire pit, driving spears of light into every corner and heat into every soul. The dwarves were in full residence, seated in places of honor with beards perfectly plaited and resplendent in gilded armor of black Dwarvish steel. Spreading from them in ripples of descending blueness of blood were the nobles of the Kingdom of Noria, the Scions of Ryan.

Every fine breast was covered in silk, lace, or velvet. Gold and silver thread surrounded pearls and jewels like the corona of frosty moons captured on dresses and doublets of the Great and the Good. Candelabras of precious metals roared like trees afire over plains of silver piled high with hills of food fitting every description. The band played sweetly and quietly in the corner, filling the air with beautiful notes. If the nobles noticed any disturbance at the main gate, they gave no sign. Conversation twittered from table to table, as each attempted to look the most cultured and civilized in front of the dwarves at the head table. Even when the sounds of shouts and screams became hints of words, the most powerful people in the kingdom ate on. Even when the cries gathered enough presence to cause all the bodyguards in the room to tense visibly, they ignored the stray cries begging for attention.

It wasn't until the cries resolved into words that a few of the highest born glanced at one another uncomfortably. There had been too much blood and too many bodies surrounding this venture for them to totally discount that they might be next. They glanced upwards, to the comforting shadows of the guards on the roof of the great hall, and to the walls, where up to ten soldiers from each entourage stood ready. But the comfort was fleeting, for the sounds got louder, and cries resolved into screams. The screams became closer, and then stopped suddenly.

The conversation inside the hall limped on for several more seconds until a resounding strike on the huge double doors echoed from corner to corner. Another strike, and another. Then the latch was finally tripped and the thick oak doors were pushed open, revealing my disheveled form to the room.

Luxuriously cared for, the doors did not creak, which was too bad. It would have made a fantastic entrance. Still, I was bloody, bruised, limping, and shivering slightly either from blood loss or from some contagion. Even Brogan's cloak, pulled closely, could not warm me nor bring color to my pallid face. My eyes had sunk into my face and the agony of my severely burnt back turned my mouth into a constant rictus of pain. I stumbled in, two sacks gripped in one defiant fist, sword hanging from the other, tip dejectedly scraping along the ground.

I paused a few steps into the Hall, more from exhaustion than design, and caught Aelia's eyes. Gelia was tense beside her, but Aelia was stricken. I glanced over my shoulder and saw myself in a large silver mirror hung upon the marble wall. I had finally become the sunken eyed demon that had hunted me across the kingdom.

Others probably found their voices first, but even though the Dwarves were given the place of honor at the high table, this was still Horatio's house, so it was he that finally managed to stand as the stunned silence was broken by a pattering of doubtful murmurs. His head whipped around to note that nobody was chasing me into the hall to tackle, beat, or arrest me. It was an obvious disappointment. Every feasting blueblood had ten men in attendance, and apparently that included Horatio. He gave one of them a meaningful look, and they started toward me from their position, comically, by the door to the kitchens. Only then did he address me with, "What is the meaning of this?"

Maybe he had seen too many plays, maybe the disease-addled bards use that line so often is it is borne out by use in reality. Still, I sighed for want of original banter, "Your Grand Grace, since she has come to your home, Her Grand Grace Aelia Conaill has been beset by assassins. I..."

"Yes! I have noticed the plague of murderers that has assailed our house since your arrival, peasant!" Down to my bones, I knew the bastard had planned his speech. "The shadow of Death himself has passed too close to our door. Or perhaps an agent of something more sinister. I heard that you were banished from the service of my sweet cousin. I notice no deaths have stained our walls since."

I had become predictable, and he had prepared for my next grand entrance into one of his feasts. He spun a tale to cast the barest shadow of doubt upon me. As a peasant, that was more than enough to doom me to execution. I looked over to Aelia and tears were already streaming down her face, utensils trembling in her hands. The soldiers were almost upon me, so it was time to stop being polite.

"Agreed. Thomorgon has hovered above this castle. He has watched carefully." The room was shocked that I would name the God here. They did not move, but they recoiled from me. The soldiers marched more intently as I continued. "But it is Isahd that has caused these miseries."

That was enough to stop even the guards as the shock deepened and became sharp. Even the most powerful in the country did not trifle with the God of Murder. Horatio sputtered, "You are mad, mad to tempt such powers with intemperate words!"

"I do not fear Isahd," I lied, "For I have penetrated his stronghold, I have faced his champions, and I have destroyed them."

Horatio forced a laugh, which dragged a half a dozen more from the mouths of lackeys and lickspittles. "You, lowly creature? Alone? You discovered the home of the assassins, danced into their lair, and killed them all? Whispers at court have said you were formidable, but now I see you are simply an insane braggart." More laughter that he started and encouraged with theatrical gestures. "How did you find a nest of vipers that the whole body of law can not?"

And, as always, the truth popped out of me at the worst possible time. "Perhaps because I looked."

And suddenly I understood, for who had means to pay the assassins but the rich? Who else had the means to hunt them down? They were like the Barbarians of the Ridge Mountains. There was no laughter anymore. Horatio inflated with wounded dignity, finding firm footing directly upon his own self worth. "Your words are poisonous, and in our mercy, we should lock you away so your madness and lies do not affect others."

The soldiers started toward me again, so I reached into the bloody bag.

"How unfortunate for you that I have proof." And I pulled

forth the letter of safe passage that had gotten me past every gate and guard up until now. It was Finnegan's head. The skin was pulled tight over nearly skeletal features. The cluster of stalks erupting from his mouth sat limp and dead, crowning eyes open, dead, and unseeing. Screams shattered against the ceiling, and two dozen nobles and half as many guards were immediately ill. Making frantic signs to ward off evil, the guards backed away, so I took the opportunity to limp forward.

Questions were flying in all directions, but one shrill cry rose above the background noise, "What is that hellish thing?"

I stumbled, Finnegan's disembodied head rocking in my hand as I reached the spot directly in front of Horatio and, as I had for his supposedly traitorous captain, placed the head in front of him. "It is the Master of Assassins, thrall of Isahd."

The imagery was clear to all assembled, and the room erupted in noise. Horatio shouted, "Silence! I will not have my Great and Grand Noble name sullied by this commoner! I demand this peasant be flogged until dead! I demand he be drawn and quartered! I demand trial by combat immediately!"

I would be unlikely to be anyone's champion at the moment, or even to be able to act as my own. I turned from him, as deadly an insult as a commoner can give a noble, when a guard pounced on me from behind. I could not fight back, could not even think, as my poor, broken body created a chorus of silent cries that blotted out the whole world. Even so, I could guess the guard had only one eye as he kicked me twice and saluted his Grand Duke. "Sir! Lieutenant Palmer spoke to me about this man. He said he saw an assassin's mark on his back!"

Horatio grasped this lifeline with obscene haste, "Very good soldier! Disrobe him!"

I struggled to my feet as the guard I had robbed of an eye ripped Brogan's cloak from my shoulders and let it flutter to the floor. The entire room erupted into gasps of horror.

I crushed my eyes shut, awaiting the order for my execution, but it never came. Then I felt the sting across my back from the clotted kisses of the coals I had been pressed into by Finnegan's thoughtless wrath. The tattoo, my mark of geas and doom, must have been erased by the uncaring claws of fire. I slowly turned so everyone could see the wound upon me, coming full circle until facing the guard who's face had drained of color. Then I lurched forward and stuck my thumb in his remaining eye. He screamed and thrashed on the ground as I limped painfully down the aisle. I could not stifle a smile.

I took another step around the great bonfire and people recoiled on all sides, as if I were tainted by the vast burn on my back, or even from touching the mutated head of the Master of Assassins. Maybe they were right, for my strength was ebbing fast and I sprawled into a table and had to blink away stars from my eyes. Almost without thinking, Right held himself out, straining across the dozen paces to where Aelia sat.

I could not see it, but I felt her jump from her chair and, hiking up her skirts, she ran to my side. Her smell smashed into me like an angry wave out on the sea, cracking walls inside and washing away a full day of misery. She cupped my dirty, bloody face in her hands and looked deeply into my eyes.

Still Horatio raged. "Cousin! I demand you renounce that villain and give him up to justice, lest you drag your family name into the vile pigpen of his baseless charges."

I stared into Aelia's eyes, glancing over her shoulder to the iron rod form of Roehm only momentarily before digging in the other sack. I pushed myself off of the table as I pulled the iron shod book from the other satchel. I held it aloft. "This is the book of the Master of Assassins, taken from his own banquet table. See how the eye of Isahd looks at you?" The room erupted into more shock and outrage. I brought it down and flipped it open, paging frantically until I had come to one in particular. The entire hall swallowed all noise as I turned the pages to the Grand Duchess and hooked my finger to the page. "See what is written there in the hand of the Master of Assassins?"

She read, and reread, her brow becoming troubled, then confused. She shook her head in denial and met my gaze. Aelia was a bright girl. She thought, well, what I had thought, and what everyone in the room thought– this was Finnegan's list of contracts and payments. Yet, as she read, it contained no more than a list of ingredients and instructions. The Master of Assassins had a terrible hunger, and this book contained his recipes for thousands of meals cooked by half dead servants.

I turned my eyes and she followed my focus all the way to where Horatio stood, sweating, pale, and lips twitching with half held back excuses. No amount of proof brought to this room, or to any court by a commoner, would ever chain his leg or free his head from his neck. Yet, there are more powerful things than the law, more unstoppable forces than evidence. Guilt is one of those.

Aelia finally understood. Understood and believed.

She glanced around the grand hall, shocked at the number of faces that were coming to understand the nature of the book and what must be written there. She looked at me, searching for some hint, some advice, but there was nothing I could say with an army on all sides, every future hinging on our next words.

Gingerly, daintily, Aelia ripped out the page I had chosen, careful to note it was blank on the reverse side. She folded it and slipped the parchment into her bodice. Then she took the book from me and walked toward Horatio. There she stood, silence ringing around her like the second before a charge is called on the field of battle, still and serene as her cousin trembled on the edge of tears. Aelia turned back to the crowd and lifted the book again. Then, without a word, she fanned out the pages and dumped the thing, spine up, onto the bonfire.

It disappeared without ceremony, without a green flash, ominous laughter, or puff of smoke. It simply sat in the hottest part of the fire, crackling merrily as all bodies in the room but one began to breathe again.

"To all things come the fire eventually, and in the flames there will be an accounting." She quoted the Amsarian holy book, her voice powerful, vibrant, and sonorous. She then impaled her childhood friend with a stare that could cave an armor plate. "There will be an accounting."

Primly she glided across the floor to where the rest of us still stood. She addressed Gelia first. "Please take him to our room and see to his wounds." She motioned for two of her soldiers along the wall to come forward and help the old woman carry me. Then, without pause, she floated onward to Roehm. "See the book burns to ashes. Kill anyone who reaches for it."

Then, with the grace of a true Grand Duchess of the Kingdom, Aelia Conaill sat back at her place and continued her meal.

I was taken upstairs and gently laid, face down, into one of the luxurious feather-and-rope-frame beds. From the sparse, military items arranged neatly in small piles, this had to be Roehm's room. It was Aelia's old room, the one with the smashed window. Even now it was covered over with greased parchment. A corner had ripped, and it was letting in a refreshingly chill breeze.

The aged cleric picked at the incinerated remnants of shirt burned into the wound. She started snapping orders like a general. The room cleared quickly, intrusion only coming with some holy or medical instrument before the bearer was dispatched again.

"What happened, Crow?"

"You weren't around. Started bleeding."

My mirth died there in the silence that followed. The cleric was crying silently at my current state. I reached out a hand to pat hers gently, but when she took it, there was a deep finality to her voice, "How did you make it back to the Grand Sage?"

"I soaked my back in icy water from the mountains until I could walk," I said truthfully. In fact, the bath had been wearing off since I arrived. "It washed the ash and burnt clothing out of the wound."

"You saw black strips in the water?"

"Yes."

Her voice cracked, "Crow, that was your skin. I don't think I can help you."

"At least the burn erased the mark," I said, gasping as the pain returned to the edges of the wound.

The next man that came in with clean bandages was tasked with lifting the mirror off of the vanity. Gelia dug inside her bag to pull out a smaller polished silver mirror and hold it up so I could see my back for the first time. It was not just the grotesque burn that made the nobles gasp, it was that the bleeding tissue unmistakably formed the silhouette of a raven in flight. I had been marked by Death Himself.

I chuckled quietly, knowing that my penance was not yet paid, that it would soon be at hand, and that the chances of healing such an open wound without infection taking me was zero. "Thomorgon has a sense of humor."

"Crow! You should not..."

"Gelia, I think it is time to dispense with superstition. The God of Death knows right where I am. He has for weeks."

The break in the conversation was like watching a grand Dwarvish bridge collapse into a cavern. Gelia fidgeted for a moment then stood up with sudden purpose. "I have some herbs to dull the pain but they must be steeped. Wait here."

I nodded, a strange hollowness taking all panic and sadness

away from me and leaving me morbidly serene. She left, keeping the door open should I call out, and I was alone with the stillness of my own mind. I glanced about and saw the Phantom Angel leaning within reach at the head of the bed, and my eyes began to tear up.

Then there was a strange, throaty trill, a flash of grey, and a warm furry presence in my face.

"Leoncur?" It was true, the little ungrateful beast that hissed, spat, and yowled at me every step from the mountains curled up in my face and purred as loud as a rockslide. I reached up and ran a bruised finger under his chin as he pushed back eagerly. There was something strangely satisfying to having made peace.

Then two perfect hands, more tan and slightly more worn than the first time I had seen them, lifted the cat from in front of me.

"You are not well, sir." Aelia's voice was like crystal, beautiful but fragile. "Sir?"

I smiled bitterly. "My apologies, Milady, I am still addled. Some dreadful creature thought I owed it a waterweight of flesh and took to collecting immediately without warning."

A small smile cracked her brittle exterior. After weeks on the road her hair was shaggy on the ends, her dress was new and obviously pinched her in many places. She had been marked for death, assaulted, hunted, and stalked, the experience did not sit well upon her. "Is it over?"

"The Master of Assassins is dead. The guild is shattered. Even when replacements grow up to fill the void, the contract will be long forgotten, as long as you have that paper you took from the book."

Gelia's voice from the doorway made Aelia jump. "What was in that book? The records of the Assassin's Guild?"

She regained her composure as she turned to her cleric. "How is he?"

The old woman was still troubled as she accepted the clumsy misdirection as a prerogative of nobility. She gave her diagnosis with a voice heavy with grief as she circled around behind Aelia to set down the kettle, "His condition is dire. The skin across his back is gone, with it so open to infection, he will most likely become gangrenous and die."

There it was. My penance was nigh.

Aelia swallowed hard. "I have scoured the city, but there are no potions, philters, draughts or tinctures to be had."

I laughed darkly, without humor. "I am not surprised." And

with so many nobles under threat of attack, I was not.

The princess turned to me, and our eyes met. Instantly all time shuddered to a stop as we allowed ourselves to feel the painful longing inside that we had shared for one another for weeks. She bent low over me, lips meeting mine. It was not a kiss; it was longing and pain, desire and loss. Complex feelings flooded through me, churning in the cauldron of my chest. In short, it was love. Pure, sweet, she tasted of strawberries and mint, both innocent and scandalous at the same time as she whispered in my ear. A gruff and somewhat indecent cough from the door announced that Roehm had seen her indiscretion.

Without a hint of modesty, Aelia stood and made to leave, barely clearing the door as Roehm turned to my prone form with his sharp demand, "What did the lady say to you?"

The voice that came from out of the room was that of a Duchess that would brook no further discussion, "Roehm! There is a small army sworn to the Conaill family without a leader. Go see to them. Now!"

He looked to me, suspicion erupting from him in professionally straight lines aimed at my heart. She had whispered, "I will always love you." Now I could die. It may be slow in coming, but at least it was all finally over. Gelia soaked her tincture onto a piece of leather and spread it across my back.

I blinked.

Evening had disappeared and dawn had arrived. Theo was sitting in the chair in the corner, sleeping deeply. I reflexively swallowed an exclamation and kneaded the bedclothes underneath me as my back erupted into pain and movement. I grunted as it felt like the skin was pulled far too tight. I strangled a cry and arched my wounded back as it seemed hundreds of needles tied to thousands of strings were wielded by dozens of rodents as they reformed my flesh.

And then, it stopped.

The very first thing I noticed was that my back was not a field of utter agony. Still, six little points stabbed into the base of my spine like gently pressed needles. Then the points moved.

I shot upright, sending the unknown visitor on my back fluttering to the windowsill. He was large and black, his glossy wings folded behind him like a gentleman's cloak. His head turned to spear me with one, bottomless, ebony eye. He was another raven, maybe the same raven. I put my feet on the floor as I breathed in the cold air coming in through the ripped parchment window. Death's Messenger shifted to look at me appraisingly, then he flapped and hopped over to the footboard. There he simply watched.

I realized that, despite the magical potion bought by Aelia's father, despite Gelia's prayers and ministrations, despite skill and luck, the only reason I had survived the journey here, the cistern, and the long walk back to the Grand Sage, was simply because Death had not collected me yet.

I should have been thankful, really, but I was still marked, owned, and bits and pieces of me inside rankled at the idea. So, no, I was not completely grateful. Still, the message was clear, though unspoken, *I am not through with you, yet.*

I considered death, my life strewn with vile sins and the debts I owed hundreds of ghosts. I nodded at the bird. "That is fair."

Theo came awake with a start, just in time to see the raven leap and flutter around the room before silently plunging through the hole in the window and out into the dawn.

"You are healed?"

I marveled as I stretched, plagued by no more than an unpleasant tightness across my back."It would seem so."

"A miracle?"

And though I said, "It would seem so," I secretly wondered if all blessings came with such chains attached.

"You came back." I turned back to my protégé, seeing the hurt and the uncertainty written there, but in a much more hidden language than before. He was learning to guard himself and his emotions.

I nodded.

He did not manage to denude all the doubt from his voice when he asked, "So who are you, now?"

I thought long about that, letting the sun come up and the castle wake up around us. My eyes kept wandering to the rip in the parchment and the wide world outside. I felt as if I had never seen it before, "I know not, Theo. All I can say is I am not who I have ever been."

His eyes narrowed, "Clever answer."

I rubbed my eyes with my palms until I saw stars, "Good that it seems so, for I am witless."

But that was not enough. Theo came to his feet, fists clenched and trembling. "I must know. Are you the man who is my friend?"

I looked him dead in the eye, watching him mature under my very gaze. "I am more that man than any other, Theodemar."

And he embraced me so fiercely I thought I was going to pass out. I wondered if this is what coming home felt like.

EPILOGUE

I SUPPOSE a hero would have died there, dark and alone in the recesses of the cistern. It would be a nice, neat ending to this story. Then again, as you know, I am no hero. And you will forgive me if there is more– this is my life, not some poxy bards tale.

Aelia had found the answer to the death of her father, as politically crippling as it was. She sent a series of masterfully worded letters to Horatio, never quite threatening him with the folded parchment near her bosom and worse (me, to be precise). Not that she asked me to assassinate him, not that I would have accepted if she had asked. I'm not in that line of work anymore. At least not directly.

Instead he gave mountains of gold to her as 'gifts' by way of making reparations and then took up the expensive task of guarding the North Ridge Mountains without the support of her troops. That would save even more carts-full of gold in the long run, but I know she would gladly become a pauper to have her father back. There would be bad blood between the O'Riagáin line and the family of Conaill for generations, even after no one remembered why.

With all those costs, Horatio could not even bid on the Dwarvish stronghold, but Aelia did not win the bid either. Aelia had fought hard for it, and lost much, but as I have said, it is neither a fair, nor often a just, world.

Horatio lived in constant fear that the parchment ripped from the Book of Assassins would surface and call for his execution. It never did. In fact, it never could. Aelia had destroyed it, lest it be found and the game given away. It would always be a much better threat than a hammer.

I traveled with Aelia in her carriage back to her castle and told her the truth– the whole truth. She took it well, and didn't pry into the details I left sketchy. Because I am not a liar, I have to say that much of my life I was trying to forget, and she allowed me that dignity. She did hug and hold me, and promised that whenever I needed a home I could stay with her.

The carriage ride beat walking, but the heat between us was

palpable. The desire for one another was growing. Then, when we got back to the castle, she disappeared like a wraith. She was always busy overseeing some facet of her lands or titles. She had to settle disputes between the nobles beneath her, make sure taxes were collected, rule in court over capital crimes. In short, I saw her less and less.

Theo was made into her high warden, trained by Roehm himself, and charged with keeping the roads cleared of bandits and worse things. He took his boys, the young men, with him, and they were happy enforcing the law.

Gelia was Aelia's nanny, and always would be. She took to caring for me as well, often coming to speak with me during the cold nights. We talked of little things, because my life was yet to be filled with anything big. I was just practicing, honing my skills with daily exercise throughout the winter, learning every brick and block of this massive castle. Now it is spring, and ravens have begun frequenting the castle in noticeable numbers. I don't feel like I can stay any longer.

I am staring now, as I pen the final words of this tale, out of a window that overlooks the fringes of the Sorrow Wood. I am wondering if the darkness inside me has been tamed, or simply sated for a time. Here is like a child's play room, safe and secure. Whether I am a good man or bad cannot be judged here, it must be out there, under magnificent wine-colored sunsets like the one before me. I don't know how I have survived so far, or how I will continue, but I will. I must. I have questions about who I have become that need answering. Of course this has nothing to do with the fact that Aelia has become engaged to be married. In the bard's tale I would be hopelessly, endlessly in love with her.

I cannot lie. For once, they would have gotten it right. And that is why my bags are packed. That's why I have to go; because she must marry for duty. But when she sees me, I know she loves me as much as I love her, and I can't let that beauty become a form of torture.

I didn't bed the girl, get the gold, or become a king. Real life is funny that way. I know there will be other girls, other tales. Looking at the bright, crisp, silvery blade of the Phantom Angel as it lays at my side, I know at least one question has been answered. I am no hero, but one day maybe I can be better than what I am. At least I killed the monster, and I will never be him ever again in my lifetime. That, at least, is something. I know, it is an abrupt end. That is because, my friends, it is an artificial one. My life went on before this story and will continue afterward. I think this is more a story of a bad man than a good one, and I know not what kind of man it will see at its end.

— FOX CROW

About The Author:

JAMES DANIEL ROSS is a native of Cincinnati, Ohio who first discovered a love of writing during his education at The School for the Creative and Performing Arts. While he began in simple, web based vanity press projects, his affinity for the written word soon landed him a job writing for Misguided Games. After a slow-down in the gaming industry made jobs scarce, he began work on *The Radiation Angels: The Chimerium Gambit* as his first novel. Soon came *The Key to Damocles, Snow and Steel, The Last Dragoon, Whispering of Dragons, The Echoes of Those Before*, as well as many novellas and short stories. Coming soon is his first fantasy/romance novel, *Elvish Jewel*, as well as the second installment of *The Legacy of Foxcrow: The Opus Discordia*.

OTHER GREAT BOOKS TO ENJOY:

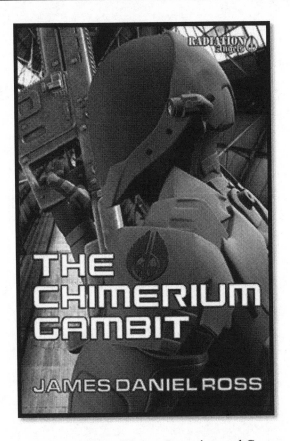

They Say You need three things: Honor, Integrity, and Courage.

What you really need is the nerve to fly half a billion light years, touch down on alien soil, and fight in a major land war... every other week.

When the enemy sets foot on your soil, when civil unrest or revolution raise their bloody hands to the stars, when governmental factions leave words behind and reach for guns and knives and bombs, there is little that the aerospace navies can do. This is when planets contact mercenaries, the last scions of professional ground troops.

Led by their Captain, Todd Rook, *The Radiation Angels* must wager their fortunes, their friends, their very lives on a plan that will make them rich beyond kings, or ensure their painful demise: **The Chimerium Gambit**

Shandahar is a cursed world. People will live and die. Wars will be fought, kingdoms built, discoveries made. For centuries, history will proceed apace... and then everything will come to a grinding halt and start all over again.

Shandahar is a world brimming with darkness, filled with no promise of a future but one. A prophecy. Spoken by the renowned seer, Johannan Chardelis, there is a divination that tells the coming of someone who can stop the curse. The snag? They have failed four times already.

Enter a world swirling with mystical realms and bloody battles, with enchanted forests and crowded cities where things are not always as they seem. Enter the World of Shandahar.

Found within these pages is a wonderful assortment of tales and adventures from some of the most memorable people in the world of Shandahar! Come and meet Sirion as a young lycan hunter, Thane before he became corrupted by the greatest of evils, Sorn as a young rogue tempted by love, and Dartanyen before he meets up with the Wildrunners! You will meet some new people too, and experience the depth and richness Shandahar truly has to offer!

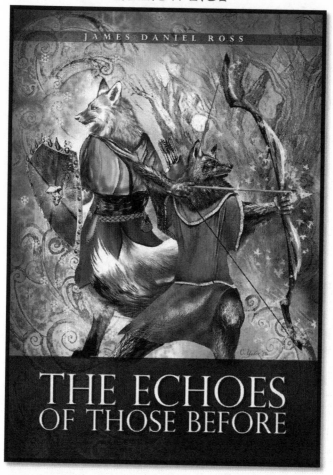

Hungry. Feral. Remorseless.

Demonic creatures have crawled from their hives for the first time in thousands of years. They seek their prey relentlessly, seemingly invincible, swarming across the world to blot out entire nations.

Two young men, and orphan and a maverick, will pick up one of the most powerful weapons ever forged by Those Before and stand against the rising tide of darkness.

Follow this pair as they venture from the safety of the Fox Vale, into the cold embrace of the big, wide world.

251

Made in the USA
Lexington, KY
11 September 2018